A TRUTHFUL MAN

A MODERN CATHOLIC NOVEL:
Book 1

HILARY WALKER

A Truthful Man

A Modern Catholic Novel

By Hilary Walker
Copyright 2022 Hilary C.T. Walker
Cover Design: 100BookCovers.com

All Rights Reserved

*****

CONTENTS

Introduction

The Background

I was lucky enough to go to a wonderful Monsignor, 95 years young, for spiritual direction. We talked for over an hour, at the end of which he asked what I do.

When I replied that I write Catholic fiction, his eyes lit up. He told me to pursue that path. "People are starving for the truth. That's your mission! It's a gift from the Holy Spirit."

Such strong confirmation of my calling as a Christian writer filled me with joy, and on the five-minute drive home the idea for this book came to me.

Although I was working on another project, I quickly wrote out the basic outline of "A Truthful Man" and continued to add details as they occurred to me over the next few months. Once my previous book was published, I was able to give this new story my full attention.

Location and Language

The novel is set in the real county of Devon, in South West England, where I went to university, although many of the towns and villages are figments of my imagination.

Devon is in the Catholic diocese of Plymouth, where the real bishop lives. However, I've moved him to the fictional cathedral city of Ruddminster, which is loosely based on Exeter, the *actual* county town of Devon. Exeter Cathedral used to be Catholic so I have unashamedly taken the structure back from Henry VIII's Church of England for the purposes of my story.

Because it is set in England, I have written it in British English for a more authentic feel.

A Church Gone Astray

It will be obvious to most that the hierarchy of the Catholic Church has completely lost its way. Over two thousand years of tradition, supported by her saints, are being threatened by a progressive agenda, and any priest who doesn't adhere to the modern narrative faces the loss of his faculties, his parish rectory and his income.

Hundreds – yes, hundreds – of good priests are being removed by their prelates and forced to find outside work or starve. They are the very shepherds we laypeople need to help us travel the narrow path, and yet these holy men are being punished for speaking God's truth.

But He hasn't forgotten them: Christ told us that the kingdom of Heaven belongs to those who are persecuted for righteousness' sake.

Role of the Laity

The following quote from Archbishop Fulton Sheen is very relevant these days: "Who is going to save our Church? Not our bishops, not our priests and religious. It is up to you, the people. You have the minds, the eyes, and the ears to save the Church. Your mission is to see that your priests act like priests, your bishops act like bishops, and your religious act like religious."

Should this book move you to help priests whose superiors have thrown them out, for caring about the souls of their parishioners and preaching the Truth, a new organization has sprung up to provide for the many needs of these hapless men.

The Coalition for Canceled Priests is "a group of committed Catholics, lay people and clergy, who came together in the spring of 2021 after one too many instances of persecution or betrayal."

Although based in the United States, they will help priests in any part of the world and are in need of funds to carry out their mission.

The Takeaway from This Book
There are many troubling things going on with the Bride of Christ today, but they are all the more reason she needs the faithful to stay and fight for her.

As Our Lady said to Pedro Regis, "Trust fully in the Power of God and all will turn out well for you. Onward in defence of the truth."

Is it easy to be Catholic? No, and it's going to get worse. But those of us who persevere to the end will win the crown of eternal life with God.

The alternative is too dreadful to contemplate!

And now, I hope you enjoy this novel.

God bless,

Hilary
https://HilaryWalkerBooks.com
Rubesca4@gmail.com

If you enjoy this novel, would you please consider leaving a review?

Reviews are the lifeblood of authors and help spread the word about their books.

For all the good and holy priests who have been unjustly removed from their priestly duties.

For all the parishes who have lost their good shepherds.

Chapter One: Cocktails
Sunday, 10th February

Mark Boulder's wife eyed him coldly over her martini. Was she onto him?

The quickest way to put a smile back on her face – genuine or otherwise – was to introduce her to one of the guests milling around the function room of Ruddminster's best hotel.

The couple were attending a lavish soirée, organized in appreciation of the top tier of contributors to Serving Seniors. Mark had formed the charity a year ago: its aim was to benefit financially struggling members of the over sixty-five community in Ruddminster and environs.

He spied the perfect candidate to present to his wife. The man next to them had just taken a flute of champagne from the passing tray and looked lost.

"Ah, Geoffrey!" Mark took the thin man's arm. "Mary, I don't think you've met Geoffrey Postleworth. He's one of our generous new donors."

As he spoke, Mark saw his brother-in-law nodding at him across the massive room. "Do excuse me, Mary, I need to talk to the bishop."

"I'm sure Mr. Postleworth will keep me *excellent* company."

Mr. Postleworth blushed with pleasure.

Mark walked the length of the Abbot's Room, crowning glory of the Monastery Hotel. It had been built in the 1700s on the ruins of Ruddminster Abbey, two centuries after its demolition at the hands of Henry VIII. The façade was a replica of the medieval exterior, but the interior had been fashioned into luxury accommodation according to the Baroque style of the day.

Multi-tiered chandeliers hung from the ornately painted ceiling. Between gilded mirrors and sconces sporting crystal lights, the walls were adorned with copies of biblical scenes by Carracci, Rubens and Bruegel.

The carpet reflected the ochre tones of the wallpaper and antique Georgian furniture lined the edges of the room: red upholstered sofas, with sleek wooden backs and thin legs. Their matching tables, currently covered in white cloth, were laden with rich food and drink being savoured by the benefactors of Serving Seniors.

Mark Boulder, Managing Director of Boulder Enterprises and well-loved pillar of the community, wove in and out of the distinguished crowd, murmuring greetings to the lady mayoress and waving to Dr. Fishbourne, a founding member. The good doctor's elderly aunt had benefitted from the Serving Seniors Charity, making her nephew an enthusiastic supporter.

Carl Hunter, chubby editor of the Ruddminster Gazette, raised his glass to Mark. "Wonderful turnout, Boulder, first class potables and edibles." The man fancied himself a literary genius and was working on his magnum opus, convinced it was destined to be an absolute gem. His host thanked him and invited him to another drink.

In addition to starting the charity, Mark was also its treasurer. The organisation was growing fast and attracting high-profile donors. Among them were his brother-in-law, Bishop Robert Marsden of the diocese of Ruddminster, who was bringing in substantial contributions from his parishes. In recognition of his positive impact on the coffers, His Excellency was now on the board as co-treasurer.

Mark finally reached him. "What's up?" he asked. They both considered small talk a waste of time.

"I need to speak with you in private, Mark." The calendar app was open on his mobile phone. "How about lunch at your club on Tuesday? Say at 12:30?"

Mark nodded. "I'll arrange it. Care to tell me what this is all about?"

Turning his face towards Bruegel's *The Tower of Babel*, the bishop said in a confidential whisper, "Something's come up, Mark, a rumour we need to scotch, and fast."

Mark swallowed hard. Surely the bishop hadn't found him out, too? He gave a weak smile. "I'll see you then."

His brother-in-law bowed slightly.

Checking his watch, Mark threaded back to Mary. It was late enough for them to leave without being rude.

She was still talking to Geoffrey Postleworth, who seemed very taken with her. She was one of those rare people who had mastered the art of listening. Anyone talking to her had the impression of being the only one in the room and found it intoxicating.

The added fact that in her mid-fifties she was still a strikingly attractive woman – slim, with soft brown curls framing a wide-eyed face – made her a real asset. Her classic clothing looked chic and, like Jackie Kennedy, she always wore her pearl earrings and pearl necklace. She had the knack of looking beautiful without making other women feel threatened. And she was brilliant at extracting confidences.

Yes, Mark had chosen well when he wooed Mary Marsden.

But recently she'd stopped paying him attention. And tonight, he was pretty sure he knew why.

*

Mary Boulder sat in rigid silence all the way home from Ruddminster to their thatched cottage in Dartleigh, on the edge of Dartmoor. Her husband parked his midnight-blue BMW in the garage, and went round to open the door for her, a courtesy he seldom observed.

She narrowed her brown eyes. "Mark Boulder, outstanding religious citizen of the year, I know all about you and your bit on the side."

He was tired. He'd drunk too much champagne this evening and was lucky not to have been caught by the police. He put on an innocent expression. "What *are* you talking about?"

"I know all about your girlfriend."

Still hoping to stop this argument, he said, "Where on earth have you got your information from?"

"You're not as clever as you think. Her name is Rita Shoreham and she works at your firm, and this has been going on for a year." Her voice held a note of triumph. "Want me to read out your lovey-dovey text messages? I've got great shots of them right here on my phone."

How had she got hold of his mobile, for goodness' sake? He was always so careful! And how had she cracked his code?

He blinked a couple of times. If this became public, his reputation in the company *and* his status with the charity would be ruined. It was unthinkable!

She stepped out of the car. He followed her to the kitchen and sat down in a wooden chair at the table with his head bowed.

"You're not denying it, then?" she snapped.

He threw up his hands. "What's the point?"

She took a deep breath. "Unlike you, I'm a *real* Catholic. Divorce is not an option."

Mark didn't want the scandal of a divorce, either.

What would the bishop, say? Defeated, he looked up at his wife. "What do you want?"

"First, your assurance that you'll finish with her. And I need to see the proof."

Mark nodded miserably.

"Second, I want you to go to confession and admit to what you've done."

"Fine, I'll go to confession."

"And?"

"And I'll finish with Rita. Look, I'm texting her now." He typed in the fateful words and held up his phone. "Happy?" he grimaced. "But I can't prove I went to confession, can I?"

"That is between you and God, Mark. But don't you *dare* go to Communion with me on Sunday with that unconfessed mortal sin on your soul."

*

Mark slept on the sofa that night.

He'd received a stunned reply from Rita, who was scathing about his cowardice in hiding behind texts instead of breaking up with her in person. Her words cut him to the quick, but it was useless to write back and explain. What was done was done.

And before Sunday, he must go to confession. That was almost harder than ending his relationship with the leggy blond in accounting.

Once as staunch a believer as his wife in the healing power of the sacrament, Mark had long ago abandoned faith in the priest's authority to absolve sins *in persona Christi.*

This lapse quickly led to the conviction that talk of sin and repentance was a repressive tactic by the Catholic Church. Mark was too smart to fall for it. And he wasn't convinced that Bishop Marsden fully embraced the

Church's teachings on the topic, either.

But until now, Mary had assumed her husband was in a so-called state of grace whenever he went up with her to receive Communion. Unfortunately, she now knew differently.

He would go to confession to stop her making his life miserable by spilling the beans about his affair – to her brother or anyone else. Contrition played no part in it.

Chapter Two: In the Office
Monday, 11th February

Mark slept badly.

The couch was too short to accommodate his long frame. He'd finally entered a REM state after a night of fitful naps when the morning alarm sounded on his mobile. He woke in a filthy mood, further exacerbated by the memory of last night's events and how he'd ended up lying here.

Some of Rita's choice phrases came to mind and he flinched at the awkwardness of seeing her in the office today.

Then there was his promise to Mary that he would go to confession before Sunday. He was furious at not having put up more of a fight, but she'd caught him with his defences down, and now he was committed.

His practical side told him to get it over with today. But why should he rush to do her bidding? It was bad enough that he had to do it at all. *He* would decide when to go.

Besides, he needed to give thought to the best priest to tell. Of course, Mary would love him to fess up to her brother as the ultimate degradation. No, he would find some other confessor. But not today.

Breakfast was a chilly affair. Mary prepared his food and coffee as though nothing had changed. But there was no conversation and Mark was glad to leave early and drive to the office.

The closer he got to the impressive building that housed Boulder Enterprises, the easier it was for him to shrug off the unpleasantness with Mary and step into his role as managing director of a successful business.

By the time he parked in his reserved space in front of

the building, he'd decided the break with Rita was a good thing. So was the fact that Mary knew about the affair. He was saved the worry about her finding out about it and she'd get over it eventually.

Rita was young and pretty. She'd forget him soon and start dating a new man.

Mark sighed at the thought.

But no, it really *was* for the best; it allowed him to concentrate on running his company.

*

Reaching his office without seeing Rita, he walked in with a renewed sense of pride at the place.

The spacious corner room on the top floor boasted a stunning view over Ruddminster, through huge windows on two sides. So stunning in fact, that Mark always sat with his back to the city to avoid being distracted.

The walls were covered in photos of Mark shaking hands with, or receiving awards from, politicians and prominent members of the community, including his brother-in-law.

A shudder went through him as his eye caught the bishop's picture. Until today, he'd derived immense satisfaction from it. But with the prelate wanting to discuss 'some rumour' with him, and his sister having discovered his affair with Rita, the man's face made him uncomfortable.

He was tempted to remove the photograph, but it would leave a mark and invite comments. Better to ignore it and get on with his day.

His plump secretary brought in a strong cup of coffee and a welcome smile.

"Good morning, sir, Mr. Waverly is outside wanting to talk to you."

"Give me a couple of minutes, will you, Brenda? Then

let him in."

Mark had hoped for an hour of solitude to gather his thoughts before dealing with the underlings.

This particular specimen was mild-mannered and amiable, qualities which annoyed Mark intensely. He resolved to keep this meeting short.

Coffee in hand, he swivelled his chair round to admire the winter sun lighting up the twin spires of Ruddminster Cathedral a few streets away. They then reminded him of his upcoming lunch with Bishop Marsden and he spun back to face his desk, just as Brenda was showing Mr. Waverly in.

"Good morning, sir," the man said.

"Yes, yes, good morning to you, too. Take a pew." Mark waved impatiently at the chair on the other side. "What's up?"

"I would like to get your input about a company I'm looking into. It might be a great addition to our portfolio."

"Have you carried out our standard investigation procedures? I assume that's why you think it would be a good fit for us?"

"Yes, sir."

"Then what *exactly* is your question?"

"I was rather hoping you'd give my plan your blessing, sir." The man placed a thick folder on Mark's desk. "I have all the details here."

"In other words, you want *me* to be responsible for taking on this company, in case things don't work out?"

Mr. Waverly blinked. "No, sir, not at all. I was simply not wanting to move forward without checking with you first."

"As I said, you're afraid to take the blame if this proves to be a bad investment." An urge to crush the man swept over Mark.

Mr. Waverly blinked again.

Mark narrowed his eyes. "How long have you been a financial advisor with us?"

"About five years, sir."

"And have you previously felt the need to come to me for my 'blessing'" – how Mark hated that word right now! – "before you proposed an investment opportunity for our clients?"

"Sir, this is the first time I've considered investing in a new company."

"After five years, you don't feel you have the expertise to make the call yourself?"

"I was just trying to be polite, sir. I don't want to jeopardise your company's reputation."

"Then make sure you don't." He waved his hand imperiously. "This meeting is over."

With a subdued "Yes, sir," Mr. Waverly took his folder and left the massive office.

"Close the door behind you!" Mark yelled.

Regret quickly set in. He shouldn't have acted in such an ugly fashion. But hey, he was going to confession soon. The priest would absolve him for that – and the other thing.

Yet Mr. Waverly got on his nerves. Everybody liked him and he didn't have a rotten bone in his body. But if he was so weak that he couldn't handle a harsh word from his boss, he was in the wrong job.

Mark looked out of the window and watched his employees filing into the building from the car park below. What a bunch of losers! There was a good reason why he was the boss and they weren't: he had the guts and vision that made this company great. They did not, and would always play peon to his lord of the manor.

Boulder Enterprises might be the youngest investment company in the UK, but it was swiftly outstripping the established big players and Mark had plans to expand into continental Europe. When he was finished, his name would be the most famous of all the CEOs in this industry.

On the only occasion when he left his office, Rita avoided him in the corridor. She also sent the financials to him as an email attachment instead of bringing them in person. Mark missed her cosy visits, but it was better that way.

After work he walked to the local pub and had something to eat. Mary was probably burning his dinner, and he knew he was headed for another night on the sofa.

Chapter Three: King's Brambling
Tuesday, 12th February

He awoke at 6 o'clock the next morning with a crick in his neck but a happy idea in his head. He needed to go to confession, yes, but it didn't have to be a priest who knew him.

Gingerly rubbing his neck, he sat up and pulled his mobile from underneath the sofa cushions to search for Catholic churches at least an hour away.

It didn't take long to find one in a seaside village he'd never heard of, exactly sixty minutes' drive from his house. Confessions were offered every weekday, half an hour before daily Mass at 8:30 a.m. He wasn't interested in who the priest was; he only cared that it not be his local pastor. Or his brother-in-law.

Deciding to get the humiliation over with today, he dressed quietly and stole out of the house before Mary came down. He'd grab a coffee on the way to St. Jude's Church in King's Brambling.

*

Mark might have been able to appreciate the beauty of the countryside through which he was passing, had he not been preoccupied with formulating the precise words to use with the priest to minimise the seriousness of his sin.

A glimpse in his rear-view mirror would have revealed the slopes of Dartmoor, covered in coarse grass and dotted with rocky tors. Ahead of him, the landscape was becoming tamer. Fields of bright green grass flanked each side of the road, bordered by dark hedges and liberally sprinkled with white sheep.

Halfway into his journey, his route took him onto a narrow lane. Deep in thought about his situation with

Mary, and failing to slow down, he just missed hitting an orange tractor lumbering towards him. His first instinct was to give the farmer the middle finger, but the already precarious state of his soul prevented him at the last moment. Instead, he made a conciliatory gesture and reversed back up the lane into a passing space.

His self-restraint was rewarded by the discovery of a café on the outskirts of a tiny village and he looked forward to a steaming cup of coffee. But it was only 7:30 a.m. and the place was closed.

Grouchier than ever, he ploughed on until he reached a modern town with a supermarket that opened early and had a café area. He ordered a large mug of coffee and sat morosely drinking it by the store window.

It was beginning to sink in that he would never again enjoy carefree hours with Rita. Instead, he would have to suffer his wife's reproaches for the rest of their married life and constantly worry about her telling the kids. Their son and daughter were grown up and leading successful lives of their own, but had always looked up to Mark and still sought his advice. If Mary spilled the beans, that would stop.

He was slowly grasping the ramifications of his sin. Everything was fine while no-one knew about it. But everyone got hurt as soon as they did. Especially him.

And now, here he was, having to find a priest in the middle of nowhere so he could go to confession about a sin he'd not intended to share with anyone – not even God, as dumb as that sounded.

He finished his coffee and walked out to his BMW.

He turned on the engine and put the sleek vehicle into first gear.

*

Father James' Border Collie was running too close to the cliff edge.

The priest whistled, afraid the stiff wind coming off the sea would drown out the sound. But the dog stopped and looked at him.

"Good girl!"

She saw his hand dive into the pocket of his black windbreaker and knew what was coming. Her dark eyes focused on the old lacrosse ball. He flung it inland and with a joyful yelp she tore off in the direction of flight, nose lifted high, watching its progress.

Father James laughed as she caught her quarry a moment before it landed, her vision unfettered by the faintness of pre-dawn light.

"Well done, Judith!" He bent over and patted his thighs. "Over here!"

Judith raced towards him, with the rubber sphere in her raised mouth, pleased with herself. Two feet in front of him, she sat and opened her jaws, eyeing him intently.

"Good girl." The pastor stroked her head. He picked up the ball and threw it again.

This was a precious morning ritual, for once the day started in earnest, he'd have little time to spend with his dog.

It also allowed him to enjoy his beautiful surroundings. He'd lived at King's Brambling for thirteen years now, but the scenery still enchanted him. Rugged grassland extended a hundred yards from his little rectory next to St. Jude's Church, halting abruptly at the cliffs, some fifty feet high. They afforded a glorious view over the beach below and the English Channel beyond.

On the right side of his modest abode, the coastline

rose more steeply. Covered in dense undergrowth over treacherous terrain, it stretched for miles along the south-western shores of England, periodically curving inland to accommodate wide swathes of sand on its way to Cornwall.

To the left, the ground sloped gently and levelled out by a half-moon beach. On this sheltered area of red earth were built the houses of King's Brambling, established 1209, population 562. Any day now, Rebecca Luckton's overdue grand-baby would bring that total to 563.

Father James smiled, recalling the mother's frustration over the delayed birth. "He's determined to make a grand entrance, Father. It's as if he's worried that being my fifth, he'll get lost in the crowd."

"Don't worry," he'd reassured her, "as much as you love all your children, he's in no danger of that."

From his perch on high, he looked out over the vastness of the sea, watching the nascent glow of dawn sprinkle sparkling gems of red and gold over the water.

At times the Channel was quiet and unruffled, and the breeze barely perceptible. At others, it hurled furious waves against the sandstone cliffs, avenging some imaginary insult. On such mornings, hurricane force winds threatened to flatten Father James to the ground, despite his tall stature. But normally it was like today, with strong gusts reminding everyone that worse could come if the sea's mood changed.

The priest looked at his watch. In twenty minutes, he needed to be in the confessional.

Judith returned. She dropped the ball at his feet and he tossed it towards the church.

*

When he walked in ten minutes later, leaving his Border

Collie flopped in her dog bed at the rectory, three penitents were already sitting near the confessional.

The old-fashioned structure was ornately decorated, with a small cross on top. Made of solid oak, it rested against the wall to the right of the church entrance. Each of its two doors had a window in the upper half, covered by a red curtain. The one on the left opened onto the priest's booth with a small wooden seat. The penitent knelt in his own booth on the other side of the centre grille.

Father James walked past the pews on his way into the sacristy and carefully refrained from looking at the occupants. He recognized them in the confessional by their voices, of course, but it was important to maintain the illusion of anonymity; it encouraged more honest admissions of wrongdoing.

He put on a long white alb with the prayer, asking the Lord to purify his heart. As he tied the cincture about his waist, he asked to be girded with purity and that the virtue of continence and chastity might remain in him.

With a final prayer, he placed the violet stole around his neck.

He left the sacristy and, eyes forward, took his place in the confessional. Someone soon entered through the other door.

*

The fifth penitent of the morning walked in with a heavy masculine tread the priest didn't recognise. The steps hesitated, then headed back out.

Father James made a silent Sign of the Cross, sensing this person's unwillingness to confess. *"Lord, please grant him the courage to approach Your Mercy."*

The confessional door closed. Had the man left?

The pastor heard loud breathing and offered a quick

prayer of thanks that God had moved him to stay.

Guessing that he was standing – perhaps reluctant to kneel? – Father James began. "May the Lord help you make a good confession. In the name of the Father and of the Son and of the Holy Spirit. Amen."

He heard a faint "Amen" through the grille.

There was a loud groan as the man knelt down. "Father, it's been a few months since my last confession and I'm a little out of practice. Could you please talk me through it?"

"Of course."

He coached the man through the process and gave him his penance. "Now please say an Act of Contrition. You'll find one pinned to the wall on your right."

Haltingly, the man recited the words.

The priest then said the prayer of Absolution over him, concluding with, "May God bless you, in the name of the Father, and of the Son and of the Holy Spirit. Amen."

This time the man's "Amen" was loud and clear.

"Go in peace," said Father James.

"Thank you, Father, thank you very much."

The man left and when no one else came in, Father James exited the confessional.

Donning his vestments for 8:30 Mass, he was troubled by a nagging suspicion that the mystery penitent had held back a major sin – even though the priest had inquired of him if there was anything more on his conscience.

Another aspect of the man was bothering the priest. Something about him seemed eerily familiar, but he couldn't put his finger on it.

*

Mark Boulder walked out of the church feeling like a new man. He'd done it – he'd actually confessed his adultery!

The whole experience was absurdly easy. Granted, the pastor had been firm in his admonishment, explaining how much Mark had hurt God and his wife through his actions, as well as everyone else involved. But he'd also made it clear that God was ready to forgive him.

There was one small point, though: when asked if he needed to confess anything else, Mark wasn't up to discussing the other matter.

Maybe later.

Baby steps.

At least he could truthfully tell Mary he'd been to confession as she requested.

The best part about all this was that Bishop Marsden would be none the wiser about his affair with Rita. Mark could still look him in the eye. He hoped his wife wouldn't be mean enough to ask if he'd confessed to her brother.

He made his way down the path from St. Jude's that threaded through the tiny cemetery and under the lychgate to the car park.

Sitting in his BMW, he recited the prayers he'd been given as his penance.

Chapter Four: Luncheon at the Club
Tuesday, 12ᵗʰ February

While Mark was enumerating his sins in King's Brambling, Bishop Marsden was standing behind a long trestle table at the Ruddminster Community Centre, doling out soup to elderly folk who'd fallen on hard times.

Outside the modern red-brick building, a large banner announced that today, from 11 a.m. through 2 p.m., the Serving Seniors Charity was providing a large bowl of nutritious broth for senior citizens in need. It was a cold day and there was a long line of people huddled in the warmth of the hall, anxious to receive said nourishment.

A reporter from the Ruddminster Gazette had perched his camera behind the line of pinched faces passing in front of the bishop, and was recording the soup recipients' grateful comments. They were a motley crew. Most had accepted their lot, but some tried to maintain a façade of respectability by donning suits that cost a pretty penny back in the day, but now looked shabby with buttons missing.

It was hard for the bishop to watch this sad section of society parade in front of him. Thankfully, he could soon escape and enjoy a good meal with his brother-in-law – even if he wasn't looking forward to discussing the topic at hand.

At noon, after an hour of playing the holy hero, he announced he had to leave.

*

At the bishop's approach, Mark rose from his chair in the corner table of his club's dining room. "I found a quiet spot for us," he said, indicating the seat opposite.

The bishop sank into the spacious chair, upholstered in

dark red satin. "I must say, Mark, this is much more like it!"

"Oh, that's right, you were at the soup kitchen this morning. How did it go?"

"Depressing, Mark, very depressing. There but for the grace of God, and all that."

"Quite," said his relative, "quite."

A waiter appeared, all deference. "What will it be, Your Excellency?"

"A large g and t, please, Matthew."

The man bowed and left as quietly as he'd arrived.

The bishop placed his large hands, palms down, on the white table cloth. "Now, Mark, I've received some very disturbing news."

"Sounds serious."

"It's *very* serious." He took a deep breath. "One of my priests has just been in touch about an allegation made by one of his parishioners."

Mark frowned. "What allegation?"

"It seems this chap has got hold of some damaging information connected with Serving Seniors."

"What information?" This was not good.

"Apparently he's come across documents proving that the higher-ups in the charity are somehow directly responsible for causing the plight of the elderly whom they're supposedly helping." The waiter handed the bishop his drink, giving Mark time to formulate a reply.

Once the man was gone, he shot Mark a piercing look. "Do you know anything about this?"

The situation was tricky. They might be related and on good terms, but his brother-in-law was a respected cleric of the Catholic Church, of which Mark was hailed as an upstanding member. And Mark had just been to confession: he must not *directly* lie.

"It would be very helpful to know the exact nature of the allegations," he said.

"Don't prevaricate, Mark. Do you or do you not know anything about this?"

Mark remained silent.

The bishop sighed deeply. "Mark, I am heavily involved in this charity. I cannot be seen to condone any wrongdoing."

"May I ask the name of the priest who told you this?"

"What difference does that make?"

"None, but surely I have the right to know who is passing on these accusations?"

His relative eyed him dubiously. "His name is Father James Stryker, if you must know."

James Stryker? Mark's eyes darted sideways. *The same man he knew at university?*

"Would you mind describing him to me?" continued Mark. "I studied accountancy with a James Stryker at Ruddminster University. If he's the same man, it could be useful."

The bishop seemed to admit that possibility, for he said, "Tall, gaunt fellow," he said. "Earnest chap, honest face. Ring any bells?"

"That's him! He was an ardent Catholic even then — very old-school. Believed same-sex attraction was disordered. And enormously pro-life. He even talked a pregnant student out of having an abortion in her second year. She had to leave university and never did graduate — ended up being a home-maker somewhere in the back of beyond. And, of course, the boyfriend was made to marry her. Her parents helped support him in finishing his degree, since *one* of the unhappy couple had to earn a living. But it wrecked her life." Mark glanced at his brother-in-law, hoping these details would put his old chum James in a bad light with his bishop.

"Oh, dear, yes," agreed the prelate, "a lot of lives have been ruined by bullying young women out of terminating their pregnancies."

Encouraged, Mark shook his head. "Misplaced compassion."

"Well, I'm sure he's learned to be more tolerant in his views, otherwise it would have come to my attention before now."

Mark nodded sagely. "Where is he based?"

"In one of my lesser parishes on the coast. A tiny place called King's Brambling. You won't have heard of it."

Mark swallowed hard and his face went purple.

"What's wrong, man? You look as if you've encountered Satan himself!"

His brother-in-law gave a wan smile. "Just a spot of bother with my blood pressure."

"You need to get that seen to."

"You're right, I do."

The bishop's eyes bored into his. "Now look here, Mark, enough chitchat. I'm asking you again, are these allegations true?"

Mark Boulder took a long sip of gin and tonic. "Some aspects, perhaps."

The prelate's eyes were now thin slits. "What aspects?"

Forced into a corner, Mark gave a watered-down version of the truth.

When he finished, Bishop Marsden leaned forward and pointed a finger at him. "Two words, Mark; damage control. For Mary's sake and the sake of your reputation and mine, we're going to have to exercise damage control."

Their roast beef and Yorkshire pudding arrived and he exclaimed, "Looks absolutely splendid!" The waiter withdrew and he said in a lowered voice, "We need to draw up a battle plan. How well did you know this priest at Ruddminster?"

Chapter Five: A Special Offer
Wednesday, 13th February

It was four days since Father James had contacted Bishop Marsden about the worrying claims. During which time the parishioner who brought them to his attention had sent him multiple texts, asking what the bishop was doing about the problem.

He's a very busy man, the pastor replied, *he'll get back to me when he's ready.*

Now, at last, the hoped-for message was waiting for Father James when he returned to the rectory at the end of another long day. His Excellency's secretary informed him that the bishop wished to speak with him in private and would he please come up to Ruddminster tomorrow?

When the priest returned the call, it went to voicemail. He left word that he would be at the appointed place at the appointed time, and texted his parishioner with the good news.

"Praise God, Judith," he told the Border Collie, "our bishop is going to take care of everything."

The allegations concerned were of an extremely sensitive nature and he was relieved to be handing over the whole sordid business to his more competent superior.

He'd never been summoned to the bishop's palace before, and was curious to see the building about which he'd heard so much, in the city where he'd spent his student days.

His time at Ruddminster held fond memories for Father James. During his three years pursuing a degree in accounting at the university, he'd enjoyed an active life on campus and, when finances allowed, would walk into the city with his friends to dine in the less expensive eateries. One or two students even had cars, a rare thing in those days, and he recalled many a weekend trip into the countryside. They would stop in one of the small villages and sit outside to eat a sumptuous cream tea. This Devonshire luxury consisted of freshly baked scones, smelling divine and warm to the touch. They were split in two and smothered with a generous portion of clotted Devon cream, then topped with a large dollop of home-made strawberry jam. This treat was, of course, accompanied by a big pot of tea.

Even in those days, when his goal was to work in London and earn as much money as possible, Father James appreciated the beauty of the red earth and verdant grass native to Devon. On the drive back to his student housing, he'd marvel as the setting sun draped a gilded cloth over the scenery, transforming the wool of the grazing sheep into golden fleeces.

Once they were back in Ruddminster City and wending through streets of historical buildings juxtaposed with new structures, his mind would slowly return to the essay assignment he must finish before the morrow.

*

That was 34 years ago, and James Stryker was now a priest only half an hour away from where he'd graduated. First, he'd followed his plan and moved to London to work for one of the major accounting firms. But the strong faith which never left him, even at university, gave him a distaste for the machinations and greed of The City.

He tried working for a smaller accountancy firm in Devon, thinking he would be happier in a rural environment. But God continued to beckon, until James the layman finally understood that the financial world was not for him. He was being called to the priesthood.

He had never been happier than now, ministering to a tiny parish by the sea in his favourite county.

Thursday, 14th February

The next morning, after celebrating the 8:30 a.m. Mass, Father James coaxed his burgundy Triumph 2000 into life. It was one of the rare models still on the road, and her engine needed a few moments before she was ready to face the trip. As always, the priest said a quick Hail Mary to encourage her, then set off northwards to the home of his alma mater.

It amused him that Ruddminster was the only city many of the locals had ever visited. To quote the words of Mrs. Luckton's husband, eloquently rendered in the Devon accent, "Oi've got everything Oi want roight here in King's Brambling. What need do Oi have to go anyplace else?"

These sentiments precisely echoed Father James'. The village and immediate environs offered all a person could desire. A scenic shoreline with beaches and cliffs; glorious sea vistas; vibrant wildlife and hedgerows strewn with bright flowers. A mere hour away lay the rough terrain of Dartmoor National Park, with its wind-hewn tors, rocky streams, rugged grass, and hardy native ponies running semi-feral over several hundred square miles of open land.

There were only roughly 300 Dartmoor Ponies left now. On Sunday afternoons, Father James loved to steal a few hours and drive away from his humble accommodation on the south coast, along the winding country roads leading to the moor, where he would park his weary Triumph. Carrying a flask of tea and a packet of McVitie's milk chocolate digestive biscuits – his sole nourishment while cramming for school finals many moons ago – he'd wander onto Dartmoor's bleak expanse and climb up a tor to watch for the little horses.

Judith stayed at home; he didn't want her frightening the animals. It also allowed him to relish the delicious combination of soft chocolate and crunchy savoury biscuit without the dog making him feel guilty for not sharing.

The parish priest felt at peace up there. It was the perfect place to pray. The constant breeze blew through his grey hair, bringing to mind the words of Christ to Nicodemus, "The wind blows wherever it pleases. You hear its sound, but you cannot tell where it comes from or where it is going (John 3:8)." And whenever he spotted a pony, he was moved to thank God for the beauty of these beings and the whole moor. He felt as if the heavens had opened for his sake alone, allowing him to feast on their glory.

But his present journey was taking him directly northwards along the A380. The road ran between undulating hills of lush pasture, framed by privet hedges, horse chestnuts and oak trees, and speckled with white ewes and the occasional early-born lamb. Every so often he'd see the spire of a Norman church standing maternally over the roofs of the stone houses huddled close by.

He wondered for the umpteenth time whether, if pressed, he was required by divine law to reveal the name of his informant? He would far rather keep the man's identity secret.

Dear Lord, please give me the right words.

He worried, too, about the major player in the allegations. The man had the same name as his old university chum, with whom he lost contact a long time ago, when they graduated.

He fervently hoped this Mark Boulder wasn't the same man he'd known back then.

The old-fashioned clock on his dashboard told him he was on time. The faithful old car soldiered on through the Ruddminster suburb of Alfredston, once a village in its own right but now swallowed up by the city, and on to the amusingly named Toad Street.

Two turns later he found himself in Cathedral Square, admiring the massive Gothic structure of Ruddminster Cathedral. Built of local limestone, it boasted a Notre Dame style rose window encased in a huge arch, which dominated the face of the building. Two tall towers protected it, one on either side. The effect was breath-taking and Father James wished he had time to explore inside. But he wasn't here as a tourist: he had an important visitor to see.

As per the bishop's instructions, he drove down the left side of the cathedral to a magnificent Victorian mansion behind. In the large cobblestone courtyard directly ahead, a few upmarket cars were parked by the red brick walls. Justifiably called the Bishop's Palace, this place was the Taj Mahal compared to his one-bedroom rectory in King's Brambling.

He parked his humble transport next to a gleaming black Jaguar, then pulled his battered leather briefcase off the front passenger seat.

He had barely reached the front door when a young man in a brown friar's habit came out to greet him. "You must be Father James. I'm Brother John. Do come in."

After a shake of hands, the two retired inside, where Father James could hardly contain his awe. Red velvet covered the hallway walls, which were adorned with expensive oil paintings. Along one side, six feet apart, stood four plinths upon which reposed marble replicas of La Pietà, St. Joseph with Baby Jesus in his arms, Our Lady of Lourdes and St. Michael the Archangel.

Brother John led him to the far end and turned right down a corridor. He opened the second door on the left and held it for Father James. "Please would you wait in here? I'll fetch you when His Excellency is ready."

Father James wasn't given long to take in the plush furnishings of his waiting room before the friar returned. "His Excellency will see you in the garden. I'll take you there."

Disappointed not to see more of the palace, the priest followed Brother John's swaying brown cassock and registered the rhythmic click-click of the black beads of the long rosary hanging from his white cincture.

They came out on the other side of the building to a magnificent garden. Brother John continued across an expanse of manicured lawn to a copse of elms and Lucombe Oaks, then through a gap in the trees to a round lawn in the centre. At the far end stood a white marble statue of Our Lady of Fatima, about six feet high. To one side of her, on a wooden bench, sat Bishop Marsden.

Brother John bowed slightly. "Your Excellency, this is Father James Stryker." To the visitor he said, "I will now leave you."

"Thank you," said the priest.

The bishop, in a long black cassock was adorned with red buttons down the front and a wide red sash, waved a magnanimous hand. "Come here, James, please, come and take a seat."

Dressed in his plain black soutane, the priest walked towards his superior and dropped on one knee to kiss the man's large amethyst ring.

"No need for that, James." He tapped the empty space next to him on the bench.

Father James rose and sat at a respectful distance.

Bishop Marsden was not as tall as the pastor and carried many more pounds. His mouth was curved in a benevolent smile, but the green eyes behind his round spectacles failed to register the same generosity.

"I hope you don't mind," he said, "but I thought it would be a good idea to have our discussion away from inquisitive ears. This is the perfect spot, wouldn't you agree?" He indicated the trees surrounding them. "I love retiring here to meditate, with Our Lady to inspire me." The bishop pointed at the exquisite statue. "This beauty was a gift to my predecessor by a prominent Vatican cardinal. She was reputedly sculpted by Michelangelo's only known apprentice, and is made of the same Carrara marble used to create La Pietà. Isn't she stunning?"

Father James murmured his admiration.

His superior continued. "I have magnificent topiaries at the southern end of the garden – descendants of the original boxwoods planted by Sir Thomas More on a visit here in 1530. This truly is paradise on earth, James."

The priest mustered a smile, envisaging the tiny rectory garden with its large plastic statue of his beloved St. Francis of Assisi by the front door – a Christmas present from his parishioners.

Behind him sounded the cheerful voice of a song thrush. He stifled the urge to turn and see the welcome songster as the bishop cleared his throat. "Now, then, James, there's something I need to talk to you about."

The priest put a ready hand on his scuffed pigskin

case.

Bishop Marsden said, "For quite some time now I've been noticing how well you're doing down in King's – um – "

"Brambling," said the pastor.

"Ah, yes, wonderful name that, isn't it?"

Father James nodded, trying to squelch a confused frown.

"I understand you're very popular with your parishioners, who are most dutiful in giving to the Church every week. You've always met your budget, unlike many other parishes I could mention."

His subordinate accepted this praise with a bow, wondering why the bishop was only now noticing the faithful discharge of his duties?

"So, to show my appreciation of your tremendous service to the Church, and to our diocese in particular, I am taking you out of that backwater and sending you to a much larger parish."

Father James could not hide his astonishment. "I'm most grateful to you, Your Excellency, but I fear the parishioners of St. Jude's may not welcome the change."

The bishop shook his head disapprovingly. "We all know it's not about the priest, James, is it? At least, it shouldn't be."

"I can't disagree with you there." *Move from King's Brambling? Why, Lord?*

"It's highly unusual for a priest to remain in one parish for as long as you have. I'd say a change is most definitely overdue. And it will mean show-casing your considerable talents to a much larger audience." He smiled at Father James. "They've been wasted on a small community for far too long, James. We can't be hiding your light under a bushel, now, can we?"

The pastor of St. Jude's wasn't aware he had been. "May I ask to which parish I am being consigned?"

"Oh, didn't I tell you? Rumbleford. You'll be exchanging your views of the sea for the magnificence of Dartmoor. And your parishioners will no longer number twenty families or so. You'll have *four hundred* benefitting from your considerable wisdom. A much better use of your natural gifts." The bishop added, "And the church grounds are delightful. They're home to a particularly beautiful fountain, adorned with cherubs, which used to stand in the herb garden of Ruddminster Abbey. Legend has it, the abbot transported it to Rumbleford before King Henry's henchmen arrived to demolish the monks' residence.

"I'm sure you'll spend many happy hours communing with Our Lord out there."

Father James attempted an enthusiastic smile. Perhaps this move wouldn't be so awful. Maybe the bishop was right, and it *was* time for a change. However, what he thought was irrelevant. Obedience was one of the vows he took when entering the priesthood and he had no choice in the matter.

The sooner he made his acceptance clear, the sooner they could discuss those damning allegations.

"Thank you, Your Excellency. I will do my best to be a credit to you and Our Blessed Lord."

"Wonderful, James! I shall also be recommending you to the Holy Father for promotion to Monsignor. As I said, it's high time you were recognised."

"I don't know what to say, Your Excellency. That's way more than I deserve."

"Nonsense! Now, shall we say a prayer to conclude?"

But they weren't finished! Frowning, the priest opened the flap of his portfolio. "With all due respect,

Your Excellency, I need to confer with you about the worrisome evidence that a parishioner has brought to my attention." He tried to sound deferential. "You will recall I left you several messages about it? I thought that was the reason for my summons."

Bishop Marsden gave a discreet cough behind his ring hand. "Yes, yes, I recall something of that nature. Do you have the documents with you?"

Father James nodded and drew a file out of the briefcase.

The prelate took it from him and skimmed through the contents. "Is this everything?"

Surprised by the question, the priest replied, "The parishioner did intimate there was more. But he wasn't ready to offer it up until he was certain that you – er, the Church – was going to look into this."

"Perfectly reasonable, of course." Bishop Marsden looked at his watch. "Oh, dear, I don't have time to discuss this with you right now. Leave these with me, and I'll get back to you."

Father James swallowed his disappointment. "Yes, Your Excellency."

"Good man!" said the prelate, rising.

Father James closed his briefcase and got up, too.

In a gesture of friendship, the bishop shook his hand. "Wonderful talking to you, James. I'll be in touch, and good luck with your new appointment. I know you'll do a sterling job."

As the great man walked out of the thicket, the thrush renewed his singing. But it now sounded mocking.

Father James made his way through the gap in the trees and across the lawn to his car. The only saving grace of this meeting were that he'd not given away the whistle blower's name.

He climbed into his old car, keen to return to the peace of his 'backwater' and ponder the meaning of this meeting.

Half an hour later, when he opened the front door of his modest dwelling, his Border Collie bounded up to him. It was good to be home!

Ruffling the animal's ears, he told her, "Judith, I think I've just been had."

Chapter Six: Lovely Rita
Thursday, 14th February – Valentine's Day

Mark Boulder was anxious to know how his brother-in-law's meeting had gone with Father James, and pounced on his mobile phone as soon as he heard a text come through.

It wasn't from the bishop. It was Rita.

Mark, we need to talk.

Mercifully he was sitting in his office at work. Mary did not need to see this, and he would have to erase it from his phone before he went home, carrying the flowers, chocolates and card his secretary had bought for him to give her for Valentine's Day.

He sat and stared at the message for a full five minutes before replying, *Why?*

I'm pregnant.

What?! The blood rushed to his cheeks and a hammer seemed to be splitting his head open. *This can't be happening!*

He took a deep breath. Then he took another.

It was low of him, but he had to ask: *Whose is it?*

Her response was immediate. *Whose do you think?* Followed swiftly with, *I'm open to a paternity test. Are you?*

Now he'd made her mad.

This mustn't leak out to Mary or her brother. If this were to come out! It didn't bear thinking about.

What was he going to do?

First, he must placate Rita.

If you think it's mine, then I believe you. There, that should do it.

Her reply took a couple of minutes.

Good! We still need to talk.

A further exchange decided the when and where, then Mark deleted their entire conversation. He also removed Rita's contact information from his phone. Knowing Mary, she'd already noticed he hadn't yet done that.

Mark felt like a Christian martyr about to be stoned. He hoped against hope that nothing else would go wrong.

His phone rang and he jumped. It was Bishop Marsden's mobile number and he'd better have some good news.

"Mark?" came the familiar voice.

"Robert, how did things go with Father James?"

"I would say pretty well. He was rather surprised by my offer, but took it on the chin."

"Good. Did he bring up the other matter?"

"He tried, but I managed to thwart him."

"Excellent! Did you get the paperwork off him?"

"Ah, that's where things become a little tricky."

"How do you mean?"

"I did get *some* paperwork – "

"But?"

"Apparently, it's only a small portion of the evidence. Our priest's whistle blower has more."

"Damn!" Mark muttered under his breath. "Have you read it?"

"Not yet. I intend to go over it this evening."

Mark swallowed. Exactly how much evidence did those papers contain? And what was missing? "We've got to get hold of the rest!" He winced, hearing the note of panic in his own voice.

"That's your department, Mark. I've done my bit. Father James is expecting me to look into these allegations and get back to him with my proposed course of action. If I insist on him handing over the rest of the proof without concrete evidence that I'm dealing with these accusations appropriately, he will smell the proverbial rat and go over my head. Then we can kiss goodbye to containing this disaster."

"But he's being promoted, damn it! He's as good as accepted a bribe!"

"Now, now, that's not how we want it to be perceived. We have to proceed very cautiously. Moving to the new parish will keep him occupied for some time. It will also physically distance him from the whistle blower – whose name you must discover, by the way – and remove the pressure on him to resolve this problem. I've found a tame priest to take his place, who'll make the necessary murmurs, and the whole mess will soon go away."

As much as Mark wanted to be reassured by this spiel, he knew he wasn't in the clear until he recovered the missing evidence from that damned parishioner. He had to find out who he was and *make* him hand it over.

"I hope you're right, Robert," he said, without conviction.

"Tread carefully, Mark."

"Of course. When can I see what you've got?"

"Come to my place tomorrow for lunch. Let's say 12:30."

Mark gritted his teeth. Things were unravelling quickly and he needed to rein them in.

He found that writing problems down often helped him solve them. They could be safely typed into his laptop and then erased.

He opened a new file and began.

- **Rita:** How do I get rid of the baby, without Mary finding out – or anyone else, especially

Robert?

- **James:** Knows too much. Probably recognized my voice in the confessional telling him about my affair. Even though he's under the seal of confession, he might squeal on me.
- **Whistle blower:** Need to discover his identity and get that proof he's holding back from James.
- **Bishop Robert:** Have to make sure he doesn't find out about my affair with Rita, or her abortion, once she's had it.

He sighed. So many problems and so many people involved!

Now for the solutions.

Rita and the whistle blower he would silence with money.

It had already proved effective in getting Dave Miller, his company accountant, to keep quiet. Dave had tried to talk Mark out of investing all their oldest clients' savings in a scheme that looked too good to be true.

But Mark was looking for a quick way to boost Boulder Enterprises' reputation. He'd told Dave that the elderly were the ones who needed the money the least, and would be the least vocal if things went wrong, so why not invest theirs?

Dave tried again to get Mark to spread the risk over other clients' portfolios, but he refused.

When the shares of the company they'd invested in plummeted, Mark's 65 years old and over depositors lost all their money.

Other investment companies also lost clients' money in the scheme, not just Boulder Enterprises, and Mark played up this fact.

But it was imperative that he hide the truth that only his oldest clientèle had suffered the loss. Banking heavily on their not being organized enough to find out, he told them he would do his level best to recoup their money.

He'd started Serving Seniors as a way of obtaining the funds to give them, without their knowing he was directly responsible for their situation. The Catholic Church was one of the biggest single donors and Bishop Marsden's support of the charity was vital.

Dave threatened to go public about the whole fiasco, and Mark had increased the man's salary substantially to keep his mouth shut and delete all incriminating emails.

Originally paid out of company cash, that extra money was now coming out of the ample charity funds. Mark hoped Dave Miller wouldn't figure that out.

But as the company accountant, Dave could see it wasn't being paid by Boulder Enterprises anymore. He confronted Mark with his suspicions that Serving Seniors was footing the bill.

Mark pointed out to Dave that he was helping these wronged elderly people through his charity. He cared about them and was doing his bit to remedy the situation. Dave had capitulated when Mark reminded his accountant that taking a bribe was against the law, regardless of where the money originated.

Rita should be easy. She was always strapped for cash, and he'd made generous payments to her while they were seeing each other. If she played ball by keeping quiet and getting rid of that baby, he would continue to do so.

But he *must* discover the whistle blower's identity. Hopefully he or she would be amenable to a bribe and hand over the missing evidence.

Mark groaned. This was about to get very expensive. The payments would have to keep coming out of the charity, but how much longer could he hide that?

And what about Robert? And Mary? Neither of them must find out about the baby. Or the bribes.

Then there was Father James. Mark needed to keep an eye on his old university friend. Even if the priest had recognised Mark's voice when he confessed to the extra-marital affair, he was under the seal of the confessional and couldn't blab about it. But he'd figure out that his old chum Mark Boulder was the man involved in the seniors' money loss.

For now, Father James had only brought it to his bishop's attention. Hopefully he wouldn't spread it any farther.

He was probably unaware that Mark and the bishop were related by marriage, but at some point, he'd find out and approach Mark about it.

Meanwhile, the priest's parish move should, as Bishop Marsden said, buy them a little time.

*

Despite the gifts of chocolates and flowers, Mary gave him a frosty greeting when he returned home, and it was clear he was destined for another night on the sofa.

After a dinner spent in uncomfortable silence, she watched him arranging the pillows and blanket on the settee. "What are you doing that for? I haven't said you need to sleep here again."

"You're still mad at me, so why pretend you intend to let me sleep in my own bed?"

Hands on her hips, she asked, "Have you been to confession yet?"

"I went two days ago." This was humiliating.

"Why didn't you say so?"

Because it's none of your business. He shrugged his shoulders.

"I bet you found some out-of-the-way priest, didn't you?"

"Wouldn't you have?"

"You're a big wimp, Mark."

He turned his back on her and plumped up the pillows.

"Fine," she said, "you can sleep in our bedroom."

He wasn't a kid and this was his house. He didn't need her permission.

Yet he would pass a sleepless night next to her, carrying the double secret of Rita's pregnancy and his appointment with her on the morrow.

Instead, he used this opportunity to make his wife feel bad. "Maybe tomorrow. I'd rather stay here tonight."

Mary rolled her eyes. "Suit yourself." She turned off the main light as she exited, plunging the room into darkness.

Mark sighed at her pettiness and groped around for the switch on the side table lamp.

Chapter Seven: Mulling Things Over
Thursday 14th February

After the visit with Bishop Marsden, Father James kept himself busy for the rest of the day.

Action was preferable to dwelling on unpleasant thoughts. He took Judith on a second walk along the cliff tops that afternoon, and threw the lacrosse ball so often that she was exhausted and ready to come home well before him.

The next morning, he paid for his excess when his pitching arm twinged in protest as he elevated the Host during Mass.

On his return to the rectory, he vigorously sorted through the accumulation of papers on his desk, paid his bills and wrote cheques to a couple of his favourite charities.

Throughout this frenzied activity, Judith lay prone on the carpet next to him, eyes closed in deep sleep.

The priest smiled. His instinct was to bend down and stroke her silky hair, but he didn't want to disturb her.

It was six years since Farmer Yarrow had needed a home for the runt of his latest Border Collie litter. The pup was an unexpected seventh, coming a full hour after her siblings and a big surprise to the farmer.

But she was half their size and his wife had to make sure the little girl got a fair share of milk when her brothers and sisters pushed her out of the way.

Russell Yarrow didn't think she was cut out for farm work. "She'll never be tough enough for the job."

And so, one Monday morning after Mass, Father James found him standing outside the church entrance. In his arms lay the now weaned pup.

He had asked the handful of parishioners filing past if

any of them would like to take the dog. They all thought she was adorable, but no, thank you.

Father James was the last to exit, and bade the man a good morning.

"Would you loik this dog?" asked the farmer. He held out the ball of black fluff with a white band around her nose and a thin strip of white reaching from there to between her ears.

"Er, no thanks."

"She needs a good Christian 'ome," pursued the man. Nestled back in the crook of his arm, the puppy regarded the priest through myopic eyes. "She loiks you," her owner said.

"She can't even see me properly!"

Yet, despite himself, Father James leaned forward and stroked the little head. Her hair was so soft! She immediately pushed her nose into the palm of his hand and the priest couldn't help smiling.

"See? Oi tole you. She loiks you."

The pastor frowned. What did he want a dog for? He'd had them as a child, but had no business buying one now, not on his meagre salary.

Divining his thoughts, Farmer Yarrow said, "Oi don't want no money for 'er. Oi just want 'er to go to someone Oi can trust. She's the runt an' won't make the cut as an 'erding dog."

Father James still hesitated and the man cannily added, "Oi don't want to have to put 'er down."

What a low blow, threatening a priest with killing one of God's creatures.

"What's her name?"

"Ain't got one yet. *You* give 'er one."

With that, Farmer Yarrow handed over the puppy and bent down to pick up a plastic bag from the ground.

"This 'as all 'er stuff: water an' food bowls an' puppy food to git 'er started till you can go buy some."

"Thank you, Russell. I think!"

"You take care of that dog, you 'ear me? She come from good stock, that one."

"I'll do my best."

Father James was in shock for the next few days, trying to accommodate the needs of his parish with those of a constantly hungry baby dog.

But he quickly found that Judith, so named to complement St. Jude's, was a big hit with everyone. Being able to carry her around wherever he went allowed him to feed her when necessary, and she quickly became a great favourite with the sick and homebound. They looked forward to visits from the dog more than him.

Judith encouraged him to take daily walks. She was someone to talk to during the many hours of loneliness and always happy to see him when he came home. She loved cuddling up with him on cold winter nights.

Stretched out on the floor, the long-haired dog, now grown into a regular-sized Border Collie, opened one eye and seemed to say, 'We've come a long way together, haven't we?'

He laughed. "Yes," he said out loud.

He knew she was now half-way through her allotted lifespan, although he could always hope she'd be the exception of her breed that reaches 17 years of age. She got lots of exercise and he was careful to add fresh food to her diet. He smiled ruefully. It was all in God's hands. His job was to take care of her and enjoy her company for as long as she was with him.

After saying his prayers, Father James went to bed too tired to worry about his talk with Bishop Marsden.

Friday, 15th February

At dawn the next day, Father James examined the implications of his conversation with the prelate, with the powerful Channel winds pushing against him as he walked along the cliffs with Judith.

Was he being bought off? He hated to think so.

His parishioner would be anxious for a report on the meeting, and would have to be told the truth.

Rather than telephone the man, he would pay him a visit. It was the least he could do, given his not-so-great news.

Dave Miller owned a small cottage by the village Post Office. A confirmed bachelor in his late forties, he was already living there when Father James arrived at St. Jude's. He kept to himself, more at ease among his books on mathematics and the evolution of accounting than around people.

Father James had recently learned the man was the Financial Director for Boulder Enterprises, founded and run by Mark Boulder. It hadn't taken much detective work to discern that Dave's boss was the same Mark Boulder he was friends with at university.

It had greatly pained him to discover what his erstwhile room-mate had been up to, but he wouldn't let on to Dave that he was personally acquainted with the man.

At a quarter to eleven, Father James parked in the village. Judith trotted happily next to him as they walked around the pond, looking expectantly at his anorak pocket. Her owner chuckled. "Maybe on the way back, O.K.?"

They walked through a gate and up a short path precisely bisecting a tiny front garden. The flagstones were laid in meticulous order, and the flowers in the beds on either side exactly matched each other, reflecting Dave's passion for symmetry and order.

The priest fleetingly thought it might explain why no eligible woman had prevailed upon him to join her in matrimony. His rigid outlook would be hard to live with and left no room for spontaneous romance.

Be that as it may, Dave Miller had brought an irregular situation to Father James' attention and the onus was on him to ensure justice was served. If only he'd gone to someone else!

Judith sat obediently next to him as he raised the wrought iron door knock and let it drop with a loud clang on the iron plate.

*

A few minutes later priest and pup were in their host's cosy sitting room, with Dave Miller pouring them tea as part of his daily elevenses. Aware of this daily ritual, Father James had deliberately arrived in time for it.

In addition to tea, the McVitie's chocolate digestive biscuits that Father James so enjoyed were also on offer.

Judith was lying by the coffee table separating the host from his guest, ever hopeful that a crumb or two might fall to the floor and need her urgent attention.

Dave passed a full cup to the priest. "So, what's the news?"

Father James described yesterday's disappointing turn of events, and expressed his deepest regrets.

The Financial Director looked at him sharply. "I get the impression you don't believe the bishop is going to do anything about this. Am I right?"

"Much as I hate to suggest anything negative – " began Father James.

"Then, yes."

"I'm afraid we must consider that possibility."

"That's a shame. I was hoping my involvement could remain anonymous, but I suppose I shall have to make the facts public myself."

"I'm sorry, Dave. But won't that mean losing your job?"

"Yes." The man's face looked more careworn than usual. "But in the grand scheme of things it doesn't matter."

"How come?"

"I don't want this generally known, Father, but I've received a diagnosis that puts things in a different light. I have stage four pancreatic cancer and less than six months to live. Losing my job is nothing compared to losing my soul by not coming out with the truth."

"Oh, Dave, I *am* sorry. Please let me know what I can do for you – besides praying, of course."

"Thank you, Father. On the subject of telling the truth, would you be willing to take my confession?"

"Here and now?"

"Yes. Unless you feel Judith shouldn't hear it." He gave a wry smile.

With a chuckle, Father James stroked the animal's head. "I can vouch for my dog's discretion."

Chapter Eight: Mark Meets Rita
Friday, 15th February

Hoping their combined absences from the office would go unnoticed, Mark had arranged to meet Rita on Dartmoor the next afternoon. There was no way to 62rganize it out of work hours without rousing Mary's suspicions.

The bleak expanse was the only place he could think of where no one might see them together or overhear their conversation.

It wasn't the most chivalrous suggestion, given her condition and the low temperatures, but then neither was the proposal he was about to make.

He would confirm himself as a heartless scoundrel in her eyes, and that was the point. She mustn't regard him as anything other than a man paying off a woman to get rid of their baby and keep her mouth shut. There should be no mistaking this for a romantic tryst.

He spotted her sitting on the lower rock of a tor, fifty yards into the rough terrain, and pulled off the road. He parked as far as possible from her white Ford Fiesta, groaning as he saw the sticker on her rear window: 'Pray the Rosary.'

Dark gray clouds laden with rain were threatening to release their burden at any moment. Better make this quick; he hoped Rita wasn't going to be melodramatic.

The biting wind was picking up. He closed the thick wool coat around him and tied his belt in a knot. He should have brought a hat.

Bowing his head against the icy gusts, he made his way uphill to the massive pile of stones.

Rita's back was turned and she was shaking. He took a deep breath and came up behind her. When he touched her shoulder, her head swung around.

From under a blue knitted hat, her golden tresses cascaded over the navy coat he'd bought her for Christmas. She was also wearing the matching scarf and gloves he'd given her.

Despite them, she was shivering. Ought Mark to take off his own coat and put it around her? Probably. But that would give the impression he cared.

He used to, but not anymore. The woman was a liability.

He sat down two feet from her on the unyielding stone. "How are you?"

"Cold," she replied, looking hopefully at him.

"Yes, it is rather chilly up here."

She scooted up and put her arm through his. "That's better."

He declined to answer. Gazing at the moors he said, "So tell me about this baby."

Rita shoved him in the side with her elbow. "You mean, *our* baby."

"*Do* I?"

She jabbed him once more, harder this time. "Yes, you do. The paternity test is still on offer."

That again! "No, it won't be necessary."

"Then what are we going to do, Mark?"

Always Mr. Boulder in the office, he didn't appreciate this reminder of their intimacy outside work.

Withdrawing her arm, he placed her gloved hand on his knee. He covered it with his own and cleared his throat. "It's more a matter of what *you're* going to do."

Her hand stiffened. "What do you mean?"

"Well, it's obvious you can't keep the baby."

"Says who?"

He struggled to keep her hand on his lap as she tried

to pull it away. "Says common sense." He patted the blue glove.

Rita snatched her hand away. "What are you suggesting *we* do?" she repeated.

"Didn't I make myself clear? You need to get rid of it."

Her face took on a vicious expression. *"I WILL NOT!"* she shrieked. A sudden gust of wind whipped up her long hair. "How *dare* you even suggest it! Even if you're not a real Catholic, I am. I won't do it."

He sneered. "How can you call yourself a 'real Catholic' when you're carrying a married man's baby?"

Rita's eyes became venomous slits and her face turned crimson.

He waited a few moments to let her think this over.

"Look, I know you need money," he said gently. "I'll pay for the, um – procedure – then you can keep your job at the company, and I'll give you a generous salary increase."

"And if I don't agree?"

Counting on her need for cash, Mark hadn't reckoned with the woman's belated scruples.

He thought fast. "You'll have to fight me in court with your limited resources. It will take you forever, and in the meantime, you'll lose your job and your income." He had no idea whether this was true. "You'll be completely alone in the world because no one will believe I'm the father. And even if it's proved, public opinion will be against you for bringing down a beloved citizen." He peered at her. "Do you understand?"

Rita stared back. "Supposing I tell your wife that you're making me get rid of our baby? Think *she* won't believe me? She already knows about our affair."

This possibility had not occurred to him. If Mary knew he was forcing Rita to abort his baby, it would be the death blow for his marriage. And his cozy relationship with the bishop. *And* his image with the charity. It would all become public.

Time to change tactics.

A dull roar from the dark horizon announced an approaching thunder storm.

Mark rose and removed his coat. "Listen, the weather's about to turn nasty. Put this on and let's go back to my car and talk there."

She allowed him to put the garment around her shoulders, but looked wary. "You'd better not get up to anything," she warned. "You've got me into enough trouble as it is."

Mark forced a benevolent smile despite the biting cold. "Don't worry, that's the last thing on my mind." He held out the coat.

Rita got up and put her arms into the long sleeves.

Lightning flashed, quickly followed by a crash of thunder.

He grabbed her hand. "Come on, we need to hurry!"

The freezing rain hit just before they reached his BMW. Rita eyed him with suspicion as he groped around in his coat pocket under her right arm for the keys.

His hands trembled with cold and he had trouble pressing the remote button. He yanked open the passenger door for Rita to climb in, slammed it shut, then ran over to the driver's side. As he turned on the engine, he prayed it would quickly circulate warmth.

Outside, claps of thunder competed with the clatter of sleet hurtling onto the windscreen.

Mark was tempted to ask for his coat. Why didn't Rita take if off and give it back to him?

Heat began to replace the cold air and when he felt sufficiently thawed out, he turned to his ex-girlfriend, determined not to blow this. "Rita, honey, I don't know what else to do. If I admit paternity, I'll be ruined and I won't be in a position to give you anything. Mary will leave me either way, if she finds out about the baby, and I'll lose everything. My reputation is all I have.

"If I can keep that intact, I'll be able to make your extra salary payments, you'll get to keep your job and you won't have to bring up a baby by yourself with no money."

Stony-faced, Rita watched the ice chips collecting on the stationary windscreen wipers. "Doesn't it bother you that you're murdering our child?"

Mark winced.

"Do you care so little about me? And are you willing to throw away an innocent life to save your precious reputation?"

"Sweetheart, this is hard on both of us. In a different life, I'd leave Mary to be with you and raise our child together."

Her face didn't soften one iota.

"We can't live on nothing," he reasoned. "And it wouldn't be long before our poverty made us start despising each other." That awful word should get her attention.

Without replying, the blonde removed Mark's coat and handed it to him. He placed the damp garment on the back seat. The car was getting very warm and he turned down the temperature a few degrees.

Rita slowly took off the blue hat and shook out her wet hair, running her fingers through it and tossing it behind her.

Mark used to enjoy the teasing way she played with those golden tresses, but now he was just impatient for her response.

She made him wait an eternity. Then, eyes still forward, she said, "How much money are we talking about?"

Mark headed for home highly relieved. It had taken more persuasion than expected, but Rita finally fell for the payout.

They'd waited for the storm to pass, during which time Mark assured her that he still cared for her. He wanted her to keep working for him, so that he wouldn't be completely cut off from seeing her and could make sure she was O.K.

The truth was, just as in Dave Miller's case, he preferred to keep his bribe recipients close by.

His façade of having feelings for her worked. By the time he'd escorted her to her Fiesta, he was confident he could rely on her to keep her mouth shut.

As long as Mary didn't find out about the abortion, he needn't worry about Bishop Robert either.

That left the whistle blower and Father James to deal with.

Chapter Nine: Bishop Marsden Pays a Visit

Friday, 15th February

When Mark walked through the front door of his house that evening, Mary greeted him with, "You've got to see this."

Since her tone didn't suggest he was in trouble, he followed her into the kitchen.

On the central island sat her laptop, and the screen displayed the familiar figure of Father James in the green Mass vestments for Ordinary Time.

"Margie from next door told me about this." Mary tapped the white arrow hovering over the video and the priest sprang to life.

"I'm being transferred to another parish, and must tell you these truths while I still can. Stick to your Catholic faith and don't be brain-washed by popular opinion. Read the Council of Trent: it embodies the truths of the Church that Christ founded.

"My dear church family, please don't be misled by the secular world into believing that hell doesn't exist.

"Hell is a real place and those who flaunt God's laws are headed straight there.

"Many saints had visions of it, including St. Faustina, the Polish nun whom Christ chose to spread the message of His Divine Mercy.

"Take heed, those of you who scoff at the notion of hell, for she noticed that most of the souls there are those who didn't believe in such a place.

"She describes the many tortures, the first being the loss of God, followed by perpetual remorse of conscience. Then comes the dreadful knowledge that one's condition will never change. The fourth torture is the fire that penetrates the soul without destroying it. It is a terrible suffering, since it is a purely spiritual fire, lit by God's anger. Then there is the torture of continual darkness and a terrible suffocating smell, and, despite the darkness, the devils and the souls of the damned see one another and all the evil perpetrated by the others and themselves. The sixth torture is the constant company of Satan and the seventh is horrible despair, hatred of God, vile words, curses and blasphemies.

"Saint Faustina says that each soul undergoes terrible and indescribable sufferings, related to the manner in which it has sinned, with caverns and pits of torture inflicting differing forms of agony.

"Another truth you mustn't distort is that God made us man and woman. There are no other genders. Marriage is between a man and a woman and sexual acts between members of the same sex are against the natural law of God.

"And remember, abortion is murder. It's against the fifth Commandment and a mortal sin.

"A society that doesn't protect the unborn is immoral and dangerous – "

Mark almost put his fist through the screen in his zeal to shut the man up.

Mary looked at him in surprise. "That's a priest in our diocese. Apparently, he's in a tiny parish on the coast, but this has gone viral."

Mark almost choked in dismay. Bishop Marsden would be livid when he found out. There was no way he could let such a pedantic dodo move to a bigger parish. The man was a menace!

Oblivious to his reaction, Mary continued, "Aren't you proud to have such a faithful priest preaching the truth?

He's an absolute credit to the diocese. Robert must see this."

Not having properly embraced the progressive teachings of Vatican II, Mary didn't appreciate how upset her brother was going to be.

Bishop Marsden may have started out as old-fashioned in his faith as Mary, but he had moved on. She hadn't.

He had to alert the prelate before he saw the video without warning.

Smiling wanly at his wife, he said, "Yes, Robert does need to see this. I'll call and tell him straight away."

*

Barely ten minutes after Mark put the phone down, the bishop called him back.

"That priest is old-school and divisive, *and* I don't like his tone. I had no idea! I can*not* allow him to spread this nonsense. He's a loose cannon and must be stopped."

Saturday, 16th February

Following his conversation with Dave Miller, Father James left several messages with Bishop Marsden, saying he needed a speedy response to the allegations, as his parishioner was about to go public with them.

Around mid-morning on Saturday, he opened his front door in response to a knock and was surprised to see his superior.

"James!"

"Your Excellency." At last, he'd come to discuss the allegations.

The priest gave a small bow, since the bishop hadn't wanted him to kiss his ring at their last meeting. But the prelate stretched out an imperious right hand.

Father James duly knelt and pressed his lips to the four-carat amethyst on the large gold ring. He then rose and invited his guest in.

He was amused by the bishop's reaction to the difference between this humble dwelling place and his own palatial accommodation.

"Tea?" offered the priest.

"Thank you, yes."

Father James ushered the great man into his tiny sitting room and went into the kitchen to put on the kettle.

Judith was in the back garden, and gave a sharp bark by the kitchen door. Father James opened it and she bounded past him into the sitting room.

"Get off me!" the bishop yelled.

Father James ran in and grabbed the Collie's collar. "I apologize, Your Excellency."

"Please remove it," the bishop said stiffly. "I didn't come here to get dog hairs all over me."

"Come on, Judith."

Disappointed, the dog padded back into the kitchen.

"Place!" her owner ordered, and Judith obediently lay down on her bed in the corner by the pantry.

The kettle was boiling. Father James poured a little hot water into the teapot to warm it, swirled it around then tipped it into the sink.

He then added the tea bags, poured the rest of the boiled water over them and put on the lid.

He arranged the pot, a small jug of milk, bowl of sugar, and two cups and saucers on a tray, together with a large plate of chocolate biscuits from his last packet.

Bishop Marsden was leafing through the parish bulletin when his host deposited the tray on the tiny coffee table.

Once the two of them were sitting tea in hand, each with a biscuit resting on the saucer, Father James ventured to say, "Your Excellency, I take it you've come to talk about the Mark Boulder situation?"

The formidable man frowned. "What? Heavens no! I'm here to discuss that video you posted online."

Father James blinked. "I'm sorry, I don't follow you."

"Come, come, James. Are you going to pretend you've no idea your last sermon has gone viral?"

The priest was confused. "I assure you, I honestly don't know what you mean."

"For heaven's sake, James! Someone took a video of your Sunday sermon and posted it online, and now the thing has gone viral."

"I truly had no idea, Your Excellency. But is there a problem with my message getting out to people other than those here in the parish?"

With a deep sigh, the bishop put down his tea. He leaned back in the armchair, hands held together as if in prayer. "The problem is with the message, James, not with the number of faithful who've heard it."

"Once again, I must confess to being at a loss as to what you mean."

The prelate drew a piece of paper from the depths of his right pocket and began to read. "'Hell is a real place where those who flaunt God's laws are headed.'" He looked up at the priest. "Then you go on *ad nauseam* about the terrible tortures of hell. What *are* you thinking? People don't want to hear about hell, James. It's too frightening. It's not what they come to Mass to be told about."

"Your Excellency, I beg to differ! Where else are the faithful going to learn that hell really exists?"

"Why do they have to have their noses rubbed in it,

James? Where's your sense of compassion?"

"Is it really compassionate, to let my parishioners live in ignorance and behave in ways that lead to their damnation, when my job is to lead their souls to heaven?"

"Talk about heaven as much as you like, James, but no more harping on hell."

Father James was blindsided.

There was more to come.

The bishop continued. "'Marriage is between a man and a woman and sexual acts between members of the same sex are against the natural law of God,'" he read. "Have you no thought for the feelings of those in your congregation who are struggling with same sex attraction?"

Father James opened his mouth to reply, but his superior interrupted him. "'Abortion is murder,' you say. Does it not occur to you that you may have women in the pews who have had abortions? That they might be feeling terrible about it, and now you're condemning them?"

This bizarre perspective rendered Father James speechless.

Bishop Marsden leaned forwards. "James, this has to stop. I cannot promote you to a bigger parish if you persist in broadcasting such intolerant, unkind views. I beg you, think about the feelings of your parishioners, and tone down your rhetoric. Remember, Jesus meets us where we are; He did not come to condemn." Regarding him with blatant hostility, the prelate pointed a stern finger at his host.

Father James summoned his courage. "With all due respect, Your Excellency, yes, Jesus does meet us where we are, and no, He does not condemn. But He does ask us to repent and sin no more. If my parishioners don't even know what sin is, how can they repent and avoid it?"

"Encourage them to read their Catechism, James. That will put them right. But don't demoralise them in church." He read again from the sheet of paper. "'Read the Council of Trent, which embodies the truths of the Church that Christ founded!' James, you're undermining the Catholic Church's ecumenical efforts. We've moved a long way from the Council of Trent. For heaven's sake, that was in 1563! We're a conciliatory church now."

Father James took a deep breath. "Your Excellency, the Truth is unchanged and unchanging. It remains constant. It doesn't move with the times. When I die, I will have to answer to Christ, not the Church hierarchy. My job is to tell the Truth, in season and out, as St. Paul tells us."

Bishop Marsden's eyes were smouldering coals.

Father James refused to be put off. "What use is it if we gain the whole world but forfeit our souls? I must respectfully decline your request, Your Excellency, and continue preaching God's Holy Word – the undiluted version."

"I warn you, James, think hard about what you're doing! Until then, don't pack your bags. You are going *nowhere*!" He rose abruptly and stormed out of the rectory.

Father James sat down again and called Judith to him, glad of her comforting presence after this unpleasant exchange. In a few minutes, he would walk next door to the church and talk to God about this mess.

Sitting in his silver Mercedes outside the rectory, Bishop Marsden spoke on the phone with his brother-in-law.

"I'm relying on you to shut that man down, Mark. Use your friendship with him. And get that remaining proof off him!"

"Leave it with me, Robert."

Chapter Ten: Old Ruddminster Chums
Saturday, 16th February

Mark Boulder was tired. Cajoling Rita into having an abortion yesterday had taken its toll, not to mention sitting with his wife at home afterwards and pretending he'd had no further contact with his ex-mistress.

And now this request from his brother-in-law.

Not only was he expected to persuade Father James to tone down his orthodox message, but he must also talk the priest into handing over the rest of his evidence of Mark's malfeasance.

This double miracle was to be achieved while talking to a man of the cloth vehemently opposed to abortion, when he, Mark, had just pushed Rita into taking their baby's life next week.

He could not, in good conscience, go up to Communion tomorrow with this sin weighing him down.

But Mary would wonder what new crime he'd committed to exclude himself from the Lord's Table. How would he reply?

He glanced uneasily at his wife, who'd walked into the sitting room at the end of his conversation with her brother. "Leave what with you, Mark?" she'd asked, and he'd answered, "Oh, just some paperwork your brother needs from me."

That appeared to satisfy her.

But he needed an excuse to go to a different Mass from her this Sunday.

First, he must arrange to see Father James. But, if he phoned for an appointment, the priest would recognize his voice from the confessional – unless Mark disguised it. But he could hardly do that when the two met in person. No, that was a non-starter.

"What's up, Mark?" Mary's voice sounded suspicious.

"Nothing. But I could do with a walk. I've spent too many hours sitting at my desk this week, and it's a shame to waste this rare sunshine."

"It's not like you to go gadding about the countryside."

"I suppose not, but it's high time I took advantage of where we live. Care to join me?"

"No, thanks, I get enough exercise tidying up this house every day." She'd been making a lot of indirect digs at him lately.

Even with the sun out, it was still a cold day. He donned the same heavy coat he'd worn for his rendezvous with Rita, but took the precaution this time of wearing a warm woollen hat.

"Bye!" he said and walked out of the front door.

Dartleigh was a pretty hamlet close to Dartmoor, ten miles east of where Mark and Rita met yesterday.

The Boulders' imposing house, on the edge of the village, stood out from the other grey stone dwellings with their tiny gardens. The front gates were of wrought iron instead of the regular white-painted wood and opened onto a wide driveway through a large expanse of lawn.

A pair of stone sculpted Seraphim – Mary's idea – stood one on each side of the entrance. Mark thought they were over the top, but her bishop brother had applauded the choice.

Aware of his wife watching him through the sitting room window, Mark set off briskly along the once cobbled drive, now covered in tarmac.

Exiting his property, he headed away from the moors with their uncomfortable memories and proceeded along the narrow lane. Lined with tall hedges, it led south through glorious countryside where he could avoid running into anyone he knew, who'd want to indulge in tiresome chitchat.

Coming to a five-barred gate between the hedgerows, he paused to watch several ewes grazing while their lambs played without a care in the world. He rested both arms on the top bar and leant his chin on them, looking morosely at the peaceful scene. How wonderful not to worry about anything.

He recoiled from a face-to-face meeting with the same priest to whom he'd revealed his marital infidelity.

Not only that, but the man now knew he was behind the company scandal – having seen the damning emails – and *that* information wasn't under the confessional seal. What prevented his old chum James Stryker from telling the world about it?

Mark suddenly had a brilliant idea. If he pulled it off, the priest would be placed in a position where he couldn't expose Mark without bringing scandal on himself.

After catching the priest in his trap, he would then warn him to obey his bishop's demands and tone down his preaching. This would conveniently segue into passing on Bishop Marsden's request to hand over the evidence that the whistle blower was holding back. He'd hit on the perfect plan.

He checked his watch. It was lunch time and Father James should be in his rectory. Mark pulled out his mobile and called the pastor. Gone were the concerns about his voice being recognized as that of the adulterer in the confessional.

Their conversation was brief and to the point.

"Father James? This is Mark Boulder. I need to see you – today, if possible, please."

The priest didn't sound surprised to hear from him.

"Of course. Can you join me for afternoon tea?"

*

Mark walked home and told Mary that an old university friend had asked him to his home on the coast for tea. He understood the village had a charming little church and thought he might attend the Saturday Vigil Mass while he was there.

Mary looked askance at him, assessing whether he was being honest. But his eyes remained steadily on hers without flinching, and relations were so strained between them, that she gave the trip her blessing.

"I'll be back in time for dinner."

Mark jumped into the BMW and made his escape before she changed her mind.

Once again, he was oblivious to the countryside as he sped down to King's Brambling, and in just under an hour he reached the pitifully small rectory next to the tiny church of St. Jude. From the outside, the priest's quarters didn't appear large enough to accommodate even one bedroom.

Mark lifted the heavy black door knock and let it fall on the plate with a loud clang that set his teeth on edge. He was not looking forward to this.

His watch read 3 p.m. He was exactly on time.

The door opened and an older version of the James Stryker he'd known at Ruddminster University stepped out.

As tall as ever, with not even the slightest hint of a stoop, the priest had not put on any weight. He had the same benign expression on his face and the only signs of advancing age were a few deep lines around his mouth and along his brow. Otherwise, apart from having exchanged his student jeans for a long black cassock, he was the same man Mark remembered arguing with all those years ago.

"Great to see you, come in! I've made us a good strong pot of tea. Let me take your hat and coat."

Mark handed over the items of clothing and followed his friend down a narrow hall into a minute sitting room. Father James indicated a sofa on the other side of a small coffee table from a cheerful fire burning in the hearth.

"How do you feel about dogs?" he asked his guest.

Puzzled, Mark replied, "No strong feelings either way."

"It's just that I have a rather exuberant Collie in the kitchen who'd love to come and say hello."

Mark laughed. "Absolutely, let her in by all means."

"Thank you." The pastor exited the room and opened the kitchen door, out of which a blur of black and white came bounding up to Mark, thrilled to see him.

Her enthusiasm was infectious. He stroked the silky head, wondering why he'd never thought to have a dog?

"What's her name?" he called out.

"Judith!"

At the sound, the dog trotted obediently back into the kitchen.

"She heard her name and thinks you want something from her," Mark said.

"Good girl," said Father James. The Collie padded behind him as he re-entered the room bearing a large tray of tea things, which he placed on the miniature table.

Judith showed an interest in the chocolate biscuits and her owner said sternly, "No, Judith, lie down."

The dog did as she was told.

"Impressive," Mark said.

"She's bred to take commands, and listens well. Milk?"

"Yes, please."

They sat and talked about the paths their lives had taken since university, snacking on the biscuits and sipping tea.

"Do you still play the piano?" asked Father James. "I remember being in awe of your musical talents."

Mark smiled, remembering how he would sneak up to the university piano rooms with James, and how much he enjoyed his friend's adulation as he recited his favourite pieces.

"I'm afraid I only tickle the ivories at Christmas these days," he said. "Mary likes to sing carols and make us all join in."

"That's a pity. I loved listening to your renditions of Saint-Saëns' Second Piano Concerto, and wishing I could play."

"Thank you, but I resented my mother for forcing me to learn the piano so a residue of bitterness hung over all my performances."

"That's such a pity! I'd never have thought it from the way you played."

"Thank you. I'm glad it didn't show."

"I always think that music lifts the soul closer to God," observed Father James.

Mark took the opportunity to say, "Do you still hang onto your old Catholic views?"

Father James peered over his cup. "How do you mean? I am, after all, a Catholic priest."

"Well, for example, do you believe in correcting sinners, showing them the error of their ways, and all that?"

"Of course, Mark. That's part of my job."

"But isn't that rather old-fashioned? Sin isn't what people want to hear about these days, is it?"

"I doubt whether the residents of Sodom and

Gomorrah wanted to hear about sin, either, and see how that worked for them. Or the people in Noah's day. Or – "

"O.K. I get it," interrupted Mark. "But can't you be more uplifting?"

The priest's knowing smile told Mark he knew he'd been sent here by the bishop. "I think preaching the Good News is uplifting, don't you?"

"Tell me the 'good' part."

"That God wants us all to be in heaven with Him and is doing everything He can to achieve that end, including sending His Son, Jesus Christ to redeem us. God is Mercy Itself and always ready to forgive."

"That's more like it!" Mark was making headway. "Your parishioners need to hear that. They don't like to be made to feel guilty all the time. It's terribly demoralising."

Father James continued. "But I can't just tell them half the message, Mark. God isn't going to forgive us unless we ask Him to."

"But you just said that He's always ready to forgive."

"He is, but first, we have to confess our sins and be sorry for them. That means acknowledging that we *have* sinned. In order to do that, we must accept that sin exists."

"It always comes down to sin with you, doesn't it James?" Mark was disappointed.

"No, it comes down to repentance. You know that as well as I do. We have to admit to having sinned, and change our ways and follow God's commandments."

Mark suddenly felt hot around the collar. "That sounds very self-righteous."

"I don't understand what you mean."

Mark didn't know what he meant, either. He'd just

thrown it out in self-defence. This conversation was making him very uncomfortable. "I mean, you sound as if any Catholic who doesn't believe in sin and confess is doomed."

"That pretty much covers it. I don't see what's so self-righteous about telling the truth." The pastor peered at him. "How well are you sleeping at night, my friend?"

The non sequitur took Mark aback. Thinking about his nights on the sofa, he snapped, "That's totally irrelevant."

"If you say so." Father James leaned forward. "But I sense things aren't going well for you, Mark. Care to share? Perhaps I can help."

Mark shifted uneasily in his chair. This wasn't supposed to get personal. "I don't need your help, thank you."

"O.K., but speaking as an old friend, I hate to see you so unhappy."

"It's nothing I can't handle, thank you." He had to get this conversation back on track.

"Well, I'm always available to talk to, if you need me."

For a split second, Mark was tempted to take him up that offer: he was feeling very alone with his mounting problems. But Father James was the enemy. He knew too much.

A voice cut into these thoughts. "Are you aware that a deliberately incomplete Confession is not valid?" His supposed friend was back in priestly mode.

Mark swallowed. "How do you mean?"

"If you intentionally omit grave sins, you are not forgiven."

"Are you accusing me of purposely holding back a grave sin?"

Father James put his cup and saucer down on the tray.

"Are you?"

Mark bristled. "You don't have the authority to ask me that and I didn't come here to be lectured, James. I have a much more pressing topic to discuss with you."

"I'm not sure what could be more pressing than the state of your immortal soul."

Mark said feebly, "Well, this is."

Father James shrugged his shoulders.

Irked, Mark said, "Look, the bishop asked me to come and talk to you about your rather – er – traditional Catholic views."

His host looked confused. "What other type of Catholic views are there?"

"Oh, come on, James, the Church has moved on since the days when you spouted your old-fashioned lines at university. You can't go around undermining the good work that's been done to modernize Church teaching."

"Can you give me an instance of how I'm doing that, please?"

"Well, that line of yours about abortion being a mortal sin, for example. I saw the video of your sermon."

"What about it?"

Mark avoided the clergyman's eyes. "There are times when abortion is the only answer."

"Could you please give me an example of when murdering an innocent baby is justified?"

Mark sputtered, "That's a rather extreme way to put it!"

"I think it's a very truthful way to put it."

The man was infuriating.

"Well," Mark said, "for example, when it's only three months along, you can't tell me it's an *actual* human being."

The priest's expression was hard to read. "You know as

well as I do, that it's an 'actual baby' from the moment of conception. And at three months in the womb, that baby is fully formed with a heartbeat. If that's not an *actual* human being, then what is it?"

Mark swallowed again. Rita was due to have the abortion next week. "What about if the baby isn't wanted?"

"What about all those couples who can't conceive and would leap at the opportunity to adopt the child?"

Honestly, the man had an answer for everything.

"What about a deformed fœtus?" Mark challenged.

Father James was unruffled. "You're still talking about a human being."

"That will have no quality of life," retorted Mark.

"*Who* will have a different quality of life from others," corrected his host, "but is nevertheless a child of God. It is not for us to decide who lives and who dies, Mark. I don't understand why you think the Catholic Church would have changed her position on that."

Mark cleared his throat. "In the past, the Church has been altogether too strict. She needed to ease up on some of her overly severe attitudes about certain things."

"You mean, she should bow to public opinion."

"That's not fair, James. The Church has been losing members over the years and we need to get people to come back."

"She's lost people because of watering down the Faith."

Mark sighed. "I can see you're not willing to even try and understand the other side of the argument."

"I'm not willing to compromise on what I know to be the truth."

Mark shook his head. "Everything was – and still is – so

black and white for you. You might live in a cosy religious bubble here in your tiny village, but life isn't so cut and dried in the real world. Is that why you bailed out on your accounting career?"

The priest frowned. "I'm not going to dignify that with an answer."

"Because you know I'm right."

"No, but believe it if you like."

"The bishop can't promote you to a bigger parish or recommend you for monsignor if you won't toe the line, James."

"So he told me. But I'm not looking for promotion or fancy titles. I'm happy doing God's work right where I am."

"Then it must be annoying that a parishioner foisted information on you that *you* had to act on, instead of handling it himself. Or herself." Mark scrutinized the priest to see if his face gave any indication of the whistle blower's gender. It didn't. "Surely whoever that person is should have gone straight to the bishop with it?"

"I grant you, that would certainly have made my life a lot easier."

"Isn't it possible for you to tell him – or her – to take the matter into their own hands and leave you out of it?"

"The individual has his own reasons for entrusting me with the mission."

Ha! Then it was a man.

"Or maybe I should say, 'her' reasons," added Father James, with a wink of his left eye.

Mark smirked. *Too late, padre!*

Or was he?

Mark finished his tea and held out his cup. "Any more in there?"

The tea pot was small and it was sure to be empty.

Father James picked it up. "I'll make another."

The priest left the room, with Judith padding behind him.

Mark rose from his chair and wandered to the kitchen. "Where can I find the men's room?"

"Down the hall, last door on your left."

"Thanks!" On the way, Mark peeked through the first open door to his left: the priest's office. He had a little time to search for that evidence before the kettle boiled.

In the tall bookcase behind the pastor's desk, he spied a thin blue file nestling between volumes two and three of Thomas Aquinas' *Summa Theologica.*

That had to be it!

He heard Father James go back into the sitting room, and hurried to the toilet, where he pulled the chain and washed his hands noisily.

As he came out again, Father James called from the kitchen, "I'll be with you in just a couple of minutes."

That's all Mark needed.

He dived back into the office, sneaked behind the desk and grabbed the file.

He'd just pulled it away from its hiding place when a voice behind him said, "I'm not sure you'll find the information in there very helpful."

Embarrassed, Mark shot back, "You're just bluffing."

"Go ahead, see if I am."

Eyeing him with malice, Mark opened the file. It contained the minutes of the last parish meeting.

"As I said, I don't think you'll find the information very helpful, but maybe I'm wrong. I can't say *I* found it that riveting."

Furious, Mark suspected the priest had put the file

there deliberately to mislead him.

Father James said soothingly, "Come and have some more tea."

Mark slammed the file down on the desk and stomped morosely out of the room. He had no desire to spend a moment more in this rectory.

But he had still not achieved his objective. He thought of his promise to the bishop that he'd retrieve those missing documents.

When they were once again seated with a cup of tea, Father James asked blandly, "What were you looking for in my office?"

Mark felt his face redden. "You know perfectly well what."

"I take it you're anxious about obtaining the rest of the proof regarding your involvement in the senior scandal. A scandal which will ruin your standing in the community and also poses serious legal questions."

Mark was again losing his grip on the situation. He countered, "How very unchristian of you, a priest of all people, to harp on the possible consequences of – er – what's happened."

"I'm just telling the truth, as I always strive to do."

"You have a pretty underhanded way of doing it."

"I can't help your reaction to how I do things."

"You *could* give me everything you have."

Father James said innocently, "I've given Bishop Robert more than enough to work with."

Mark decided to be direct. "Who's the parishioner who came to you?"

"I'm not at liberty to reveal his identity. He came to me in confidence."

Ha! It *was* a man! "I'm going to find out, you can be sure of that."

The priest smiled. "You will, when he's ready to come forward."

"When will that be?"

"That's up to him. I have no influence over his timing."

Mark stood up. "I'm wasting my time talking to you, James. You're the same narrow-minded man you were back in uni. I don't know why I thought you might have changed."

"Neither do I." The tall pastor rose from his chair. "I'll get your hat and coat."

Out in the hallway by the front door, Mark fairly snatched them out of his hands. "Good bye!"

He climbed into his BMW having accomplished none of what he set out to do. He was no closer to retrieving the rest of those documents, and how would Robert receive the news that his rural priest still wouldn't sit down and behave?

Mark definitely wasn't going to attend the Vigil Mass at St. Jude now. He'd just have to lie to Mary and tell her he had. After the other sins he'd already committed, what difference did one more make?

Chapter Eleven: Rita's Loss
Saturday, 16th February

Still thawing out from her freezing rendezvous with Mark, Rita crawled under the bed covers in her little flat on the outskirts of Ruddminster.

How could she have let herself be trapped and blinded by the boss's flattery? See where it had landed her!

If only she could turn to someone for comfort and advice; but no one must know. She wanted to pray, but why would God listen to the likes of her?

The bed's soft warmth lulled her into an uneasy sleep, where she dreamed of giving birth to a monkey with little red horns on its head and a menacing spike on the end of its tail.

*

Early the next morning, she brewed a strong cup of coffee, then sat bleary-eyed in front of her laptop, searching for the nearest abortion clinic. Hopefully one would be open over the weekend.

She was in luck. Ruddminster Women's Health was open 24 hours a day, with consultations between 9 a.m. and 7 p.m.

The online photo of a drab one storey building did nothing to raise her spirits as she scrolled down to read about 'available procedures.'

Being over 9 weeks and under 19 weeks pregnant, she was eligible for a surgical abortion. The site assured her it could be done in one appointment and she should rest at home for at least a couple of days afterwards.

There was no reference to a baby, but frequent mentions of 'womb contents.'

Did the use of this euphemism mean the staff knew abortion was wrong? Or was it to save the sensitivities of abortion-minded women and make it easier for them to choose this gruesome method?

No matter how they glossed over the truth, Rita couldn't pretend not to know exactly what happened during the 'removal of the womb contents.'

It sickened her. But what was she supposed to do? Mark was right. If she kept the baby and lost her job, she would have no income to pay for her child. Her parents, strict Catholics living in the north of England, would be too ashamed of their daughter to take her in. They were both active in their local church and reputation was everything to them.

The only pregnancy crisis centre in the area had been forced to close down for lack of local support.

She dialled the clinic number.

Monday, 18th February

Rita couldn't bring herself to plan an abortion on the Lord's Day, so she drove to her appointment at the clinic on Monday after work.

"How far along are you?" the lady doctor asked.

"Three months."

The woman noted this in her pad. "Then you're still eligible for a surgical procedure." She beamed while imparting this wonderful news.

Rita managed a faint smile. "Shouldn't you do an ultrasound, just to make sure I'm right?"

"Oh, dear, no! That would not be good. If your GP has told you you're three months along, I believe you."

"Oh, O.K."

After that, she was very kind. She avoided any unpleasant details, just as the website had done, and played up how Rita would soon be free to enjoy life to the full, with no tiresome responsibilities.

The woman's upbeat attitude was more uplifting than the thoughts that had been swirling around Rita's head during the past few days. Maybe this wouldn't be so bad after all. Maybe it *was* the right decision.

Tuesday, 19th February

The surgery was scheduled for 9:30 a.m. the next day. Rita texted Mark to let him know she wouldn't be in the office until Friday and why.

If only she had a friend to drive her to the clinic, as their paperwork recommended!

Parched and hungry from having no food or drink since last night, she arrived half an hour early, as instructed, and parked on the side of the building where her car didn't risk being seen by anyone who knew her.

The long line of women waiting outside the clinic worried her. She should have come sooner; it would take way longer than thirty minutes for all these ladies to be processed ahead of her!

As she walked to the front of the building, she noticed all those women were praying the Rosary together. They weren't here to have an abortion. About twenty of them were standing on the pavement, careful not to block any visitors or trespass on clinic property.

They were reciting Tuesday's Sorrowful Mysteries.
How apt!

She slunk along the grass by the wall to avoid interaction with them. But one of them turned and locked eyes with Rita. The woman's expression was of compassion, not reproach. "Holy Mary, Mother of God," the woman was saying, "pray for us sinners, now and at the hour of our death."

Without thinking, Rita said "Amen."

Then she hurried into the building.

*

The next hour was a blur. Before she was put under, she handed over the referral letter from her doctor, hastily faxed to her flat yesterday, her blood group card and health insurance details. When asked if she had anyone to drive her home, she nodded.

Sixty minutes later, she was lying on a narrow hospital bed in a small room, feeling very sore down below. A nurse stood over her, telling her it 'had all gone extremely well. Your friend can come and take you home in forty minutes.'

The nurse left.

Rita gasped for breath, overcome with anguish at the horror of what she'd done, and wept bitterly.

*

She left the building forty minutes later, having assured the staff that a friend was standing outside. Her right hand clutched a sheet of instructions: 'Shower instead of taking baths, use sanitary pads instead of tampons, avoid swimming, and avoid sexual intercourse for at least two weeks until the bleeding has stopped.'

Even if the physical bleeding stopped within two weeks, Rita knew the emotional bleeding would take much longer – if it ever stopped at all.

The same woman whose eye she'd caught earlier was still standing outside. Surely this pro-life person hadn't been watching out for her all this time?

Staring at the ground, Rita weaved her wobbly way across the front lawn and was about to turn the corner to the car park when a gentle voice said, "Are you alright, dear? Who's taking you home?"

Rita leaned against the wall for support and tried to sound defiant. "I'm perfectly fine, thank you! Please leave me alone."

"I'm sure you are, dear," the lady replied, "but let me accompany you to your car and make sure you get in O.K."

"If you insist." She was too feeble to argue.

"Give me your arm. That's better."

Rita allowed herself to be led like a little child to her Fiesta.

The lady waited for her to pull the car keys out of her handbag, then helped her in. "Would you like me to drive you home? One of the other ladies can follow us and bring me back."

Feeling more in control now she was in her own vehicle, Rita shook her head. "No." Her voice softened. "But I appreciate the offer." This lady's kindness had come exactly when she needed it.

"Then I'll leave you, dear. You take care of yourself." She smiled broadly. "And don't forget to follow the advice on your rear screen."

The woman walked away, leaving Rita confused until she checked in her rear-view mirror and saw what she meant.

She sent a quick text to Mark. *It's done.*

Then she pulled a Rosary from the outer zipped pocket of her handbag. Fingering the pearl beads, she hesitantly prayed, *Our Father, Who art in heaven, please forgive me, for I have sinned! Our Lady, please intercede for me!*

*

So busy reciting the five decades of the Sorrowful Mysteries while she drove, she was back at her flat before she checked her phone for Mark's reply.

The thumbs up emoji.

Chapter Twelve: The Bishop Gets Angry
Wednesday, 20th February

Until now, Mark had skilfully deflected Bishop Marsden's numerous texts demanding an update on the "Priest Problem."

But this morning he received a phone call from his brother-in-law's secretary.

"Mr. Boulder, the Bishop requests your presence at the palace at 11 o'clock this morning."

Not a friendly lunch invitation, then.

He told Brenda that he was meeting with a business associate and was only available to answer urgent calls. He fervently hoped an office emergency would cut short his uncomfortable session with Robert.

On arriving at the Bishop's Palace, Mark was led by Brother John, not into the lavishly decorated parlour as on previous occasions, but across the garden to a circle of tall trees enclosing a hidden lawn. Within, Bishop Marsden sat on a long wooden bench, by a marble statue of Our Lady of Fatima.

His expression was not inviting as he motioned impatiently for his visitor to come and sit down. Mark was in audience with a peeved prelate, not popping in on a close family member.

He approached with dread as Brother John discreetly withdrew from the copse.

"Now then, Mark, no more prevaricating. What's the situation with Father James?"

Mark reported the details of his meeting with the priest, carefully highlighting the pastor's obstinacy and playing up his own defence of the bishop's position.

The bishop's face went through deepening shades of red during this recital and settled for a purplish hue.

Barely able to contain himself, he asked, "When *exactly* did you visit Father James?" His eyes narrowed. "And don't lie to me."

Mark mumbled, "Saturday."

"Saturday?" roared the cleric. "You've known all this time and didn't think to tell me?"

"I've been extremely busy."

"What is more important than handling this mess?"

The other mess I'm in, thought Mark. "You're right, this should have been my top priority."

"You never said a truer word."

The bishop snapped open the locks of a dark red leather briefcase. Crafted by Swaine Adeney Brigg, makers of the attaché cases used in the James Bond films, it was allegedly given to him by a grateful parishioner, but Mark always suspected the man of having bought it himself. His heart sank as he watched him pull out a file.

"I've been through this and it's a lot worse than I thought." He looked menacingly over the rim of his tortoiseshell glasses. "You're in a great deal more trouble than you originally let on, Mark."

His brother-in-law put on a hurt face. "How so?"

Bishop Marsden's green eyes were scornful. "Not only are you implicated in the reckless investment of your older clients' funds, but there is also the troubling suggestion that the charity's finances are being used to pay bribes." He took on a bland expression. "Care to elucidate?"

Mark didn't care to at all, but he had no choice. "Look," he began, "things got tricky very fast and I had to do something to protect the company, to protect us –

to protect Mary."

"Spare me the soppy speech and tell me the truth."

Speaking more to the grass underfoot than to the angry man, Mark confessed to having used charity money to stop his Financial Director from blabbing the truth. And he didn't want those payments – "Bribes, Mark," the bishop interrupted, "let's call them what they are," – to show up on the company books. They were described in the charity files as donations and were made in the name of a non-existent sponsor.

It occurred to Mark that his FD was the only one with access to both sets of accounts. He also knew about the bribes, being the recipient.

Was Dave Miller the mole? If so, why would he jeopardize his substantial extra income by risking discovery as the bribe taker? And why had he gone to Father James?

Mark needed to check up on the quiet man who made such a show of caring about nothing except his accounting library.

As for Bishop Marsden, he was co-treasurer of the charity in name only. He had no signatory powers and never became involved in its transactions. Mark had made sure of that. But now the cat was out of the bag.

The furious bishop enunciated his words very slowly, as though speaking to a dim child or a foreigner. "If you don't put a lid on this charity scandal before it breaks, I'm going to distance myself from it and resign. And if I do that, people will ask why. Especially Mary."

The noose was beginning to tighten.

Mark tugged at his collar uncomfortably; where was the money going to come from to keep Rita quiet?

Chapter Thirteen: Devon Cream Tea & Sympathy
Friday, 22nd February

Rita was sore and miserable during the two days following her surgery. Any movement was painful.

But by Friday morning she was sick of her own company and needed the companionship of other people. 'Other people' meant Mark, from whom she hadn't heard, and from whom she still hoped for sympathy.

She dressed carefully and paid special attention to her makeup, determined to appear fully recovered.

Her given reason to human resources for not coming into work since Monday was food poisoning, so when she stepped into the office, the staff expressed hopes that she was feeling a lot better. Had she eaten out somewhere? If so, which restaurant? They must all be careful to avoid it!

Rita attributed her illness to a bad piece of fish, but declined to give the grocery store a bad name by saying which one she'd bought it from. It could happen anywhere, she said magnanimously.

Happy to be told she looked as amazing as ever, she took her seat in accounting, anticipating a visit from Mark. It had been a whole week since she'd seen him, and despite everything, she missed him.

She waited in vain. Mark didn't come near her. When she walked past his open office on the way to the water cooler, his eyes were glued to the papers on his desk.

Even when she stood talking with a colleague outside his door, laughing more loudly than usual to make sure he heard her, there was not an iota of interest. He remained engrossed in his work.

She knew then that he was avoiding her. Did he worry she'd say something to embarrass him? Or was it out of guilt? Hopefully the latter.

His behaviour hurt badly and she was tempted to shout out the truth and to hell with the money!

But she needed it, and he knew it.

Rita was desperate for comfort, but she wouldn't find it here.

Unable to witness Mark's callousness any longer, she feigned a sudden attack of nausea. Looked like she wasn't completely over her food-poisoning after all, she told everyone, as she grabbed her coat and exited quickly, feigning a woman running for the bathroom to throw up.

Tears ran down her face as she ran into the car park, where the Rosary decal on her Fiesta reminded her of the only person who *had* shown compassion.

That lady at the 'health' centre was obviously Catholic and knew Rita was as well. Yet she'd still extended sympathy to her, despite knowing she'd just killed her baby. She'd understood the bereft mother's need for solace, even though Rita had rudely dismissed her.

She grimaced at the memory. If she met her now, how differently she'd act!

She got into her car, craving the relief of sobbing right there. But an office employee might see her and offer help and ask awkward questions. She must wait until she was well clear of the parking lot.

At the exit, she instinctively turned south to avoid heading towards Dartmoor and its horrible memories. Soon she was out of Ruddminster and on the way to the coast.

The trip began with her feeling mad at Mark for

putting her in this position. That turned into fury at herself for not being strong enough to stand up to him right at the beginning of their liaison. Where were her religious principles when Mark asked her out for that first drink? She'd been so stupid, taken in by the handsome man's sweet talk.

And now she'd destroyed an innocent life. For thirty pieces of silver from Mark, she'd betrayed and killed her own baby.

What kind of person had she become? Vain and weak and selfish, she'd gone against everything she knew to be right and true.

How could she call herself a Christian?

God must hate her; she certainly hated herself.

Twenty minutes farther down the main road, a sign told her the exit for King's Brambling was coming up in half a mile.

She'd never heard of it, but the name sounded charming and it was as good a place as any for an escape.

The exit took her onto a much smaller road, flanked by elm hedgerows resting on turf-covered banks of earth, with barely enough width for two cars to pass each other. At intervals, the shrubs parted to accommodate a stile or a gate, affording room for a vehicle to stop and allow the one travelling in the opposite direction to drive past.

The ground rose steadily, then levelled out briefly, before beginning a steep and winding descent. A mile later, the road flattened again and Rita passed the village sign. Lined with medieval red brick houses, the road continued for another quarter of a mile until it stopped at a T-junction, where a lane ran left and right along a stunning half-moon beach.

Beyond it she could hear the crash of waves as the grey waters of the Channel pummelled the sand.

She turned right. The road rose sharply, following high cliffs along the coastline and the Fiesta's engine complained loudly as it strained past scattered stone dwellings and red brick houses. Finally, the roadway petered out halfway up the ascent into the small car park of a little church with a diminutive graveyard. A sign by the lychgate proudly declared this to be St. Jude Catholic Church.

Next to it stood a tiny rectory, with a tiny front garden and a large plastic statue of St. Francis of Assisi with a bird in his hand and a deer pressing into his right leg.

Rita pulled in next to the only vehicle in the lot, a burgundy specimen that belonged in a museum. She got out and read the name *Triumph* on the rusting boot. She'd never heard of it. Was it a foreign car? Did it even work?

The heels on her shoes were too high for comfortable walking on the gravel surface, and she was glad to enter through the lychgate and step on the smoother flagstones of the path leading to the church door.

She meant to go in and see if talking to God would ease the terrible ache. But when she reached the studded wooden door, her courage failed. God didn't want her anywhere near Him.

She continued to the rear of the building and was met with a rough expanse of grass extending to the cliffs.

Now she knew what had compelled her to come here: this was where it was all supposed to end. She took off the cumbersome heels and strode purposefully towards the edge.

*

Father James saw a disturbing sight through his kitchen window.

He was pouring the boiled water he'd used to warm the tea pot into the sink when his eye caught a woman moving rapidly in the direction of the cliffs, holding high heels in her left hand. He didn't like her demeanour; her head was bowed low and he feared the worst.

"Come, Judith!"

He grabbed his coat and jammed his arms through the sleeves while running out of the back door. The Border Collie bounded beside him, thrilled to be going on another walk.

"This is serious, girl." He stopped and pulled the lacrosse ball out of his pocket. *Please, Lord, make this a good one!*

He flung the ball as far as he could, aiming for the narrowing gap between the woman and the cliff edge. With a high yelp, Judith flew after it.

Yes, Lord, thank you! The rubber orb was poised to hit the ground just in front of the mystery lady, when Judith intercepted it.

The woman gave a startled cry and Father James, jogging along the ball's path, yelled "Sit!" to his dog.

Judith immediately complied, facing the woman. She bent down to stroke the animal's head then looked up and saw the priest loping towards her. "Is this your dog?"

"Yes, I hope she's not bothering you."

"No, not at all." She continued to pet Judith, avoiding his eyes.

What was such a pretty lady doing on these cliff tops? She seemed disinclined to talk.

"I don't remember seeing you in St. Jude. I'm Father James, the pastor."

The woman stood up and appeared to register for the first time that he was a Catholic priest.

"Yes?" he asked, sensing a question.

She faced the drab waters of the English Channel. "Is it true that God can forgive all sins?" She glanced at him, then looked away again. "I mean, the really, really bad ones."

"God is omnipotent and all-loving. He can and *wants* to forgive absolutely anything."

"But I thought there was an unforgivable sin?"

"True, the sin against the Holy Spirit."

"Which one is that?"

"Lack of repentance," replied the pastor. "Refusing to acknowledge that we have sinned and refusing to ask God for His mercy and forgiveness."

The young lady blinked several times and wiped her cheek with a blue-gloved hand.

Judith had dropped the ball at her feet and was staring up at her.

"She'd like you to throw it for her," explained her owner. "Preferably not into the sea."

A smile crossed her face. She reached down and picked up the ball. "Where should I throw it?"

He pointed behind them. "How about towards the rectory? I was just brewing a mean cup of tea." He added, "I also have a new packet of McVitie's chocolate biscuits."

"How can I refuse *them*?" She laughed and hurled the ball inland.

As an ecstatic Judith bolted after it, the lady took off her right glove and stretched out her hand. "Rita Shoreham."

Father James pressed it firmly. "Very glad to meet you, Rita. Now let's get warm by my fire."

Rita found herself seated on the sofa of a small sitting room with a fire blazing in the hearth and a cup of tea on the little coffee table in front of her. She nibbled on a chocolate biscuit and looked across at the kindly priest in the armchair. His dog was lying on his polished black leather shoes, but he didn't seem to mind that or the hairs accumulating around the base of his soutane. She imagined his parishioners must be used to seeing them, too.

"What brings you to these parts, Rita?"

What was the point in lying? She'd already asked him if God could forgive anything. "I've committed a mortal sin, Father, and I'm not sure God will forgive me."

Father James gave a paternal smile. "And what is so special about *your* sin that God won't forgive it?"

Rita frowned. Was he making fun of her? But his face showed otherwise. "What you're saying is that my sins are no different from anyone else's?"

"Precisely. There is nothing about your particular sins that prevents God from being able to forgive you. Remember, He's All-Powerful."

Rita put her biscuit down on the saucer and summoned every ounce of courage. Making the Sign of the Cross, she began, "Bless me, Father, for I have sinned. It has been over a year since my last confession."

Father James lay his cup and saucer on the coffee table and drew a purple stole from his pocket. Placing it around his neck, he murmured a prayer, then said, "May God help you make a good Confession."

"I had an abortion on Tuesday, and I feel horrible about it," she blurted, and the tears burst out of her.

Father James was gentle and understanding, while at the same time making it clear that what she had done was wrong. "Do you sincerely repent of your actions?"

"More than anything in the world, Father. I can't believe I murdered my baby because the father paid me to."

They talked for a while longer, during which Rita confessed her affair with a married man, then Father James coached her through the long-forgotten words of the Act of Contrition and gave her Absolution.

"For your penance, I want you to pray for your baby's soul – and the soul of the man who pushed you into this. You must forgive him, too."

Rita bridled. "Father, I can't forgive Mark – I mean the baby's father – for what he's done."

"You must, Rita, if you want to be forgiven. Remember what it says in the Our Father: 'forgive us as we forgive those who trespass against us.' I know it's hard, but it's essential if you want God's complete forgiveness."

He made the Sign of the Cross over her to conclude. "Let's finish our tea, shall we?"

Rita's soul was wiped clean, as long as she carried out her penance, and she was elated. "Thank you, Father, you've no idea how timely your intervention was."

"Oh, I have a fair one. But isn't reconciling with God by far the better course of action?"

Rita nodded, blushing as she recollected her walk to the cliff edge.

Father James poured her a second cup and asked, "Would you like to talk to a lady who can help you feel better about yourself? It'll be in the strictest confidence."

Rita's eyes widened. "You know someone?"

"Oh, yes. Let me give her a call. She lives here in the village."

Less than ten minutes later, a rap on the front door

announced the arrival of a visitor. Father James went to let her in, and brought her into the sitting room.

"Rita, this is Rebecca Luckton. Rebecca, meet Rita Shoreham."

Rita jumped up in astonishment. The lady standing before her was the one who'd been praying the Rosary outside the 'health' clinic and accompanied her to her car.

Rebecca gave her a huge hug. "My poor lamb!"

She was very motherly. Rita thought she must have a lot of children.

They sat down on the sofa and Father James picked up the teapot. "I'll brew some more and bring in a cup and saucer for you, Rebecca."

"Thank you, Father."

When the priest was out of the room, she asked Rita, "It's so good to see you again! How are you feeling?"

Rita's answer surprised even her. "Much better after talking to Father." Her eyes dropped to her hands, folded on her lap and she reddened a little. "And after making my confession."

Rebecca touched her arm lightly. "I'm very glad to hear that. It's wonderful what a good confession can do for the soul, isn't it?"

Rita glanced up at her. "I never realized how lucky I am to have that sacrament."

"Yes, and we're very fortunate to have Father James to turn to in times of need." She paused. "I hope you don't mind my asking, but did you give your baby a name?"

Rita was puzzled. What good would that have done?

"I know it seems a rather moot point, but I assure you it isn't. Do you know whether you were carrying a boy or a girl?"

Why did this otherwise caring lady keep talking about

her baby, when the subject was so painful?

Rebecca continued, "The reason I'm asking, you see, is because many women find comfort in having a ceremony to commemorate their unborn child, and committing him or her to God. I thought maybe you'd like that for your baby?"

Rita pondered Rebecca's words. Mark's reaction to the premature death of their baby had been a thumbs up emoji. This lady embraced the reality of her lost child, and wanted to honor him rather than pretend he never existed.

It would be hard, having to admit to what she'd done all over again. But she knew in her heart it was the right thing to do. She owed it to her baby.

In a strong voice she told Rebecca, "I was carrying a boy."

The older lady beamed at her.

"And I was going to call him Mark."

Father James walked in with the full teapot and set it down in front of Rita, together with Rebecca's cup and saucer. "Would you be so kind as to pour it for us?"

Rita smiled. He was asking her to 'be mother.'

*

Father James drank his tea in silence, allowing Rebecca to explain to Rita how they would organize the memorial service for baby Mark.

Halfway through he announced, "I'm going to take Judith for a walk and let you ladies finish working out the details."

He thought it better to leave the two of them alone. Rebecca was a compassionate confidante, having herself been on the verge of aborting her baby in university, until James intervened. She understood the dilemma and knew plenty of ladies in Rita's situation. She would put the grieving mother in touch with a group where she would be among women – and some men – who shared her anguish. They would accept her and make her feel less alone.

To Judith's great joy, Father James again pulled the lacrosse ball from his pocket.

He looked at it for a moment. Less than an hour ago this little sphere had prevented a woman from jumping off the cliff to certain death.

He threw it and the excited Collie raced to catch it.

Despite his thankfulness at having prevented a tragedy, Father James was disturbed by something Rita said during her confession. She'd mentioned Mark as the father's name. And it was going to be the baby's name, too.

Mark Boulder had confessed to adultery – the priest recognized his voice at their subsequent meetings – so could *he* be the man Rita was talking about? And might Mark be paying her to keep quiet? After all, he had a history of bribery.

Father James hoped he was wrong, but a troubling suspicion told him he wasn't.

His university pal was fast heading for the hell he didn't believe in.

His old room-mate wanted to help him, but for the time being all he could do was pray that Mark would confess to this abortion – and his other misdeeds – and save his soul.

Chapter Fourteen: Mark Confesses
Sunday, 24th February

A week after his meeting with Father James, Mark was still smarting over how the priest had got the upper hand and sent him away with nothing.

If not for that meddling cleric, Mark would merely be handling the discomfort of life at home in the aftermath of his affair, paying Rita off like Dave Miller, with no one any the wiser.

But the man insisted on pursuing justice for the old people, divulging the use of charity funds to bribe Dave Miller, refusing to give him the missing evidence or the name of the whistle blower. If this double scandal ever came to light, Father James was going down with him.

Mark wasn't being vindictive; his actions were driven by the behaviour of those around him, and Bishop Marsden's threat to withdraw from Serving Seniors was the final push. By fair means or foul, Mark must get that priest under control.

His last attempt failed because being a decent sort he'd tried to reason with his old friend. This time would be different.

He told Mary her brother was sending him on a mission. She didn't give him any sceptical looks and even wished him a good trip.

Brimming with confidence all the way down to the coast, by the time his BMW passed the first cottages of King's Brambling, he was actually looking forward to surprising the priest with this second visit.

He was thoroughly piqued when Father James opened the door with the words, "Welcome back, Mark! I've been expecting you."

Forbearing to ask why, he stepped past him into the

hallway and down to the shabby little sitting room.

The priest's tea tray sat on the coffee table, and a newly poured cup rested by his armchair.

Mark sat down in the chair, picked up the cup and sipped daintily from it.

Father James cleared his throat delicately. "I hope you're not afraid of my germs. I've already drunk some of that."

Mark smiled sweetly. "No worries. We didn't catch anything from each other back in the day. I trust you're not carrying anything infectious."

"So do I," said his friend.

Mark forced his smile to widen.

"As you're happy drinking out of that, I'll fetch myself a clean cup," said the priest.

Mark would dearly have loved one, too.

Round One to Father James.

The humiliation hardened Mark's resolve.

A few minutes later, the priest was raising a fresh cup of tea to his lips, when Mark announced, "I've thought a lot about what you said last time, and I want to make a full confession."

Father James took a slow, deliberate drink then put his tea down on the table. "I rather thought you might."

Irritated, Mark asked, "Any chance we could do it now? I really would like to get it over with."

"Of course." He pulled a purple stole from the depths of his cassock and placed it around his neck, murmuring a prayer as he did so.

"Shouldn't I kneel or something?"

"No. Continue as if we were in the regular confessional."

"O.K." Mark coughed. "Bless me Father, for I have sinned. It's about two weeks since my last confession."

Injecting as much remorse as he could into his voice, Mark came clean about mishandling the seniors' money, setting up the charity as a cover and bribing Dave Miller, whom he named, out of its funds to keep quiet.

That was enough. He didn't need to mention Rita and the abortion. Or the fact that he'd gone up to receive Communion with his wife this morning, when he was no longer in a state of grace: he feared Mary's ire more than God's.

Father James looked straight at him. "Is that your full confession?"

"Yes."

"You don't have any other major sins on your conscience?"

"No, Father, isn't that enough?" Mark retorted. "That's all I have."

There was an awkward silence, and Mark could sense the priest didn't believe him.

Father James shook his head sadly. "Mark, I know you *haven't* made a full confession. You're withholding serious sins and therefore I cannot absolve you."

Mark frowned. "But what I said is still under the seal of confession?"

"Yes."

Mark smiled triumphantly. "Then if you or your whistle blower repeat anything I've just said, I'll happily expose you for breaking the seal of secrecy. You know Bishop Marsden will back me up on this. It will be the end of you as a priest. If you or your informant know what's good for you, you'd do well to keep quiet and hand over the remaining documents."

Chapter Fifteen: Letters from the Bishop

Monday, 25th February, a.m.

Mark's triumph was short-lived.

From his car outside Father James' rectory, he texted his brother-in-law that he had happy news.

If it's about Father James, you're too late, came the reply.

What do you mean? Mark typed.

You'll see.

Mark dialled the bishop's number, but he didn't pick up, leaving Mark to fret all the way back to Dartleigh and suffer a sleepless night next to his wife.

*

He drove to the office the following morning, still wondering what the bishop had meant. He sincerely hoped Rita wouldn't be moping around the water cooler today. He had enough on his plate without that.

He'd been at his desk no longer than twenty minutes when a courier came in with a slim overnight package.

Mark pulled out an envelope and instantly recognized the bishop's seal on the back. His heart sank; this formal missive wouldn't contain anything good.

He told Brenda to hold all calls and closed his office door.

Sitting down, he swivelled his chair round and looked out of the window onto the company car park. This time he envied his employees as they walked from their vehicles into the building for a normal day at work.

Mark would never again enjoy a normal work day.

He turned his leather chair to face his desk and forced himself to read the letter.

Dear Mark,

Upon further consideration after our talk on Wednesday, I find myself unable to continue my association with the Serving Seniors Charity and hereby resign my post as co-treasurer, effective today.

I very much regret having to take this step, and wish you the best of luck moving forward with your charitable work.

Yours in Christ,

Robert Marsden.

Mark was appalled. Why hadn't the bishop waited? They'd spoken only five days ago!

But that was just it. After giving him several days' grace, the bishop had heard nothing. This letter was already on its way when Mark visited Father James.

No wonder his brother-in-law hadn't answered the phone.

*

Father James was leaving church at 9:05 a.m. after Monday morning Mass, when a courier ran up and handed him a thin package sent overnight.

"Sign here, please, Father," requested the thin young man with bicycle clips on his jeans.

Baffled, the priest did as asked.

"Thank you, Father!" The youth ran off through the lychgate to the car park, leaving Father James wondering what on earth he'd just signed for.

He walked the few yards to his rectory. When he opened the front door, Judith raced up to him, tail wagging furiously, as if the man had been gone for several hours instead of sixty minutes.

"I wonder what this is all about?" he asked, showing her the delivery.

He'd not eaten or drunk before celebrating Mass and was hungry for his scrambled eggs on toast.

Placing the mystery correspondence on the kitchen table, he went about the business of preparing breakfast. In his experience, rushed mail was never good, and he wasn't going to let it ruin his first meal of the day.

Fifteen minutes later he was sitting in front of a hearty plate of food and a large mug of coffee.

But his curiosity got the better of him halfway through the scrambled eggs. He wiped the knife on his napkin and used it to slice open the package.

His appetite vanished when he saw his bishop's seal on the envelope. He pulled out the enclosed letter and read,

Dear James,

Effective immediately, I must ask you to step down from your position as parish priest of King's Brambling, due to your divisive and ineffective preaching. You must also vacate your present accommodation as I am sending a new priest to take over your duties.

I have attached the decree pertaining to your situation, but here is a brief summary.

You may not offer public Mass in your home diocese or any other diocese. You are not permitted to baptise people unless they are in danger of death. You may no longer preach. You may only celebrate the Holy Eucharist in private.

Further, at a time yet to be decided, you will attend a thirty (30) day retreat to spiritually heal and address the issues that led to this decree.

These ministerial restrictions are imposed for an indeterminate amount of time, until the cause for such restrictions ceases to exist, and you must live within the

boundaries of the diocese.

I very much regret having to take this step, but have no alternative given your refusal to comply with my request to tone down your inflammatory rhetoric from the pulpit.

If you choose to recant and follow your vow of obedience, I shall be more than happy to reverse my decision.

Yours in Christ,

Robert Marsden, Bishop of Ruddminster

Father James sat in stunned silence. First Mark, and now his own bishop!

He pushed back his chair and stroked Judith's silky hair. "Looks as if you and I are in for a change of routine, old girl. But one thing's not going to change, and that is your need for exercise."

He had already taken his dog out early that morning, before the pre-Mass confessions. But she was always up for another walk, and it would help him ponder the repercussions of this letter.

A strong north-easterly wind was blowing off the Channel. It buffeted his tall figure as he walked parallel to the cliffs, away from the village. Ahead of him stretched miles of glorious wild terrain.

He threw the lacrosse ball, given to him years ago by one of Rebecca Luckton's daughters, as far as he could into the tall grass and hoped Judith would take a long time to find it.

If only Dave Miller hadn't come to him with those documents!

But if he hadn't, then what? Father James would have lived out his days peacefully by the sea, never knowing any real strife and never having his faith put to the test.

Had he been ordained to be quiet, to 'tone down his

message' when Our Lord was relying on him to shout the truth from the rooftops?

No! Now, more than ever, it was vital he tell the truth. The world contained too many timid priests; he mustn't be one of them.

But he'd just lost his parish. How would he get Christ's message out?

He decided to talk to Rebecca Luckton. He didn't know who'd shot the first video, but her son Dan was a whiz at technology. Perhaps he could produce and upload his sermons? They wouldn't be from the pulpit so they wouldn't count as actual preaching, and the Gospel message would reach farther than the parishioners of St. Jude.

Lord, I need your help!

This was going to be hard. But it was more important to have a clear conscience and do his utmost to lead as many people as possible to Jesus, than enjoy a comfortable existence.

Speaking of which, he needed to find new accommodation.

*

That afternoon Father James received a phone call from a Father Gregory, who explained in embarrassed tones that the bishop had appointed him administrator of St. Jude parish.

The man sounded young and inexperienced. How were the parishioners going to cope?

He added, with a self-conscious cough, "Unless, of course, you've changed your mind about your – um – preaching style?"

Father James replied, "No, I haven't."

"Er, then, well, the thing is, the bishop wanted me to come down today. Does that work for you?"

What was Father James supposed to say? 'No, it doesn't, so don't come'?

But the youthful priest was simply obeying his bishop, as he was bound to do.

"That will be fine. What time should I expect you?"

The rectory only had one bedroom. Father James had to immediately vacate the building he'd called home for fifteen years.

The obvious choice was Mrs. Luckton's B&B. It would serve him well until he found more permanent lodging, and he could use the opportunity to ask her help with producing those videos.

*

Late that night he was wondering how to break the news of his abrupt dismissal to his parishioners when Dave Miller phoned.

"How are you?" the priest asked.

"Father, Mark Boulder wants to meet with me. I think he knows I'm the whistle blower."

Chapter Sixteen: Mark Goes A-Visiting
Monday, 25th February, evening

Once over his initial shock, Mark left the office and slipped into his BMW to phone the bishop. He was going to fight this.

"Yes?" said Bishop Marsden.

A little small talk wouldn't have gone amiss on this occasion. "I received your letter."

"Good."

"And I was hoping you'd be willing to reconsider."

A heavy sigh could be heard at the other end. "What I have written, I have written."

Mark resented this Scripture quotation. It was uncalled for.

"That's settled, then," said the bishop, when Mark didn't respond.

"Not *entirely.*"

"What's that supposed to mean?" Bishop Marsden's voice had acquired an edge.

"It means I think it only fair you let me read those documents. Surely, it's not too much to ask? Am I not allowed to know exactly what I'm being accused of?" *Or exactly what those documents reveal?*

There was another sigh. "It won't change anything, Mark."

"I don't expect it to."

After a pause, Bishop Marsden said, "Fine. Dinner at the palace this evening. 7 p.m. Don't be late!"

Was the man perhaps relenting a smidgeon?

Full of hope that this was the case, Mark phoned Mary to tell her of his plans. They met with no resistance, since they were verifiable.

In need of Dutch courage before meeting the bishop, Mark drove to a pub on the outskirts of Ruddminster after work.

He downed a couple of neat whiskeys with water on the side, then got back into his car and made his way to Cathedral Square, and along the left side of the magnificent edifice to the regal Bishop's Palace. He wondered irrelevantly why the cobblestones hadn't been updated like his own driveway, to better serve the modern luxury car?

The bishop's Mercedes had pride of place by the front door. Normally Mark parked next to it, but the idea was distasteful to him and he took a space as far away as he could.

*

Brother John escorted Mark to the private dining room at the rear of the building, with a view over the pristine Palace lawns.

The tapestried walls were rumoured to be sound-proof and Mark hoped having no witnesses to their conversation would not work against him.

The monk opened the door and announced Mark's arrival. The bishop remained standing with his back to his guest, pretending to admire the grounds, even though it was pitch black outside.

Brother John didn't appear perturbed. "Dinner will be served in ten minutes, Your Excellency."

"Thank you, John." A wave of his hand dismissed the man, who withdrew and closed the door silently behind him, leaving Mark staring at his brother-in-law's back — or was it his cold shoulder?

Still without turning around, Bishop Marsden said, "Take a seat, Mark." His voice carried the regret of a headmaster steeling himself to thrash an errant pupil. "You'll find a neat whiskey at your place setting."

Mark sat down by the full glass, wishing he hadn't imbibed so much on the way here. He would have to drink slowly to keep his wits about him. "Cheers," he said without enthusiasm, and took a sip.

The bishop finally turned to face him, holding a glass of sherry in his right hand. He walked over to the table and sank into the chair opposite his brother-in-law. On his left lay the file.

At the sight of it, Mark took a longer draught of whiskey.

"How's Mary?" asked the bishop.

"Doing well."

"I'm anxious she not get hurt by this whole sordid affair."

There was no answer to that.

"You do realise, don't you," the bishop continued, "that I'll have to tell her about my resignation from the charity?"

Mark coughed. "Is that really necessary?"

"Why, were *you* planning to tell her?"

"When the time is right, yes."

"Now is the right time, Mark. You've dithered long enough. Tell her tonight, or she'll be unpleasantly surprised by my text tomorrow, telling her how sorry I am to have had to step down."

Mark's shoulders slumped in defeat.

The two men sat in silence, sipping their drinks and avoiding eye contact until Brother John opened the door to admit a server carrying a tray, followed by a sommelier with a white cloth over his left arm, bearing a bottle of red wine.

Mark knew without looking that it was Châteauneufdu-pape, his brother-in-law's favourite. The wine steward stood by the bishop, opened the bottle, poured some into his glass, then waited for his approval.

Meanwhile, the other server was depositing a red beet salad with arugula and warmed goat cheese to the left of the two men's folded napkins.

Bishop Marsden tasted the wine and nodded to the sommelier, who bowed slightly and poured it into both glasses. Then he left the open bottle on the table by the bishop and wrapped the white cloth around the neck.

He stood back while the waiter served two large plates of beef Wellington, roast potatoes, carrots and sugar snap peas.

The servers left the room and Brother John closed the door softly behind them.

"I hope you don't mind having the entrée served at the same time as our salads," said the bishop, "but I'd rather we not be disturbed for a while and this seemed to be the most expedient way of guaranteeing it."

"Not at bit. This all looks delicious."

Omitting to say grace, the bishop picked up his knife and fork and began eating.

Mark followed suit. The food was delicious, but he was too tense to enjoy it. His eyes kept wandering to the file and he wondered how much longer before the bishop let him see its contents?

They continued to eat without speaking. At times Mark could feel the bishop's eyes on him, and knew they weren't friendly.

Half-way through the meal, Bishop Marsden raised the wine bottle and gave his brother-in-law an inquiring look.

After a nod in reply, the bishop poured him another glass.

Perhaps the prelate was trying to get him too drunk to remember why he was here? He decided to broach the subject of the papers now.

"When can I look through that file?"

"I thought you'd never ask."

Mark wanted to spit. "Dammit, Robert! I don't appreciate your playing games with me. Please hand it over."

Bishop Marsden looked blandly at him. "Maybe you now understand how I feel about the games you've been playing with *me*." He slid the file across the table.

Mark could feel his blood pressure soar as he opened the file. On the first page was Dave Miller's email to him expressing concerns about Mark's investing all the older clients' money and no one else's, and expressing his reservations about the company in question. 'It looks far too risky to me.'

The second page contained a short email from Mark, saying he had it all under control and Dave wasn't to worry. If this worked, they would then invest money from other accounts.

That was the extent of their email exchange. All other discussions about the situation had been conducted face to face in Mark's office. There was no physical trail.

And yet he was staring at what appeared to be transcripts of snippets of those conversations. Had someone wired his office?

Mark winced at his response to Dave's repeated misgivings.

'Dave, we stand to make a huge gain. Isn't that what we're all about? If this pays off, they'll thank me for providing them with a comfortable income in their golden years, as well as decent capital to pass onto their nearest and dearest after they're gone.'

But Dave had again protested against Mark's not spreading the risk across all their investors.

And again, Mark had pushed back. 'Look, unlike our younger clientèle, the seniors won't need their money for much longer. They can take a hit better than anyone. Anyway, stop worrying. It won't come to that. We've always done well with our more adventurous deals.'

Then came his directives not to let anyone know that only the seniors' funds were being used.

Next came his instructions after the dicey company went broke and the elderly lost all their money. 'The official storyline will be that the seniors were hit hardest – not that they were the *only* ones hit.'

Now came his later conversations about setting up a charity to help the seniors whose money he'd lost, by giving them grants to get them back on their feet. 'This is a win-win for us, Dave. It'll help them and make us look good.'

Certain conversations were missing, namely those telling Dave he would make it worth his while to set up the fund and keep quiet about the investment gaffe.

There could only be one reason why the communications incriminating Dave Miller weren't included. There was no wire in Mark's office, the informant was Dave himself.

A copy of a typed memo was included, that Mark had never seen before. It mentioned monthly payments by the charity, each in the same amount, to an unidentified senior, who didn't exist.

Despite the strong inference that funds were being misappropriated, there was no concrete proof that bribes were being paid. For that at least Mark was glad. But it all pointed to Dave being the whistle blower.

Although why the man should come forward and

divulge everything was a mystery. He stood to lose everything, too.

He closed the file and glanced across at the bishop. "How do I explain your stepping down from the charity to Mary? Are you going to tell her the real reason?" He didn't want to discuss the file contents.

"You tell her tonight that I'm leaving and make up the reason."

"I'll say that you're too busy to continue."

Bishop Marsden smiled insincerely. "That will work for the time being."

Chapter Seventeen: Mark Pays Another Visit
Monday, 25th February

On the way home, Mark stopped off at a late-night café. While waiting for the waitress to notice him, he sat at a dark corner table and pulled out his phone.

Convinced now that Dave Miller was the culprit, and not caring that it was after 9 p.m., he dialled his employee's number.

A groggy voice answered. "Yes?"

"Dave, this is Mark. We need to talk."

The man was supposedly on sick leave, but now Mark suspected the real reason was that he was too embarrassed to show his face at work after his treachery. He felt no sympathy for him.

"Why?" Dave sounded nervous.

Good. "I'll tell you when we meet."

They arranged for Mark to visit Dave's house the next day.

The waitress was now hovering and he ordered a large mug of black coffee. He needed to cover up his alcohol breath before breaking the news to his wife about her brother.

She'd know he was telling the truth about visiting the bishop tonight, but would she accept the official version of why he was walking away from the charity?

He mustered the nerve to tell her just before bedtime, and as soon as the words 'your brother's too busy' came out of his mouth, Mary looked askance at him. "*Why* is he suddenly too busy?"

Mark's eyes swerved to the right. "I've no idea, you'll have to ask him."

"What have you been up to?" Her hands were on her hips now.

"Having dinner with your brother, what else?"

"You know perfectly well what I mean, Mark."

He sighed. "Does this mean another night on the sofa?"

"Only if you're lying to me."

Tuesday, 26th February

Mark lay next to his wife that night, his head churning over the evidence pointing to Dave Miller as the whistle blower.

*

The next morning, he told his secretary he planned to pay Dave Miller a visit that afternoon. It was, after all, the decent thing to do. The man had been home sick for quite a while.

At 3:30 p.m. he asked her to take messages if anyone called and he would get back to them tomorrow.

Human Resources had given him Dave's address that morning and he lived in King's Brambling. Dave was his man.

The BMW's SatNav took him along the familiar road, past the sign reminding visitors that the hamlet was established in 1209. The number of inhabitants had been crossed through, and 562 replaced by the number 563. Underneath hung a banner reading 'Welcome Baby Brendan!'

At the T junction facing the English Channel, the navigation told him to take a left instead of turning uphill towards the rectory.

He followed the coastline for an eighth of a mile before the road curved away from the sea for a hundred yards and arrived in the village. It comprised a tight group of squat Medieval homes in a wide horse shoe around half an acre of green grass, leaving the view of the beach unobstructed by buildings. Mark was impressed; even back then, the planners had had foresight.

He spotted the Post Office in the middle of the arc of buildings and drove along looking at the house numbers.

Number 11 was to the right, with Dave Miller's grey VW diesel Jetta out in front.

Mark imagined the man at a desk in his dressing-gown, poring over books on the history of accounting and salivating over the intricacies of double entry book-keeping.

He couldn't imagine what Dave was spending his bribe money on. It certainly didn't show in the car he drove or his modest abode.

He parked behind the Jetta. As he stepped out of his vehicle, a vaguely familiar lady walked by him. She gave him a second look, as if she, too, thought she knew him, then went on her way.

Quickly forgetting her, Mark unlatched the gate that opened onto Dave's short flagstone path, lined on either side with magenta, purple, and yellow winter pansies. It struck him that the flowers were spaced identically, with each colour exactly opposite its counterpart on the other side.

The flagstones were the same size and shape, no mean feat, and a matching close-cropped lawn lay to the left and right.

A man who paid meticulous attention to symmetry and detail lived here.

Mark lifted the heavy door knock as high as he could,

then dropped it, hoping the loud clang would startle his host.

The door was opened by a pasty-faced version of the employee who'd gone on leave a month ago. He'd also dropped a lot of weight.

Mark had planned to greet him with a quip about how healthy he was looking for a sick man, but the man appeared deathly ill.

"Hello, Dave. How are you feeling?"

"So-so. Why don't you come in?" A hand bordering on the skeletal ushered him in.

The front door led immediately into a pretty sitting room, and Mark was surprised by the bright chintz curtains and bold colours of the upholstery. Like the pansies outside, they indicated a cheerful side to the owner of the house.

"I've made us some tea," Dave said. "Would you care for some biscuits?"

"No, thanks, but tea would be great." Mark suddenly felt guilty about making the man go to such trouble.

"Back in a sec." Limping, Dave disappeared from the room, and Mark forced himself to remember why he was here. That man was trying to ruin him. There was no room for sentiment!

While Dave poured the tea, Mark asked whether he was getting any better?

Dave replied that things weren't good right now. He didn't seem to want to elaborate, although Mark would have liked to know whether the man was expecting to come back to work any day soon.

Dave handed him a full cup of tea and Mark sat back, sipping on it for a moment, assessing his opponent. The Financial Director didn't appear to have any fight in him, so this should be easy.

Peering at the accountant, he said, "I know you recorded the private conversations we had in my office about the senior investments as well as the charity. And you gave damning evidence about me to Father James."

Dave looked at his boss with blank eyes. "Did I?"

"Don't prevaricate," said Mark, stealing the bishop's useful word. "Everything points to you. Otherwise, how come my financial offer to you to keep quiet about it isn't included in that evidence?"

Dave stared at the thick red carpet and said nothing.

"Unless you take back your accusations and say you made up those transcripts, I have no choice but to cut off your extra money."

Dave's eyes met his. "I've been putting that money back into the charity for a long time now, via my sister, Joyce Renfrew. Haven't you seen the amounts coming in?"

"Why would I? I'm not in charge of the book-keeping. Don't expect to come back to work. You're fired!"

"I don't care. I can't stand having this whole mess on my conscience. Losing my job is worth it." He gave a lopsided grin. "Although there's probably some law preventing you from firing me when I'm sick."

Mark snorted. "Even so, *no one's* going to give credence to supposed evidence given to your parish priest by a disgruntled employee. Neither is anyone going to pay attention to documents handed over by a disgraced priest to the bishop."

Dave looked up sharply. "Did you have anything to do with Father James' removal?"

"No, he did it to himself." Mark leaned back to observe the effect of this statement.

But the man quickly rallied. "I don't believe you. And how are you going to explain the extra payments to me?"

Mark's expression was blasé. "I'll say you stole the money from the company. When you thought you'd get caught, you then took it from the charity."

Dave's laugh was hollow. "Don't forget, I can prove they were bribes. I still have the recording of you offering them to me."

Mark lunged at him. "I'll ruin you!"

Dave didn't move a muscle. "Go for it."

Envisaging the headlines, *Bullying Business Tycoon Strangles Sick Employee*, Mark backed off. "I hope you never get better!" he yelled, and stormed out of the house.

Mark drove quickly away from the horrible village. He realised that he'd never stood a chance of getting the original evidence and disposing of it. Having already threatened to stop paying the bribes to Dave Miller, and now fired him, he had no more leverage against the man.

He cursed. Instead of losing his temper, he should have looked for another way to silence him. With nothing to lose anymore, the man would go public with his information.

All Mark could do now was research the best company law firms.

Chapter Eighteen: Rebecca's Bed & Breakfast

Wednesday, 27th February

Father James sat on the bed of his room on the first floor of Rebecca Luckton's Bed & Breakfast. Hers was the last house in the horse shoe around the green and the priest's accommodation was at the front of the building.

He gazed out of the window at the beach; a big change from his view of the Channel from the rectory.

Up there, he'd become used to the incessant crash of waves dashing against the cliffs below. But here they broke gently onto the sand and provided a soothing background.

He was now on day three of his ousting.

Father Gregory Baker had arrived on Monday afternoon, full of apology, and accompanied Father James on a short tour of the rectory and church before sitting down to tea with the priest he was replacing.

While imparting as much information as he could, Father James' thoughts drifted to the four packets of McVitie's chocolate biscuits in the pantry. He hoped it wasn't wrong of him to have packed a couple to take to his temporary home.

After the two men had cleared away the tea things and washed up, he wished the new administrator good luck and piled his suitcases into the old Triumph.

Judith walked under the lychgate with him to the church, and lay next to him while he prayed for strength.

Please, Lord, don't let me be swayed from proclaiming the Truth, whatever the cost!

The dog lay motionless for twenty minutes while her owner knelt in the back pew.

She recognised the Sign of the Cross that ended the session and rose before he did.

Then she jumped into the passenger seat of the old car and peered intently through the windscreen, tail wagging in excitement at this change of routine.

*

Father James immediately adopted the habit of saying his morning prayers from the comfort of an old armchair in the corner of his new room.

Afterwards, he'd take Judith for a walk along the beach. The Border Collie would rush into the water to fetch her ball, then dig in the sand, and he watched her enjoy her new environment with no concern for tomorrow.

Once he'd dried her off, he would say Mass in private at the little makeshift altar Rebecca had set up in his room on the antique chest of drawers.

Hound and human would then descend the rickety wooden stairs and part ways at the bottom.

Judith padded off to eat in the kitchen and Father James walked to his table in the breakfast room. Soon Rebecca would appear, bearing bacon and eggs with toast and marmalade.

This ritual was the highlight of his day. After it, he felt rather lost. There were no confessions to hear, no parish office duties to perform, no sermons to prepare, no baptisms, First Holy Communions or Confirmations to plan. It was disorientating.

But he wouldn't go back to St. Jude and become a tame priest to please his bishop. Obedience had its limits and Father James must remain loyal to his mission of saving souls by telling them the Truth.

He'd continue to say his daily prayers at the prescribed times, celebrate Mass in private, and look for a new way to serve the Lord.

Which reminded him; he must ask Rebecca about helping him video what would have to be renamed 'talks'. Unless or until the bishop banned him from that activity, too.

He could, of course, ask his superior's permission. But he was inclined to seek forgiveness after the event, rather than risk prohibition ahead of it.

This morning, however, he had something to look forward to.

Rita Shoreham was coming to see Rebecca and him about the memorial service for her baby. It was unlikely that the bishop would let Father James preside over the ceremony and he wasn't going to risk going ahead with *that* without permission, but Rita had specifically requested he be part of the planning process.

He saw her white Fiesta drive by from his perch on the bed. He got up and Judith padded over to him from her bed.

"I'm sure you're invited, too. Come on!"

They descended the stairs to the small lobby, where Rebecca was opening the front door and Father James thought the striking blonde's face appeared less haggard.

"Hello, love, do come in!" Rebecca extended a welcoming arm as the dog ran up to the newcomer.

Rita fawned over her and looked up. "Hello, Judith! Good to see you, Father James, I'm so glad you could make it."

Rebecca gave him a meaningful look; the girl didn't know what had happened to the priest since their last meeting. "Come into the breakfast room," she said, "I'll bring in our elevenses, and we'll catch you up on the latest."

"Oh? What's been going on?"

Father James ushered her into the room. "Rather a lot, I'm afraid."

"That doesn't sound good."

"And it isn't, my dear. But it doesn't change things for you and your little one's memorial service."

He motioned for her to sit down at a table in the alcove with the same view of the beach that Father James had upstairs.

Rebecca Luckton had laid three places for them. Cream napkins in a blue seashell pattern were rolled into white china rings, each adorned with a single blue seahorse.

She brought in a large tray and set it down on the neighbouring table. Father James put the coffee pot by her place setting, together with a milk jug, sugar bowl and three sea-themed mugs.

These were followed by a plate of steaming hot crumpets with butter melting on top, a honey pot in the shape of a beehive, and a jar of strawberry jam.

"This is a veritable feast!" exclaimed Father James, savouring the smell of home baking.

"Thanks ever so much, Mrs. Luckton," said Rita, "I skipped breakfast this morning, and I'm not half hungry!"

Their hostess beamed. "Help yourself to everything," she said, pouring coffee into their mugs. "And I do think you should call me Rebecca, love."

Rita smiled. "Thank you, that's a lovely name."

Soon they were biting into crumpets dripping with honey or piled high with jam.

"Absolutely divine," said the priest. "And now, my

dear," turning to Rita, "I have some sad news for you."

He proceeded to tell her about his eviction, keeping the details factual and his voice unemotional.

"But Father, does that mean I can't come to you for confession anymore?"

"I haven't been specifically excluded from that, if you come to me outside the church building. But you really should go to Father Gregory."

"What about my baby's ceremony? Can you do that?"

Rebecca laid her hand on the girl's arm while Father James explained. "I'm sorry, Rita, I'm no longer allowed to perform public rites."

"Then let's do it here! This doesn't count as public, does it?"

Rebecca came to the rescue. "I tell you what, love, why don't you have the ceremony in the church with Father Gregory? Father James can be present, I'm sure, and afterwards we'll have a little get together back here."

"Thank you, Rebecca, that's really kind of you. Oh, Father, how awful for you! I'm so sorry!" Rita got up and hugged him right where he was sitting.

He was very moved. "You're most kind, my dear. But with God's help, I'll get through this. Don't worry about me."

Rita sat down again and the discussion turned to organising the ceremony.

That done, she gazed at the ceramic bee on the honey pot lid, eyes misting over. "You know, if only *one* person had told me not to – you know – I wouldn't have. But I couldn't talk to anyone about it." She looked at Rebecca. "You're so lucky you had Father James to persuade you not to!"

That lady glanced at the priest. "God was watching out

for me when he put Father James in my path, that's for sure."

"And here you are with five grown children! I hope one day I get married and have a big family, and put all this behind me."

"We hope so, too, dear. Now, Father, there was one more thing I wanted to talk to you about. We've been talking in the village; you need to warn that Father Gregory not to expect any money from us in the collection box."

Father James frowned. "What do you mean?"

"You need to fight your case in Rome and come back to us, Father. That takes money. So, we're going to create a fund for you to pay a Canon lawyer and do just that."

"My dear Rebecca, that's enormously kind of you all, but – "

He was interrupted by a swarthy man bursting into the room. "Father James, you gotta come quickly! Dave Miller's asking for you! 'E needs the Last Rites!"

The priest crossed himself. "Have you told Father Gregory?"

"Oi can't get ahold of 'im, Father, an' at any rate Dave don't want 'im. You gotta come – now!"

"Tell him I'll be right over, Malcolm." He rose from the table. "Excuse me, ladies, we'll continue this conversation at a later date."

Surprising himself with his sudden agility, Father James ran up the rickety stairs two at a time, with Judith at his heels. Grabbing his prayer book, and checking that his purple stole and car keys were in his pockets, he and the dog tore back downstairs and out to his car.

Ten minutes later, he was at St. Jude's, hoping the sacristy was open and he could find the sacramentals he needed.

He rushed into the church to find Father Gregory praying in the back pew.

"Father, you're needed to give the Last Rites to a dying parishioner and you need to hurry."

A look of terror crossed the priest's face. "I – I've never done it before. And I've never been with a dying person, either. Can't *you* do it?"

Resisting his urge to shake the man, Father James said, "I'll do it, but you need to come and cover for me. If anyone asks, I was assisting you for your first time. Do you think you can manage that?"

"So, *you're* going to perform the actual rite?"

"Yes, I'll do everything. But watch closely, and learn!"

*

The two priests gathered up the necessary items and climbed into Father James' car, where Judith was waiting patiently in the back seat.

In seven minutes, he was parking behind Dave's Jetta. The three of them walked up to the man's front door.

Malcolm was already opening it and before he could object to the presence of the new priest, Father James said, "Father Gregory will be assisting me."

Malcolm looked dubious, but nodded and led them to Dave's bedroom at the back of the house.

The once strong man's appearance shocked Father James. His emaciated face and thin arms resting on the bed spread told of impending death, yet he managed a smile at the sight of his pastor. "You made it, Father!"

"You bet I did."

"Who are you?" Dave raised an index finger towards the unknown man.

"This is Father Gregory," his ex-pastor said. "He's going to observe, if you don't have any objections. But he won't be able to hear what you say during your confession. Are you alright with that?"

"Two priests have got to be better than one, Father!"

Dave tried to laugh but coughed up blood. Father James gently wiped it off the counterpane with a towel lying by the sick man's hand. With a grin, he said, "We'll get right to it, then, shall we?"

Dave nodded. "Fire away, Father!"

From out of his black bag, Father James took a holy water sprinkler, oil stock, a glass dish and a pyx containing the consecrated Host.

Then he drew the purple stole from his pocket and placed it around his neck with the usual prayer. "Are you ready to make your confession?"

Dave nodded weakly and Father James leaned in to hear him.

It was short, since Dave had already confessed his major sins a few days ago. The priest absolved him in the Name of the Father, and of the Son and of the Holy Spirit. Next, he poured some oil into the small glass dish. He dipped his right forefinger in it and drew a cross on Dave's forehead and the palms of both his hands with the words, "Through this holy anointing, may the Lord in His Love and Mercy help you with the grace of the Holy Spirit. May the Lord Who frees you from sin save you and raise you up."

As he uttered those words, Father James felt a strong presence enveloping the bed, as he often had before in these circumstances. The angels and saints and the Blessed Mother were gathering to take Dave Miller to eternal life with God the Father and Son, safely away from Satan's attempts to snatch his soul in his final moments.

The priest raised the Host and said, "The Body of

Christ."

"Amen," said Dave.

Father James placed the wafer onto his tongue then pointed questioningly to a glass of water standing on the bedstand. Dave nodded. The priest put his hand under the dying man's head to raise it up a little as he offered him the water.

Thus propped up, Dave took a sip and chewed on the Host. Then he closed his eyes and pressed against Father James' hand, wanting to lie flat again.

Father Gregory sat motionless throughout this ritual, on the chair farthest from the bed.

Father James hoped the inexperienced priest was now in a better position to administer the Last Rites himself. But God help the faithful of King's Brambling under the care of this newbie!

He remained kneeling by the bedside until Dave's last breath. He made the Sign of the Cross over him when his soul departed from his body, and thanked God it was a peaceful passing as he bent over to close the dead man's lifeless eyes.

"Is he gone?" asked Father Gregory anxiously from his corner.

"Yes, God rest his soul."

The young priest shuddered and crossed himself. "Can we leave now?"

Father James tried to remember his own emotions when performing the Last Rites for the first time. Had he been as nervous and callous? He didn't think so, but his memory might be playing tricks.

Lord, please grant Father Gregory a sense of compassion. Otherwise, he won't last long!

⚖️

Chapter Nineteen: Mark and Father James Reconvene
Thursday, 28th February

On Friday morning, Linda from Human Resources phoned Mark to ask if he'd heard the news about Dave Miller?

"No. Why?"

"Yesterday we sent him the paperwork as you requested, but when the courier knocked on the door to get Mr. Miller's signature, some priest opened it and said that Mr. Miller had just passed away."

Mark swallowed hard to prevent himself from letting out a loud whoop. "That's *terrible* news!" he managed to say. "I suppose there are no details yet about the funeral?"

"No, sir. But I'll find out and let you know."

"Thank you, Linda. His death is a sad loss for the company."

"Yes, sir, we were all very fond of Mr. Miller. He had his funny ways, but then he was an accountant, so it was to be expected. But he was a very kind man."

"Yes, indeed, I shall miss him very much. Let me know about those funeral arrangements when you get them."

"Yes, sir. Good bye."

For a brief moment, Mark was torn between elation at the whistle blower's demise and irritation that the man hadn't had the decency to hang on until he'd received his dismissal papers.

Elation won. With a loud laugh, he threw a victorious fist into the air. His troubles were over! The man who'd ratted on him was dead, and the priest championing his cause was a discredited has-been, whom no one would take seriously.

Mark laughed again; he could now pay those bribes to Rita out of charity funds.

Nevertheless, he *would* like reassurance that Father James was going to drop the accusations against him. Supposing Dave Miller had told him how to access the recordings of their conversations?

But it would be amusing to see how exile was treating the self-righteous priest.

Telling his secretary that he was off to King's Brambling to convey his condolences and offer financial assistance with Dave Miller's funeral arrangements, he power-walked out of the building to his BMW and jumped gleefully into the driver's seat.

Unbridled joy made it hard to obey the speed limits on the way down. But he became increasingly hampered by a descending mist, which was a thick fog by the time he turned towards the village. He could barely see the beach on his right, although it was only a few hundred yards away, and when he reached the village green it was impossible to see more than ten feet ahead.

Mark slowed to a crawl and followed the road until he found the Post Office. He had no idea where Father James was, but the priest wouldn't be far away from his ex-parishioners. A quick inquiry of the postal staff would tell him.

Dave Miller's Jetta was still outside his house. Why that should surprise Mark, he didn't know. There was no room behind it, so he drove farther along until he came to a little parking lot and stopped.

He got out of his car and pulled up the lapels of his wool coat. That wasn't enough protection, so he reached inside the vehicle for his grey lambswool scarf before setting off through the dense fog towards the

Post Office.

The first house he walked past was a quaint building, sporting a sign on the gate that read, "Rebecca's Bed & Breakfast." He paused a moment to look at it.

Looks like a friendly place to stay, he thought idly, *if you happen to want to spend the night in this village – although it's hard to see why one would.*

The front door opened and Father James stepped out onto the garden path bordered with seashells.

Mark waved. "Just the man I was hoping to run into!"

Father James' face didn't register the same sentiment. "What brings you here?"

"I heard about poor Dave Miller. Sad business."

"Yes, it is."

"Were you with him when he died?"

"Thankfully, yes."

"Giving him the Last Rites, were you?"

The priest's eyes narrowed and Mark could tell he sensed a trap.

"I assisted the new priest, who hadn't administered them before."

"I see." Mark winked gauchely. "Any chance we could have a cup of coffee together? It's beastly cold out here."

"What do you really want, Mark?"

"Well, first to offer my sincere condolences. I know Dave lived here for many years and I'm sure his death has come as a blow to the village residents."

"But not to you, I imagine," the priest said. "Come to see if he's really dead?"

"Father, how uncharitable!"

"And yet, how true."

"I understand you told the courier yesterday that he had passed away, and I have no reason to doubt your word."

"When it's convenient."

"I say, old chap, being removed from active duty has removed your sense of humour." Mark rubbed his hands together for warmth. "Any chance of that coffee?"

Father James appeared about to refuse, then said, "Of course. You'll find an old friend of yours lives here."

Mark wondered who that might be.

He stepped inside the boarding house and the familiar looking lady, whom he'd seen outside the Post Office the other day, walked out of the dining room into the hallway.

Father James closed the front door behind them and said, "Rebecca, we have a visitor. You remember Mark Boulder, don't you?"

So *this* was the Rebecca who ran the bed and breakfast. Mark automatically put out his hand.

Rebecca didn't return the favour. "Only too well. I hope you don't plan to stay?"

"No, don't worry. This is a flying visit."

"Good."

"Might I prevail upon you for two cups of coffee?" asked the priest.

"I'll do it for you, Father."

"Thank you so much. I think the breakfast room would be the best place to drink undisturbed at this time of the morning, do you agree?"

Rebecca nodded. "I'll have it ready in about ten minutes."

"Thank you, Rebecca," said Mark.

"Don't thank me. I'm not doing it for *you*." She walked off, leaving Mark suitably chastened. But he knew the feeling wouldn't last long.

Father James ushered him into a small room

decorated with cream wallpaper covered in blue cockleshells, scallops and seahorses. He was led to a table with napkins that matched the walls, tucked inside white ceramic rings with a single blue seahorse on each.

Mark thought the nautical theme rather overdone, but it was cheerful.

The two men sat opposite each other at an alcove table and Mark supposed the view outside must be pretty, but with this infernal fog he couldn't see a thing. It was going to make the drive home difficult.

Before Rebecca arrived with their coffee, he said, "She really doesn't like me, does she?"

"And that's just based on the past. Imagine how much more she'd dislike you if she had any idea what you've been up to more recently."

Mark squinted at him. "I suppose you're going to tell her?"

"You suppose wrongly."

"Ever the decent chap."

"I try."

"Hasn't done you much good, has it?"

"I like to believe it has done me a great deal of good in the eyes of Our Lord and Saviour."

Rebecca came in and made short work of serving them coffee and placing a plate of the priest's favourite biscuits between them.

Father James smiled up at her. "Thank you, Rebecca, that's very thoughtful."

"*You* are very welcome, Father." She nodded to him and left the room.

Mark stirred a spoonful of sugar in his coffee, saying, "So, with Dave gone, are you still going to pursue the charges against me?"

The priest glanced through the window at the

worsening fog and drank his coffee. Mark's bile rose at this delaying tactic.

His old room-mate sighed. "I'm afraid it's too late. Dave's sister has already gone to the authorities. He gave her everything in case he died before you were brought to justice." He raised his eyebrows. "I believe she's also alerted the newspapers."

Mark clenched his jaw. His eyes took on a vicious expression and suddenly he understood why people commit murder.

But he couldn't do that in broad daylight at a respectable boarding establishment. Or ever, for that matter.

He rolled his tongue back and forth over the teeth under his upper lip. "How are you enjoying your little vacation from the priesthood?"

"I am never on vacation from my vocation," Father James responded evenly. But he appeared puzzled that Mark knew about his demotion.

Mark pressed his advantage. "Can't do any preaching now, though, can you?"

"Never fear, there are plenty of other avenues open to me for spreading God's Word."

"Such as?"

"Why are you interested?" said Father James. "You don't seem to want to hear His Word anymore."

"Maybe I do."

"In that case, Father Gregory the new priest will take your confession."

Mark's face dropped. "Why can't you? Aren't you allowed to hear confessions anymore, either?" He only wanted to go to this priest for confession; he already knew the worst.

"The bishop hasn't expressly forbidden it, but I doubt

he would approve, especially since he's put another priest in my place." Father James looked at him sideways. "And you don't have a history of making truthful confessions to me."

"What makes you think I'll be truthful to Father Gregory?"

"That's on your conscience, not mine."

*

Mark was a bundle of nerves when he drove home through the thick haze. He worried about having a bad accident and across that the huge bombshell that Father James had announced was about to explode in his life.

He wished he hadn't come. Once again, the priest had gained the upper hand.

How did the man manage to remain as peaceful and recollected as before his removal from parish life?

Chapter Twenty: The Ruddminster Gazette

Saturday, 2nd March

Mark rose early on Saturday morning to find Mary sitting at the kitchen island in her dressing gown. Her fingernails tapping on the marble surface sounded like glass splinters falling from a great height onto corrugated iron.

Today's Ruddminster Gazette lay in front of her, with an open laptop next to it, and her eyes narrowed as he approached. She shoved the newspaper in his direction and turned the computer screen towards him. Both of them were screaming the same terrible headlines.

"Take your pick," she hissed.

Mark grabbed the newspaper and hastily exited the room, sensing Mary's hatred follow him out. He leaned against the hall wall with his eyes closed, fighting off increasing panic, before squinting at the front page.

Above a photo of him looking cynical, ran the first headline: *Financial Director Wrecks Hundreds of Seniors' Lives*.

Underneath came a second article entitled *Bogus Charity Set Up to Pay Boulder's Bribes*. Inset was another picture of him, taken at the charity function in the Monastery Hotel. He was holding a glass of champagne with a smug expression.

Gulping, Mark reached for his coat and car keys. He had to escape the house.

Mary appeared in the hallway. "Look at my brave husband running away."

He gave his best attempt at a scornful smile and slammed the front door behind him.

The sun was not yet fully risen as he drove east along the edge of the moors, looking for a parking spot.

He must stop soon or he would burst; he felt as if a dozen hippos were sitting on his chest and rats were gnawing at his stomach lining.

He found a space. Staggering out of the car he ran, clutching the newspaper, to the nearest tor. Too breathless to climb up the stones, he sat on the base.

Head flung back, he gasped for air, trying to push away the heavy mammals and subdue the malevolent rodents.

When his breathing improved and his pulse had settled into a calmer rhythm, he looked out across the moor.

Shafts of dawn light were piercing through the mist and a single ray of gold came to rest on a rabbit chewing grass in front of him. Mark could see the delicate veins running through the animal's translucent ears.

The tableau portrayed the innocent side of life now closed to him and stirred up an unbearable longing.

Taking a deep breath, he flattened the paper on his knees and forced himself to read it.

It was all there. How he'd 'allegedly' been reckless with the funds of the senior investors in his company and lost all their savings. How he'd set up the Helping Seniors Charity to make himself look good, even though his own actions were responsible for their plight.

In the second article he was accused of bribing the deceased, Dave Miller, to keep quiet about his actions, and an unnamed source even suggested that the accountant's 'sudden' death was not from natural causes.

It got worse. A rumour was circulating that Mark had

conducted an affair with a female employee at the company and got her pregnant, then forced her to have an abortion and accept bribes to remain silent. The payments to both parties had allegedly come out of charity funds.

Upon learning this, the article continued, Bishop Robert Marsden, Mark Boulder's brother-in-law, had abruptly withdrawn his support from Helping Seniors and stepped down as co-treasurer. The bishop was quoted as saying, 'Of course, these are only accusations at present, but I feel it wise not to involve the Church in even a whiff of possible scandal.'

Under any other circumstances, Mark would have laughed out loud at such hypocrisy.

He let the paper drop to the ground. Elbows on knees, he held his head in his hands. Everything was collapsing on top of him, but he had no one to blame but himself.

He was stunned by the all-encompassing nature of the accusations. How, for example, had they found out about Rita? He'd made the first payment to her only yesterday!

He remained at the tor a long while without reaching any firm plan on how to proceed from here. The only thing he *was* sure of, was that his wife would not be lost for words.

Feeling the tip of his nose go numb, he headed back to his car.

*

Mary was in the sitting room with her mobile phone next to her on the sofa.

Mark stood in the doorway. "I imagine you have a lot to say."

"Where do I start?" Her voice sounded rough and he could see she'd been crying.

"Where would you like to start?"

"By telling you that you've brought utter disgrace and humiliation to our family – to me, to the children and to *their* families. You've shown total disregard for anyone's feelings but your own and proved what a selfish bastard you are, over and over again. You're not fit to be a husband or father."

"You're not choosing to presume me innocent until proven guilty, then?"

She picked her coffee mug off the side table and threw it at him. "Get *out*!"

The mug missed him and hit the wall behind, sending a cascade of brown liquid down the satin wallpaper and breaking into myriad shards on the oak floorboards.

Mark looked at the mess then back at his wife, and a broad grin stretched across his face. Her loss of composure was oddly satisfying, not to mention the stains on her precious wall.

But she wasn't finished. "Don't expect the children to want anything to do with you, either!"

Mark blinked.

"Not so complacent now, are we?"

He couldn't think of a response.

In an even voice, she said, "I repeat, get out of this house. I stand by my earlier statement that I will not divorce you, but I refuse to spend another moment under the same roof."

There was nothing Mark could say. He nodded and went to the bedroom.

*

He packed his bags swiftly.

Mary stood in the doorway to make sure he got into his BMW. He turned on the engine with no idea where to go. It needed to be a place where no one knew him, and that ruled out Devon.

Heading north, he found a roadside café on the other side of the county line where he could have breakfast and think things over.

The waitress took his order and poured him a mug of inferior coffee. He sipped on it and attempted to hide his disgust as he pondered where in England he'd like to visit.

By the time he finished his bacon, eggs, sausage and fried toast, he'd made a choice.

Feeling more like himself again, he climbed back into his car and typed a destination into the SatNav.

Chapter Twenty-One: Father James
Saturday, 2nd March

That same Saturday morning Father James sat down at his usual table in the breakfast room of the B & B to find a copy of *The Ruddminster Gazette* resting on his napkin.

A brief perusal revealed that Dave Miller's sister had lost no time in letting the press know about Mark Boulder's activities.

Rebecca came in to pour his coffee and pointed at the broadsheet. "I always knew he was no good, even back then."

Inclined to agree with her, Father James nevertheless managed to say, "We still need to pray for him."

"You're too good for this world, Father."

She was about to leave, with the paper still lying on the table, but Father James handed it to her. "I'd rather not read this."

She tucked it under her arm. "Can't say as I blame you, Father. It's all pretty depressing."

"Now, on a completely different topic, there is something I'd like to discuss with you – when you have time."

"Oh, what's that?"

"I'd appreciate your help with a project."

"Then how about elevenses back here this morning?"

The priest laughed. "Sounds divine, Rebecca. I'll see you then."

He felt guilty about his hostess adding extra comforts without adding extra charges, and elevenses was a frequent one. He had broached the subject of additional payment with her once and been met with high dudgeon that he should even suggest it. "It's that bishop as should be paying the extra, Father, not you. But we all know *that'll* happen when Farmer Russell's Gloucester Old Spots sprout wings and fly across the Channel and home again."

Father James had smiled at this interesting image. Forbearing to comment on her opinion of the bishop, he'd expressed his deep gratitude for her kindness.

Judith had finished licking out her bowl in the kitchen and trotted in to see him. The few human guests who came and went had no problem with this, and most of them thought her charming. Father James hoped no one would report this breach of health and safety to the Food Standards Agency.

"Come on, Judith, let's go for another walk on the beach."

The earlier mist over the Channel had dissipated and bright sunshine reduced the chill in the air. While it didn't create warmth, it spread a welcome cheerfulness over the seascape.

Throwing the lacrosse ball into the water, Father James wondered how his university friend was faring after this public humiliation. He was tempted to reach out to him, but Mark might take it the wrong way, and see it as self-righteousness rather than genuine commiseration.

He moved on to more productive thoughts.

In the short time away from his church duties he'd not been idle. When he wasn't praying or exercising his dog, he was jotting down ideas for his video 'talks.'

He planned to write several series on different topics and perhaps even put them in a book.

Judith carried her rubber ball out of the water for the umpteenth time. She dropped it at his feet, shook herself vigorously, splashing drops of water on his cassock, and lay down panting.

Father James squatted beside her for a few moments, drawing idly in the wet sand with his index finger. The action brought to mind Jesus writing in the sand when the crowd was poised to stone the adulterous woman, and this gave him another idea for one of his talks.

His thighs began to ache and he stood up. Checking his watch, he saw there was ample time to sketch out another essay around this new inspiration before his meeting with Rebecca.

Back at the Bed & Breakfast, he rubbed Judith down with the towel Rebecca left hanging by the rear door. He fetched his pad and pen from the bedroom, then settled at his table in the breakfast room alcove with the Collie lying beside him, and scribbled down his latest thoughts.

The aroma of warm crumpets and melted butter an hour and a half later announced the arrival of Rebecca and their elevenses.

God was taking care of His humble servant and for that Father James was thankful.

He explained his plan for a series of videos and asked if her son-in-law might be able to help him produce them.

Rebecca smiled. "Dan's the one who made the video that went viral, Father."

"So, *he's* the one I have to thank!" He looked at her hopefully. "Do you think he'd be willing to continue making them?"

"I'm sure he'd be happy to."

"God bless you both. Hopefully this project will bring souls to God and make me feel useful again."

"I'll talk to him today." She offered him another crumpet. "Speaking of doing useful things, have you done anything about getting your old job back?"

Father James nodded. "I've contacted a priest with a good reputation in these matters."

His ex-parishioners had strongly urged him to contact a Canon lawyer to take his case for reinstatement to Rome. He was deeply touched by their insistence on creating a fund to pay for these professional services, yet wished they weren't so angry at the bishop for removing him.

This had led to a stipulation of his own: he insisted they pray for Bishop Marsden's soul every day, and to this end had drafted a prayer for them to recite.

He helped Rebecca clear the table and carried the tray back to the kitchen. There she dismissed his offers of further assistance and told him to get back to his talks.

She bent down to stroke Judith. "I'll let you know as soon as I've talked to my Anna's husband."

"Thank you – and for the wonderful snack."

Father James arranged his writing pad and pen on the table again. He was working on paragraph subheadings, when Rebecca came back into the room to tell him that Anna's husband was very pleased to be asked to help with the project. "Just let him know when, Father."

"That's great news! I'll work out a schedule and run it by you."

Rebecca remained standing.

The priest looked up. "Was there anything else?"

"Oh, just that I'm surprised to see someone writing by hand on real paper these days. It's so unusual. Don't you use a laptop?"

Father James sighed. "Alas 'my' laptop," he put air quotes around the word, "belongs to St. Jude Church and as such is only available to the incumbent parish priest." He smiled. "But it's always good to improve one's handwriting."

Rebecca peered at his notes. "Is that so? What did your writing look like before it improved?"

The priest laughed.

"Your school teachers must have dreaded reading your essays!" Rebecca said.

"I confess to receiving many uncomplimentary comments regarding their legibility."

"Well, as long as *you* can read it, that's the main thing, Father. I'll leave you to it."

He sighed. A laptop would really be useful for this project. But he had no idea what income to expect while he was in this state of limbo, or whether he could hope to receive any salary at all. He must summon the courage to contact the bishop about it.

In the meantime, he must be frugal. He couldn't afford to live at Rebecca's forever. Never would he have imagined the day would come when he'd ask himself what else he was good for besides being a Catholic priest.

With that question unresolved, he turned his attention to his current task. Here, at least, was something he *could* do.

He'd just finished the layout of the talk inspired by this morning's doodling in the sand, when a text came through on his phone – another expense he must monitor.

Father Gregory was inviting him to the rectory for lunch after noon Mass tomorrow. He had a few pressing things to discuss.

Father James agreed. *May I bring Judith?* he added.

The reply was immediate. *Of course!*

Chapter Twenty-Two: The Lake District

Sunday, 3rd March

When Mark awoke on Sunday, it took him a moment to remember he was in the Lake District.

He'd driven six hours the day before, mostly up the M6, and stopped for the night in the picturesque town of Kendal.

As he snuggled under the heavy duvet in his room at Allhallows Inn, Mary's last words rang in his ears, accusing him of running away. She didn't understand. This wasn't running away; he needed time alone to work out his next steps. Putting as many miles as possible between him and the scandal would give him a better perspective and allow him to think more clearly.

One thing he already knew. Going into the office this week was out of the question; he'd have to talk to his number two man about managing things in his absence.

He grimaced. Would the company survive this?

But first things first: a hearty breakfast – hopefully less greasy than yesterday's and with better coffee – then a look at the map to find a charming village with an equally charming bed and breakfast where he could spend a few days in blissful anonymity.

Mrs. Parkson, the proprietor of Allhallows Inn, was most helpful. Once he'd cleared his plate of scrambled eggs and spicy Cumberland sausage served in a long coil, she sat next to him and went through a list of potential candidates.

"If you're looking for the most out-of-the-way places, these should fit the bill. It's the off season, so you won't have a problem finding a room."

She gave her personal opinion of each, free of charge, then poured him a second cup of excellent coffee, also free of charge, and left him to choose.

It occurred to Mark that such remote locations might not take credit cards. This wasn't the city of Ruddminster. He surreptitiously counted the notes in his wallet and decided there was enough for a couple of nights if he couldn't use plastic.

He planned to take a leisurely drive to Keswick, have lunch there, then travel the short distance to the Westfell Bed & Breakfast in the village of Fellstock, Mrs. Parkson's personal recommendation.

He went up to his room to call and reserve a room for three nights. "Do you take credit cards?" he asked the thick-accented woman at the other end.

"Oh, no sir, they charge us too much. Cash only, I'm afraid."

"That's O.K." said Mark and she told him the room rate.

He checked out of the inn, where he could thankfully use his credit card, then put his bags in the BMW.

He went back in to use the cash machine in a small area leading off the foyer.

It only allowed him to withdraw £200. Mark frowned. He wanted £500. He tried again and was told he couldn't take any more money out today.

With the cash he had on him, he could only last a few days. He needed to sort this out quickly.

On a whim, he asked for the balance in his current account. The machine told him he had precisely £200.

What the – ?! There should be at least £5,000 in there! Where was the rest?

A horrible thought occurred to him as he requested his savings account details.

The machine let him know he had £0.

He spat.

Mary!

Boy, had she been busy the moment he left the house! Although the bank closed at 3 p.m. on Saturdays, she'd made full use of the available time.

It was *his* money, dammit! He'd earned it, not her!

Seething, he made his way back to the car and left Kendal.

The drive along the A591 took him along beautiful lakes with soaring peaks on either side, and through old villages delightful even to the spoiled eye of a Devon man. But the whole experience was marred by the spiteful actions of his darling wife.

Thirty minutes into the journey, when he trusted himself enough to control his temper, he called her.

"How's my fugitive?" she asked.

He counted to five, fighting the urge to yell obscenities. "What did you do with my money?"

"It's *our* money, Mark, and I've put it somewhere safe."

"Why?"

"Because you're soon going to have to part with most of it."

"What do you mean? You said you weren't going to pursue a divorce."

"And I won't. But, unlike you, I didn't run away. I've had an interesting chat with a solicitor who handles company malfeasance. You're in big trouble, Mark."

He tried to laugh this off. "What's the worst that can happen to me?"

"You won't find it so amusing when I tell you you're facing huge fines and a prison sentence. If you're lucky that sentence will be suspended – *if* you behave yourself. But you won't be able to head a company again, or be in charge of public or corporate funds."

Mark's heart was racing. "What about the charity?"

"My brother and I have stepped in. We'll make the necessary apologies for unknowingly being a part of your deception, and distribute the funds among all the seniors you defrauded."

"Maybe that money will be deducted from the fines."

"Or maybe you'll have a lot of angry donors wanting their money back after I've given it all away."

"You're deliberately trying to ruin me!"

"Oh, please, Mark, don't make me laugh."

The only silver lining to this massive cloud was that now the scandal was out in the open, he didn't need money for paying Rita off.

"What am I supposed to live on if you keep all my money for fines? How am I supposed to earn a living?"

"The same way as Father James, I imagine. And I expect you'll forfeit your pension."

Mark had paid the highest possible amount into the Boulder Enterprises' pension plan, and a significant sum was waiting for his retirement. He could barely prevent himself from screaming. "I suppose *you* get that?"

"I am entitled to the widow's portion."

"How nice for you."

Mary was silent for a few seconds. "None of this is nice for me, Mark."

"Look, I earned that money and it isn't fair for you to steal it. You've got to let me have *something*."

"I suppose I could give you a small stipend. I expect that's what Father James is getting."

"Why do you keep whittling on about a Father James? Who's he?"

"Don't play the innocent. I know *you* are responsible for his ousting. Yet another person you've hurt, Mark."

"Where did you get *that* idea?"

"My brother told me you fed him stories about the priest and forced him to take action."

Mark didn't know whether to believe that or not. But the bishop certainly wasn't above lying to Mary to preserve her good opinion of him.

"Is your brother going to reinstate Father James?" he asked.

"I didn't inquire. Why do you ask?"

"Because, if I lied to him there's no reason not to put him back in his parish, is there?" Mark added, "Especially now that *I've* been disgraced."

There was a long pause at the other end.

Mark asked, "How much will this stipend be?"

He flinched, remembering Rita's capitulation to his offer of a bribe.

After bickering back and forth, Mary agreed to give him enough to stay in the Lake District for the week. After that he must come home and face the music.

"Before you get any ideas, by 'coming home' I don't mean living in this house, Mark. I mean staying close to Ruddminster. Once you return, we'll renegotiate the amount of money you'll need for that."

Mark bit his lower lip as evil thoughts about his wife ran through his head. He slowed down for a forty mile an hour limit and the physical reduction in speed calmed him enough to say, "Fine. I'll call you next Saturday, when I'm on my way back. *Please* don't forget to deposit that money!"

It was only a temporary solution, but it afforded Mark time and space to lick his wounds.

Fifteen minutes later, he wound down the car window and let in the country air. He'd left the A591 and was now on the Penrith Road leading west to Keswick.

The view was magnificent. To his right flowed the River

Greta towards the lake ahead. Beyond it towered the Northern Fells, their snowy caps rising above the low clouds as they kept watch on the town below.

The beauty of his surroundings mesmerised Mark. He found the Lake Road which led to the massive Derwent Water extending south from Keswick. He passed a café and restaurant and decided to stop there for lunch after checking out the lake.

He drew into a small car park opposite four jetties projecting into the water and several canoes pulled onto the shore.

A large commercial boat with a wooden keel was tied to the jetty directly in front of him. Passengers were boarding, while others were coming off and strolling towards the car park.

Mark observed the carefree attitudes of these travellers, wishing he could join them.

Eyes closed, he reclined his seat and reflected on Mary's comment about Father James. Had Bishop Marsden reduced his salary? Priests earned very little as it was. Had he perhaps cut off *all* his income? Was Father James now penniless because of him?

Of course, if Father James hadn't been stubborn and old-fashioned, the bishop wouldn't have had an excuse to fire him. The man had brought it on himself.

But if Mark hadn't behaved so recklessly and covered it up, there'd have been no need for his brother-in-law to find an excuse in the first place.

His conscience, dulled though it was, still admitted to playing a huge part in Father James' demise. It irked him that Mary was right.

Changing his mind about having lunch, he pressed on past the café and restaurant to Fellstock. The village was on the other side of the huge lake, right on the water.

The Northwestern Fells provided an imposing backdrop, and Mrs. Parkson had promised him a stunning view looking back across the Derwent Water to Keswick, 'especially at night.'

Mark had missed Sunday Mass, but he wasn't going to find a Catholic church out here. Oh, well, he'd already skipped it once. Another time wouldn't be the end of the world.

Westfell Bed & Breakfast came up on his left. Two storeys high, with a back garden leading down to the water's edge, the grey stone building must have weathered centuries of storms brewing across the lake or descending from the Fells.

Mark smiled. It was the perfect sanctuary.

Chapter Twenty-Three: Father Gregory

Sunday, 3rd March and the following week

Father James' old Triumph groaned its way over the crest of the hill.

His heart ached at the sight of his old rectory.

Judith's tail was thumping loudly on the passenger seat when he parked outside St. Jude. He'd hardly opened his door before she leaped over him and bounded off to her old home.

He caught up with her. "Sorry, old girl, we don't live here anymore."

He opened the gate and she trotted up to the front door. When he knocked instead of producing the key, she looked up in confusion, which only deepened when Father Gregory appeared on the threshold.

"Come in, come in! Good to see you. Hello, Judith." He leaned down to stroke her.

He led them into the sitting room, where on the tiny coffee table lay a tray with two small glasses and a bottle of cheap sherry. "You'll need something to help you cope with my cooking."

"I came for the company rather than the food," Father James said, "but I'm always ready for a pre-lunch drink."

Father Gregory pointed to the armchair. "Please, I imagine that was your usual spot."

"Thank you. Yes, it was." His guest sank into his old chair and Judith sprawled next to him.

Father Gregory handed him a full glass, and sat on the sofa looking uncomfortable.

"How are things going?" asked Father James.

The young priest took a quick gulp. "Not well," he

confessed, "not well at all. I need your help."

"I'm all ears. What's the problem?"

Father Gregory reddened as he admitted his devastation at the parishioners' refusal to give to the collection basket. "Bishop Marsden will not be impressed when I tell him the sum of my first week's offerings is zero." He glanced at the older man. "Is it true that you're receiving money from the parishioners to finance your cause for reinstatement?"

"Yes. I'm afraid that's why your collection baskets are empty. The people are very upset with the bishop, and I can't say I blame them."

"You're lucky, Father. Such loyalty to one's parish priest is very rare."

"Luck has nothing to do with it. If you lead your flock with integrity, and equip them with the truths they need to travel the narrow path to heaven, you will also gain their trust." He smiled. "And discover how naturally generous they are."

Father Gregory grimaced. "I understand you were also bequeathed half of Dave Miller's estate."

"Yes," said Father James. "He was so upset at my removal that he changed his will at the last moment. It was a big surprise when his sister told me about it."

"If there's any surplus, would you consider giving that to the Church?"

"I have to honour my parishioners' wishes. They feel they've been badly let down by the diocese, so I'm bound to use the money as they direct.

"I've promised that any extra funds will go to the The Coalition for Canceled Priests to help other unfairly dismissed clerics. I'm sad to say, there are hundreds of us." Father James peered over the rim of his sherry glass. "But remember what I said. Your parishioners are not going to hand over their money if you water down the truth. They want to hear the undiluted Word of God."

Father Gregory couldn't know that several attendees of the 7:30 a.m. Mass that morning had already been to see Father James to complain about the new priest.

Said Mrs. Newman from the Post Office, "He's saying 'dare we hope that everyone gets to heaven?' and that Purgatory doesn't exist, and that Hell is hopefully empty."

"Why bother to be Catholic – or even Christian," chimed in her husband, "if there's no cause to worry about going to Hell, Father?"

"And why did Christ have to die on the Cross for us, if we don't need saving?" asked Bill Crowther, owner of the Brambling Butchers.

Mary Bellham, who ran the village grocery, shook her head. "It's not right, what he's saying, Father, especially as we're going into Lent this week."

"We're not going to give him a single penny for his nonsense!" added Mrs. Newman.

Father James told them he was seeing the new pastor for lunch, and would voice their concerns.

"How about writing his sermons for him?" suggested the butcher, eliciting 'Hear, hear!' from everyone.

Father James now said to his host, "I know you're under pressure from Bishop Marsden to preach a low-key message, just as I was. But you have already seen it doesn't pay – literally."

"How do you know my message was low-key? Has anyone said anything to you?"

Father James couldn't lie. He nodded.

"I see. Well, do you think the bishop will allow for more – um – forthright sermons when he sees he's losing money?"

"I do think he'll be surprised at the reaction of the parish to my removal. Perhaps you could point out to him exactly why you have no collection to offer the diocese this week, and ask if you can continue preaching in the manner to which the good people of this area are accustomed?"

"But in that case, he may as well reinstate *you*, Father."

Father James smiled sadly. "Logically, you are correct. But logic has little to do with it, I fear. I'm handing over the baton to you, as a younger, more energetic priest, to carry on the good work I began and which the Church so desperately needs you to do."

He was laying a heavy burden on the newly-ordained cleric, who had doubtless hoped to make a good impression on Bishop Marsden and place himself on the fast track in the Catholic hierarchy. But priests aren't supposed to strive for earthly recognition; their job is to lead souls to heaven, and thus ensure their own entrance through the pearly gates.

"Forfeit the glory of high posts, or forfeit Heaven," Father James warned, "you can't have both."

He watched his host's face fall.

Father Gregory poured them both another sherry and said, "Is that why you were so happy here in King's Brambling? You never had any ambitions to go higher up the ranks?"

"I had everything I could possibly want. The love of my parishioners, a beautiful location, my trusty dog," he bent down to stroke Judith's back, "a beautiful old church and quaint accommodation. Why would I exchange that for the cutthroat world of clerical ambition?"

"When you put it that way, I suppose I am lucky to be

here."

"You have no idea just *how* lucky." Had Father James himself appreciated this parish when he first replaced the deceased pastor fifteen years ago? He couldn't recall.

"Are you ready for some terrible food?"

Father James grinned. "Always."

Over a meal of almost burned roast pork and potatoes, Father James could see the man was lonely. No villagers had offered hospitality to the priest they blamed for the ousting of their beloved pastor and Father James must do what he could to change that.

He was also at fault. He should have set aside self-pity and extended a helping hand, for here was an ideal opportunity to train this priest to be a proper shepherd, Bishop Marsden notwithstanding.

Over a soggy trifle, Father Gregory asked if his guest could be prevailed upon to help draft the sermon for Ash Wednesday? "The bishop was most emphatic that there be no mention of sin or doing penance during the season of Lent. Perhaps you could give me some pointers on how to keep the parishioners *and* the bishop happy?"

"I'd be most glad to. We'll tread a careful path between traditional orthodoxy and the bishop's leniency."

Father James agreed to come back the next day and give his assistance. He then broached the subject of baby Mark's memorial service. "Rita was hoping to have it this Saturday. Would you be willing to officiate?"

"What exactly does one *do* at a memorial service for an aborted baby?"

"How about letting me give you some pointers on that tomorrow, as well?"

Father Gregory was looking a good deal happier when the older priest and his dog left some time later. And on the short drive home Father James remembered his resolve to do what he could to ease the new priest's loneliness.

Chapter Twenty-Four: Rabbit Prints
Sunday, 3rd March and the following week

Mark was pleased with his upstairs bedroom at the back of the Westfell Bed & Breakfast, which afforded a view of Keswick across the lake and the Northern Fells beyond.

He was hungry and asked his landlady about restaurants in the area that took credit cards.

"Well, sir, there's always Lingholm Kitchen, just south of here." Mrs. Bothart looked at her old-fashioned wrist watch. "They're open till 4:30 and serve hot food until 3:30. If you go soon, you'll make it in time." She pointed to a framed print on the wall. "See that?"

"Yes," said Mark, peering at a sketch of three fictional characters from his youth; Flopsy, Mopsy and Cotton-Tail.

"That was drawn by Miss Beatrix Potter when she spent her holidays at Lingholm," Mrs. Bothart proudly explained. "They say as the walled garden there was her inspiration for Mr. McGregor's garden in *The Tale of Peter Rabbit*."

Mark rolled his eyes. What did he care about the tale of a silly rabbit?

Suddenly remembering a long pair of sun-kissed ears attached to another rabbit on Dartmoor, he frowned. Was this some kind of God moment? But seriously, *rabbits*?

He shook his head.

"Don't think the place'll suit you, sir?"

Mark smiled. "Not at all. I was reminded of when her books were read to me as a youngster. I think the place will do very well."

It was too cold to sit outdoors this time of year, but the Lingholm café's large glass wall afforded a splendid view of the craggy mountains beyond the vegetable garden mentioned by Mrs. Bothart.

The only other people there, an elderly couple, had finished their lunch and were leaving, but were soon replaced by several walkers arriving for tea.

Mark ordered smoked chicken and avocado sandwiches, and a glass of Prosecco, the only alcohol on offer.

Gazing at the walled garden, Mark imagined Peter Rabbit hopping around the cabbages. Beatrix Potter's stories had enthralled him as a boy, when life was a well-regulated series of Sunday Masses, monthly confession, and receiving Communion in a state of grace. In those days he had no inkling about upcoming temptations and his future fall.

His mind turned to Rebecca's little B&B by the sea, and the sacked priest currently residing there.

He thought about the seniors whose money he'd squandered, and Rita and the baby, and Dave Miller. He even spared a thought for Mary.

How could one man create such a trail of wreckage? It would be impressive, if it weren't so depressing.

Monday, 4th March

Fortified by a hearty breakfast on Monday morning, he forced himself to check his emails.

Linda in HR informed him that Dave Miller's funeral was this coming Friday. He was too embarrassed to attend – especially after the rumour that he may be responsible for the man's 'sudden' death.

She made no mention of Friday's breaking news.

It was time to talk to his number two man. Not wanting anyone to overhear the conversation, he drove to a quiet spot by the lake.

Ordinarily Dave Miller would be his right-hand man, but when he became ill the job went to Gustav Branstrom, of Swedish descent, who had worked for Dave and was a whiz with numbers.

"Hello, Gustav, how are things?"

"Not good, Mr. Boulder, not good." He pronounced it 'gud.' "A lot of clients have already closed their accounts with us. The staff are worried about their jobs – and wondering where you are."

"I've had a family emergency up north," Mark lied. "I shall be back in the office next Monday."

"A bigger emergency than this one?"

"I'm afraid so. How many accounts are we talking about? And how much money?"

The figures Gustav gave him were alarming. If the company continued to bleed like this, the whole business would collapse by the end of the week.

Mark must think of something to stem the haemorrhaging. "Gustav, tell all our investors that we will add an additional percentage point to their investment earnings, if they agree not to withdraw their money."

It would mean robbing Peter to pay Paul, but might just save the company.

"O.K., sir, I'll do that."

"Call me this evening, would you, and let me know how that's working?"

After the call, Mark sat staring at the lake, absorbing this bad news and worrying about Mary's predictions of going to jail, as well as being fined out of existence. He needed a good solicitor.

Thinking of Mary reminded him to drive to the branch of his bank in Keswick and check whether his wife had done as promised.

She had been true to her word and sent him more money. He could now stay until Saturday. He wasn't sure how he would spend the week, but it beat being in the line of fire back home.

He stopped for a bite in town, and used his phone to research reputable solicitors in the Devon area who'd dealt with cases like his. He was well into a delicious dessert of sticky toffee pudding before he found the right man.

After lunch he sat in his car and called Mr. Tibbett, of Tibbett, Tibbett & Treyman, in Ruddminster. Then he left Keswick and followed the lake road towards his lodgings.

Mr. Tibbett informed him that since this was his first offence, it was reasonably certain he wouldn't get a custodial sentence, but, he added, "there's no avoiding the fines, Mr. Boulder, and they will be heavy. Then you have to consider the possibility of a class action suit against you by the seniors. It's not looking good, I'm afraid."

Mark thanked him for his advice and they arranged to talk again the next day, once he'd absorbed this sobering information.

The mighty Fells mountains rose to his right, standing impassively over the minutiae of human existence and he wondered idly when the snow on their peaks would thaw.

Sleepy after his heavy meal, he went back to Westfell for a long nap and a break from his growing angst.

Two hours later, the strident tones of his mobile woke him.

It was Gustav.

Mark said in a cheerful voice, "Did our clients take the bait?"

The Swede sounded tired. "No, sir, they didn't. They're all bailing."

"*All* of them? Couldn't you think of *something* to stop them?" Holding clients' hands wasn't his forte – he hired people for that and clearly they weren't doing their job.

"All of them," repeated Gustav. "We've spent the whole day closing accounts and organising the return of our clients' investments."

"But that's *terrible*!" Mark said with a soupçon of reproach to suggest the blame for this catastrophe lay on shoulders other than his own.

Gustav gave a polite cough. "I feel I ought to warn you that reporters from the Ruddminster Gazette were here today with their cameras. Several investors called the paper to announce that they're pulling out. We tried to put as good a spin on the situation as possible. But it'll be on the local channels this evening, and national news tomorrow."

Mark had forgotten about the press and forced himself to keep his voice even. "Thank you for the heads up, Gustav."

"Does this mean you'll be back before Saturday, sir?"

"No, it doesn't."

No sooner was that conversation over, than Mark's phone rang again. A reporter wanted to interview him about his part in the Boulder Enterprises scandals. Mark was irked the man put the word in the plural – it made the situation sound so much worse.

"Innocent until proven guilty," he told the man.

"Then why are your investors abandoning your

company, Mr. Boulder? There must be a good reason."

"You know how it is with rumours. People panic. Once this whole thing dies down, they'll be back."

"I admire your optimism, Mr. Boulder. And – "

Mark cut him off.

That evening he was careful not to watch or listen to the news and congratulated himself on making a good move, by leaving Devon. Here he could pretend that nothing was wrong.

Chapter Twenty-Five: A Helping Hand
Monday, 4th March

Father James was as good as his word and returned to the rectory the next afternoon, bearing a packet of his beloved biscuits.

Delighted to see him, Father Gregory ushered him into the sitting room and motioned for him to take his old armchair again. "I've just got off the phone with Bill Crowther the butcher. He and his wife have invited me over to dinner tomorrow. They say it's to take advantage of the last chance for a good meal before Lent begins. Isn't that kind of them?"

Father James had spoken that very morning with several prominent members of the village, asking them to receive the new priest into their homes, and pointing out that "he didn't *choose* this assignment and *he* didn't get me kicked out. You need to help him become a good parish priest. Showing hospitality is a first step, whatever your feelings. Then he'll be able to serve you better."

He was proud of the butcher and his wife for heeding his request so promptly. "Excellent! I'm very happy for you."

Father Gregory arranged Father James' chocolate biscuits around the plain ones already on the large plate; then he set to pouring the tea.

That done, he indicated a pad and paper on the small table next him. "I'm ready to take notes if you want to get started."

"A keen pupil, I like that."

Over the next thirty minutes, Father James coached the young pastor in writing an Ash Wednesday homily that would go a long way to satisfying his audience. "It'll be an improvement on what you said at the Sunday Masses. But mind," he warned, "you can't steer a middle course for too long. They'll want to see that you are genuinely orthodox and not pandering to the progressive powers that be."

His pupil nodded. "Duly noted, Father. Do you mind if I run all my homilies by you for the foreseeable future?"

"I'm happy to look them over, but remember why I got kicked out. I could also get *you* into trouble."

"I just want to be a good priest, Father."

"You and I both."

"Why is the hierarchy preventing it?"

"It's very baffling. But we must stick to the one true Faith, even if it means being side-lined."

"I'd hate to be side-lined after only one assignment!"

"I'm afraid that's a chance you may have to take." His host sighed.

Father James didn't envy him. "Shall we discuss Saturday's ceremony for baby Mark?" he said.

*

Father Gregory called his new mentor late that Tuesday to say that the assigned altar server was unable to attend Ash Wednesday Mass tomorrow. This was a disaster. Did he know of anyone who might be willing to step into the position?

After a moment's hesitation, Father James offered himself.

"Do you really want to do it, Father? Won't it be strange for you?"

"Yes, it will, I won't deny it. But my job is to serve where I'm needed, and right now I'm needed in a different role."

"I can't thank you enough! Father, you're a saint!"

"Let's not get carried away, but it's good to be

appreciated. I'll be there twenty minutes before Mass tomorrow morning. Does that work for you?"

When the call was ended, Father James checked the exact wording of Bishop Marsden's decree. Nowhere did it say he wasn't allowed to serve in a non-priestly capacity at Mass. Therefore, he wasn't directly disobeying his superior.

Ash Wednesday, 6th March

He remained hidden in the sacristy with Father Gregory until Mass began, not wanting the parishioners to see him and get excited, thinking he'd been reinstated.

Mrs. Cotteshall, church organist on Sundays and village librarian during the rest of the week, struck up the notes to Number 463 in the hymnal, *From Ashes to the Living Fount.*
Father Gregory began his procession up the aisle.

Ahead of him walked Father James, carrying the crucifix on a long shaft. He felt everyone's stares as he placed the cross in its holder on the back wall and stood by the kneeler near the altar, with the hand bells on a cushion next to him.

Fresh-faced and nervous, Father Gregory began Mass as if nothing out of the ordinary were happening, and soon the pew members settled down and uttered the responses.

Roger Bellham, husband of Mary and co-owner of the grocery store, was today's lector. He walked up the altar steps to the pulpit and read the first reading from the Prophet Joel, in a sonorous voice.

"Even now, says the Lord, return to me with your whole heart, with fasting, weeping and mourning."

Afterwards, he stood back while the organist played

and sang Psalm 51. The congregation joined her in singing the response between each verse; *Be merciful, O Lord, for we have sinned.*

Roger then read the second reading, an epistle of St. Paul to the Corinthians.

The blood pulsed faster through Father James' veins at the saint's apt words; "We are ambassadors for Christ, as if God were appealing through us."

He said a prayer for Father Gregory, the new ambassador for Christ at St. Jude, that he might have the fortitude to lead this little flock along the narrow path of righteousness and truth, and away from the broad road of secularism and watered-down Catholicism that led to Hell.

Roger Bellham returned to his pew. Mrs. Cotteshall sang the verse before the Gospel and the congregation rose as Father Gregory bowed in front of the tabernacle and walked across to the pulpit.

Today's Gospel was from Matthew, in which Christ was admonishing his disciples to "take care not to perform righteous deeds in order that people might see them; otherwise, you will have no recompense from your heavenly Father."

The new priest's voice was clear and easy to understand, a bonus for the older laity.

"The Gospel of the Lord," he concluded.

"Praise to you, Lord Jesus Christ," they responded.

Seeing the resignation on everyone's faces as they sat down in anticipation of the sermon, Father James felt bad for the pastor. He had an uphill struggle ahead.

"Friends," began Father Gregory, "I need to make an admission. This homily," he held up several sheets of paper, "was written with the help of your former pastor, Father James." He glanced at his stand-in altar server. "I got off to a bad start on Sunday, and he was kind enough to give me assistance in producing words that are closer to those you are used to hearing.

"He advised me to tread carefully, after what has happened to him. But I did not become a priest to dilute the message of the Gospel."

Father James watched the parishioners staring in amazement, as he himself was doing.

Father Gregory continued. "As we are about to be reminded, we are dust, and unto dust we shall return. We came into the world with nothing and will leave with nothing except our faith and good works.

"We must take care not to let the values of the world influence our thinking and our actions. Jesus warns us against performing righteous deeds in order that others may see them. We owe our Creator all glory and allegiance. Therefore, do everything for His greater glory and not for human approval.

"The Truth is unchanged and never changing, it does not – it *cannot* bend to current whims or pander to political ideals.

"The Ten Commandments are as binding on us now as they were in Moses' day. We shall be held accountable for any and all infractions of that code handed down to us by God millennia ago.

"Remember Christ's words; we must love our neighbour as ourselves. This means not being afraid to admonish, with charity, anyone who is not walking in the way of the Lord, and urging them to come back into the fold. God will remember such acts of kindness on our deathbed.

"Ash Wednesday reminds us of our mortality, and our need to repent of our sins and turn back to God through the Sacrament of Reconciliation, which returns us to a state of grace.

"If you have a mortal sin on your conscience, I urge you to go to Confession as soon as you can. This is essential preparation for receiving the Eucharist, for 'he who receives unworthily eats and drinks condemnation upon himself.'

"My friends, let us use these forty days of Lent wisely, and be mindful that unless we come back to the Lord and openly acknowledge Him, He will turn His back on us.

"Aim high, aim for Heaven. The alternative is too awful to contemplate. God bless."

He made to leave the lectern, then stopped. "Normally we would take up a collection today, but I am not going to do that, as I know you wish to save your money to help Father James and other cancelled priests like him."

There were nods of approval from the pews. The man was learning fast.

Father James rose to hold the bowl of ashes for Father Gregory to bless. The congregants then formed a queue down the centre aisle and came forward to have a cross drawn on their foreheads by the priest's finger dipped in the ashes.

Mass continued as usual after that, with Father James assisting Father Gregory by bringing the chalice and the water and wine to the altar at the appropriate times, and washing the priest's hands.

It was humbling work, yet the demoted pastor was at peace. He thought of St. Padre Pio, the wonderful stigmatic priest, who was banned from saying Mass in public for many years because of falsehoods spoken against him.

I am in good company, he thought.

While Father Gregory said the prayers of Consecration

over the bread and wine, he imagined choirs of angels carrying both species to Heaven where they became Christ's Body and Blood, and returned to their place on the altar in an unbloody re-enactment of Jesus' sacrifice on the Cross.

When Mass was over, and the two men were processing down the aisle, Father Gregory whispered, "Do you think I should stand and greet everyone? Or will they prefer me to disappear?"

"Stand and be counted, Father. I don't think you'll regret it."

"O.K., but I want you next to me. We're in this together."

Chapter Twenty-Six: Bail
Tuesday, 5th March

At breakfast the next morning Mrs. Bothart gave Mark a strange look while pouring his coffee, and again, when she brought his scrambled eggs and Cumberland sausage. Her manner was decidedly off.

As she was clearing his plate, she asked, "Aren't you the Mark Boulder who was on the news this morning?"

"No." He shook his head.

"But you look a lot like him," she persisted.

"Coincidence."

"If you say so." She looked unconvinced and picked up the rest of his breakfast things without offering him a second cup of coffee.

So much for anonymity. Mark went upstairs and packed his things, then told Mrs. Bothart that he had a family emergency and needed to leave a day early. Looking relieved, she readily refunded the third night's money.

He sat in his car, wondering where he could go without being recognised. If somewhere this out of the way wasn't safe, then nowhere would be.

He wasn't ready to face the storm brewing back home, and desperately wanted to remain away until the last possible moment.

He decided to take the long route south, travelling on minor roads and stopping at tiny overnight places, in the hope that no one else would spot his similarity with the criminal on the news.

The kids hadn't called – for sure Mary had turned them against him. A crushing loneliness overcame him.

He thought about Father James, ousted from office yet beloved by his ex-parishioners, who were fighting his corner. Unlike Mark, the priest was on God's good side and it was paying off.

Travelling back and forth to Keswick almost daily, Mark had noticed a little Church of England chapel along the shores of Derwent Water.

Perhaps it was time to pay a visit to the Creator of translucent rabbit ears and put in a word or two on his own behalf.

*

Ten minutes later he was kneeling in the back pew of the ancient stone building, afraid to raise his eyes towards the large wooden cross hanging over the altar.

He wanted forgiveness, but how was he going to get it? Everyone hated him.

He mouthed a prayer asking God to show him the way out of this mess.

Mark walked out of the chapel shortly after, unsure that God had listened to a single word, yet clinging to the hope that He would quickly help him.

An unfamiliar Ruddminster area number rang on his mobile; it must be Mr. Tibbett, and he answered with a sinking heart as he got into his car.

"Mr. Boulder? This is Ronald Tibbett. Do you have a moment?"

"Yes."

"The police are looking for you, and I strongly advise you to go into the nearest station right away.

"You *will* be arrested, but they'll release you on bail after charging you. Call me when you get back out."

Arrested?

Stunned, Mark hunted in his SatNav for the directions to Keswick Police Station.

*

It was dark outside when he left Cumbria Police custody.

They had been perfectly polite, but the whole experience was mortifying.

He'd been searched, had his wallet, watch, belt and car keys taken away, and been put into a cold cell. Then interviewed and shown the charge sheet detailing his crimes.

It was a long list – they hadn't missed anything.

Finally, he was released on bail and given back his possessions.

The conditions of his freedom were that he live at his house in Dartleigh until his court date (Mary was going to love that) and hand in his passport at Ruddminster Police Station by Friday.

Also, he may not spend a single night outside the County of Devon and must report to Ruddminster Police Station once a week in person until his hearing at the magistrates' court.

Since it was late, he was allowed to spend one night en route before returning home, but must call Keswick Police Station to let them know where he was. A squad car may come round to verify his location.

Would the humiliation never end?

Mr. Tibbett, whom he called immediately afterwards, told him that the magistrates' court hearing was only the first step. Due to the severe nature of his crimes, he would be tried later in Crown Court.

If he obeyed the restrictions placed on him, there was a good chance his bail would be renewed after the hearing until his trial.

"You mean, if it isn't, I could languish in prison for *months*?"

Who would visit him? No one.

"Calm down, Mr. Boulder and just follow the conditions of your bail."

Mark found a cheap motel close to the M6 and called the Keswick Police to give his location.

He was grateful when no panda car appeared outside to embarrass him.

Wednesday, 6th March

By 6 o'clock the next morning, he was placing his suitcase in the BMW and debating whether to go back inside for his 'free' breakfast. He thought better of it and stopped at an eatery just off the motorway, an hour into his trip home.

He had the full works, which would keep him going until he reached Dartleigh.

Before setting off again, he looked inside the centre console for a cloth to wipe the condensation off the inside of his windscreen. He pulled out a large yellow duster and something fell onto the floor under the brake pedal.

He reached down to pick it up.

It was the rosary his daughter had given him for his last birthday. The beads were sapphire, his September birthstone. Was this a sign from above?

Fine, God, I'll do it! But I warn you, I don't remember all the prayers.

Mark made the Sign of the Cross and recalled that, being Wednesday, he ought to recite the Glorious Mysteries, when Christ rose from the dead. But he wasn't feeling glorious.

I hope you don't mind, but I'm more in the mood for the Sorrowful ones.

He had trouble remembering the Apostles' Creed at the start of the rosary, but knew the other prayers and hoped he was getting the order of the Mysteries right.

Five decades of the Rosary didn't make up for the missed Masses, but surely, they would earn him *some* Brownie points with God?

*

Four hours later, as he turned into his driveway, his throat constricted when the remote opened the garage door. He was not looking forward to seeing his wife.

Predictably, Mary was annoyed when he explained his bail conditions. "How long will you be staying here?"

"I can't say. I imagine the hearing in magistrates' court will be pretty soon, but afterwards I'll be out on bail again, waiting for my arraignment at the Crown Court."

"*Crown Court?*" Her eyes widened. "Then what?"

"I live here until my trial."

"So, you're going to be tried in front of a jury?"

"Unless I plead guilty."

"Are you going to do that?"

"I don't see any alternative. I have to talk to my solicitor again."

Mary scowled. "You could be living here for months, then?"

"Yes. But it is my home, too, don't forget."

"You forfeited your home when you decided to play nasty tricks on everyone, Mark."

"We'll just have to make the best of it."

Her eyes were hostile. "I already told you, I can't live under the same roof with you."

"What do you propose then?"

"I'm calling Robert."

*

She made him his last supper. While he ate it, she was in their bedroom packing two large suitcases.

Bishop Marsden had room for her at his palace and

invited her to stay there indefinitely. But she also planned to visit the children.

After refusing Mark's offer to put the cases in her Volvo, her parting shot was, "Enjoy the house while you can, Mark, *before you lose it.*"

He shut the side door to the garage and leaned back against it with a sigh of relief. No more snide comments – *and* he could sleep in his own bed again.

He grabbed a bottle of red wine from the rack to keep him company for the evening.

Thursday, 7*th* March

He woke up with a sore head the next day. It took two strong coffees before he could summon enough courage to call the office, after seeing online that his company's stock had plummeted even farther.

Gustav told Mark that Boulder Enterprises would probably go into administration and management would be taken over by an insolvency practitioner. If the company couldn't be rescued, the business would be broken up and the proceeds distributed to creditors, most of whom were the employees. "Since you're not here, I had to get legal advice on the company's behalf myself."

Mark ignored the man's petulant tone. "Do the staff know about this?"

"Not yet, sir. But you need to come and talk to them. They're really worried about their jobs."

Mark was afraid of being mugged if he went into the office. "Let's do a video conference with everyone this afternoon. Can you arrange that?"

Gustav's voice was strained. "I'll send you the link when it's been set up."

The Swede organised the meeting for 1 p.m.

Mark was tempted to start drinking beforehand, but appearing drunk would only increase the employees' ire. He needed to keep his mind clear – although he had no idea what he was going to tell them.

During the conference, his staff hurled invectives, calling him a coward and a swindler and telling him he should be in jail. Gustav tried to keep the conversation civilised, but there was no holding back the collective anger.

Then a man from accounting said the fatal words, "I hear the company is going into administration. What does that mean for all of us?"

This brought on a renewed spate of insults, and Gustav closed down the session for everyone except him and a grateful Mark.

Gustav said, "It looks as if administration means we all lose our jobs. The staff won't be happy."

"Let me look into that. This is new information for me, too. I'll call you when I've spoken to my solicitor and we'll put together an official message for the staff."

His next unpleasant task was to stop in at the Ruddminster Police Station and hand over his passport to the Devon & Cornwall Constabulary.

"See you next Thursday," the uniform behind the desk said amiably.

Mark managed a return smile and walked out, hoping no one he knew would see him, and doing his best not to look like a criminal.

On the way home, he called Mr. Tibbett. "What do you know about administration? I need to know the implications for my staff."

"I'll add that to my list of items to research." Ronald Tibbett coughed. "Now I need to let you know what this means for *you*."

By the time their phone conversation was over, Mark understood all too clearly what awaited him. After paying the fines and repaying moneys he owed to the seniors he'd robbed, he would be bankrupt.

Mark Boulder, founder of Boulder Enterprises, was poised to lose his house and his car, as well as his job and end up with nothing except the proverbial shirt on his back. And hopefully his trousers, too, he thought wryly.

His life was in ruins, as were his friendships and he had no one to turn to.

St. Peter's words came to him, when the disciples were deserting Jesus *en masse* because of His teaching on the Eucharist. Jesus asked the twelve apostles if they, too, were going to leave?

Simon Peter said: "Lord, to whom shall we go? You have the words of eternal life."

Chapter Twenty-Seven: Baby Mark
Saturday, 9th March

Rita sat nervously in the front pew of St. Jude, wearing a black coat, and a black veil draped over her blonde hair.

Father James was by her side, patting her on the arm. "You'll be fine."

It was 10 o'clock on Saturday morning, and the church was rapidly filling with villagers paying their respects to the unknown baby whose life had come to a premature end.

Rebecca had asked Rita's permission to open this ceremony to everyone. When the grieving mother had baulked at the idea of their knowing what she'd done, Rebecca told her she wasn't the only woman in the area who regretted her abortion. By allowing a public funeral she'd be doing a service to other mothers, who were consumed with guilt and silently mourning their loss. Her example would inspire them to come forward and arrange for their own unborn children to be acknowledged before God.

Now, as she heard the seats filling up behind her, Rita wished she hadn't agreed.

She glanced at the tiny coffin on a trestle next to her in the aisle. On top rested the few things she'd bought for baby Mark when she discovered she was pregnant. A white hooded snowsuit, a minute pair of yellow knitted socks and a blue woollen hat. He was due in September, when the weather turned cold, and would have needed the warm clothes.

The items reminded her of what would never be. After the service, they would be placed in the coffin and buried in the cemetery, where a headstone would later mark the spot.

She bowed her head to hide her welling tears from Father James.

The first few notes of 'Abide with Me' played on the organ and she stood up, shaking. The priest's reassuring arm gripped her elbow and together they sang the first two verses.

The funeral Mass had begun.

Rita had been given the choice of reading her chosen Bible excerpts. But she knew she wouldn't manage and had asked Father Gregory to take her place.

He read from the book of Lamentations and her heart broke all over again. Her soul, too, was bereft of peace and she had forgotten what happiness was.

She sat floundering in the misery of irreparable loss and Father James handed her a tissue.

Then, Father Gregory recited Psalm 25, reminding her that those who hope in the Lord will not be disappointed.

Rita squared her shoulders, telling herself to be brave for the sake of her baby boy. She needed strength to read her tribute to little Mark after Mass.

She was filled with gratitude to the villagers who'd come here to help her heal. She felt unworthy of their kindness, yet knew something good was coming out of the evil she'd perpetrated. Perhaps God truly *had* forgiven her?

But her grief quickly returned during the Eucharistic Prayer when Father Gregory asked God "to give baby Mark kind admittance to His kingdom."

She struggled for composure as she went up to Communion and offered it for her son, numbly hoping God would accept it.

Mass ended and Father Gregory followed the final prayer with the announcement, "Rita would now like to say a few words."

He took his seat on the left of the altar and she walked up to the pulpit.

By some miracle, she read her short speech without breaking down, and concluded by saying, "Thank you all for coming here today and supporting me in my grief, even though I'm an outsider and a complete stranger. You are now all invited to attend the committal at the grave."

"Wait!" a voice shouted from the back of the church. Rita looked up to see Mark Boulder.

She stared in disbelief as he made his way up the aisle, saying, "I want to say a few words, too, please."

He stopped by the coffin and touched the tiny booties.

Father Gregory stood up and made his way to the altar steps with raised palm. "Stop." He turned to Rita. "Are you comfortable with him speaking? If you want, I can ask him to leave."

Rita felt dizzy. What was Mark doing here? Part of her wanted him to go away – the other wanted to hear what he had to say.

He looked at her. "*Please* let me say something, Rita."

Why should I? You didn't listen to me when I wanted to keep our baby!

"Rita?" nudged Father Gregory.

She glanced at Father James, who mouthed a single word, 'forgiveness.'

With reluctance, she nodded.

"Thank you," he said.

As she came past him down the altar steps, he repeated, "Thank you, and God bless you."

She didn't react and took her seat.

"Well done, my dear!" whispered Father James.

But Rita already regretted her decision.

Mark stood at the pulpit, surveying the villagers and hesitating.

"Did you want to say something?" Father Gregory prodded.

"Yes, Father, I'm sorry. It's just that I'm amazed to see so many people here.

"For those of you who don't know me, my name is Mark Boulder and I am – was – the father of baby Mark whom you are honouring today."

There was a collective gasp.

"Yes, I know, I have a lot of gall coming here today. It's thanks to me that Rita was pushed into ending the life of our son.

"Not only did I not support her desire to keep our baby, but I didn't let her tell anyone about him, and made her go to the abortion clinic by herself."

Sitting behind Rita, Rebecca leaned forward to squeeze her shoulder.

Mark continued. "I also offered her money to keep quiet about the abortion, because I'm a married man."

"You bastard!" yelled one woman.

"Be *quiet*, Ethel!" hissed her husband.

"You're absolutely right," said Mark, "I *am* a bastard."

But at least you didn't tell everyone I accepted the bribe, thought Rita.

He looked straight at her. "I know you can't forgive me, Rita, but please know that I am sincerely sorry. I also beg baby Mark's forgiveness.

"Thank you for listening, and God bless you all for supporting Rita and paying your respects to a little boy you never met."

No one said a word as Mark bowed to the altar and descended the steps.

Rita watched him touch the coffin again, then walk

down the aisle and out of the church.

Chapter Twenty-Eight: At the Graveside

Saturday, March 9th

"Are you alright?" Father James asked Rita. "I'd like to see if I can catch up with Mark."

"Go ahead," she said, "I'll be fine."

The recessional hymn was beginning as Father James left in pursuit of the deceased baby's father.

Mark's stooped figure was passing under the lychgate on the way to the car park.

"Wait!" called the priest.

Mark turned and Father James hurried over to him. "Come back! You can't just walk away. You need to talk to Rita."

"I just did." Mark pointed to the church. "In there. Weren't you paying attention?"

"It was an excellent public performance, but was it for her benefit or yours?"

"Why can't you ever take my actions at face value, James?"

"Because I know you too well. And it's *Father* James now. Or haven't you been paying attention?"

Mark shifted uneasily.

"You want people to forgive you because you feel sorry for *yourself*," said Father James. "No one likes you. You want to be accepted back into the community, but you don't care one fig about the people you've hurt." The priest paused. "Or feel any remorse over the death of your baby son."

Mark snapped, "I'm leaving now."

"Not so fast." Father James pointed to the side of the church. "I want to show you something."

Mark raised his eyebrows. "What?"

"You'll see."

Father James led him to a small rectangular hole, freshly dug. Next to it was a little mound of earth.

Mark pulled back with a start.

Father James grabbed his sleeve. "Look at it, Mark! Look!" He pointed at the grave with short stabbing motions. "The people who aborted your son threw away his tiny mutilated body, probably after selling his organs. So, there's no corpse to bury here today. There shouldn't have been one at all, but Rita has taken the brave decision to acknowledge what she did, and honour her baby with this celebration."

"And I've acknowledged what *I* did, James – I mean, Father."

The priest nodded approval at the correction. He wasn't fixated on being called 'Father,' but Mark needed to learn respect for others. "That was a great first step, yet that's all it was."

"What do you want from me?"

Before Father James could reply, the new parish priest rounded the corner, and behind him a pall bearer carrying the tiny coffin. Rita walked alongside, face drawn and largely covered by her veil, and the villagers made up the rest of the procession.

Mark backed away from the grave, and Father James drew him to a spot where they could observe from a respectful distance.

He was deeply concerned for his old room-mate, who seemed incapable of genuine compassion for the woman and child whose lives he'd shattered. Did Mark really believe one quick, public apology would repair the damage?

During the committal, Rebecca put a motherly arm

through Rita's and the latter leaned her head briefly on the woman's shoulders.

Mark's expression remained wooden.

Father Gregory recited the final prayer: "In sure and certain hope of the resurrection to eternal life through Our Lord Jesus Christ, we commend baby Mark to Almighty God.

"May the Lord bless him and keep him, and make His Face to shine upon him and be gracious to him. May the Lord lift up His Countenance upon him and give him peace. Amen."

The tiny coffin containing the few baby items was lowered into the ground.

When Father Gregory invited Rita to throw the first clod of earth over it, Father James felt Mark's shoulders shaking next to him. Perhaps there was hope for the man, after all.

Once the grave was covered, several villagers placed flowers on the pitiful mound before walking away.

"There's a reception at Rebecca's Bed & Breakfast," said Father James. "It would be a good opportunity to talk to Rita face to face."

Mark didn't respond.

In silence, the two men watched the procession leave the gravesite. Rita threw an angry glance at Mark as she passed by and Rebecca gave him a furious glare.

Soon a long motorcade was making its slow way down the hill towards the village.

Father James waited quietly next to the hated man.

When the last car was out of sight, Mark said, staring ahead, "Father, I need your forgiveness."

"What you need is to go to confession."

"No, you don't understand. I need *your* forgiveness."

Father James stifled a sigh. "Mark, before you seek my

forgiveness, you need to apologize to God."

"Why?" His voice sounded whiny.

"Because you need to express real regret for the hurt you've caused others – not the hurt your actions have caused *you*. You need to repent of your sins, change your ways and make reparation."

Mark gave a hollow laugh. "I'm already making reparation!"

"To whom?"

"The seniors whose money I lost and the other investors in my company - they've all taken their money out, you know."

"What about your employees? And your wife? What about Rita and your aborted son?"

"Stop!" Mark put his hands over his ears.

Father James removed one of those hands. "You need to empathize with the people whose lives you've destroyed, Mark. You need to feel *their* pain. Not yours. Theirs."

"How's confession going to help?"

"A genuine confession will require true contrition. Father Gregory will be able to tell if your confession *is* genuine."

Mark groaned. "Oh, tell me he's not another pastor like you!"

Father James smiled. "You could always go to your brother-in-law."

Mark grimaced. "I need to find another out-of-the-way place."

"Suit yourself." Father James began walking towards the lychgate. "Are you coming to the reception?"

Chapter Twenty-Nine: By the Sea
Saturday, March 9th

Mark rolled his eyes. The last thing he wanted was to walk into a roomful of people who despised him and talk to the woman whom he'd bullied into killing their baby. They would lynch him.

It was hard to feel genuine remorse when his life was on the line.

Father James patted him on the shoulder. "It'll be fine, I promise you."

Mark pouted. "I don't know why I'm putting myself through this."

"Because you know it's the right thing to do."

"I'm a little out of practice."

"Oh, I don't know. Your speech in church fits the description."

"But you called it an excellent public performance."

"I also called it a great first step. It's time to take the next one."

Mark followed him to the last two cars in the parking lot. "Why do I listen to you?"

Father James grinned. "Because I'm the voice of your conscience."

"Conscience is over-rated."

"You don't believe that."

Mark avoided a response by pointing to the dilapidated Triumph. "When are you going to get a decent vehicle?"

Father James sighed. "Probably never, with my income situation."

"Join the club."

Driving behind Father James down the steep hill, Mark reminisced on their many trips to a café on Dartmoor during their university years, and indulging in delicious cream teas, with clotted cream oozing out of their scones and jam dribbling down their chins.

How precious were those days! And how stupid of him to ruin his friendship with James Stryker.

For two long years the faithful Catholic had tried to keep Mark on the straight and narrow, explaining the dire consequences if he didn't.

But Mark had resisted his efforts, arguing that James was old-fashioned and needed to move with the times. Life was for the living, and Mark fully intended to enjoy his time here on earth.

The tension between them came to a head, when James begged Rebecca to reconsider aborting her baby and Mark laughed at him for being a relic.

He still remembered his own words: "It's none of your business what Rebecca does. Her body is hers to do with as she likes. You're asking her to give up her whole life for the sake of a blob in her belly!"

To which James replied, "Mark, I fear for your soul if you really believe that."

Mark had laughed it off. Angry with his friend, the next day he took Rebecca to the abortion clinic just off campus and stayed with her while she made an appointment to rid herself of the unwanted thing inside her.

That night, he triumphantly told James that Rebecca was due to have an abortion in a couple of days.

James was horrified. "How do you know?"

"Because I took her to the clinic myself to arrange it."

James picked up his Bible and read "(I)t is necessary that temptations come, but woe to the one by whom the temptation comes! (Matthew 18:7)."

Mark howled with laughter. "Seriously, James, you

think a stupid Bible verse is going to put me off?"

"Beware of Satan, my friend. I have done all I can to save you, but you've hardened your heart against God."

Was James now giving up on him?

That didn't sit well with Mark, who'd grown curiously accustomed to his pious room-mate having his back.

James left the room. When he returned two hours later, he looked exhausted.

"Where've you been?" Mark asked

"To undo the damage you've done."

"What do you mean?"

"I don't want to talk about it. Now or ever."

The next day Rebecca told Mark she'd changed her mind. She was going to keep the baby, and leave university, and later he heard that she'd married the father, who stayed on at Ruddminster to get his degree.

James moved out of their shared room with the parting words, "I will pray for you, Mark, every day."

The only time they saw each other after that was in lectures, but they no longer sat together. Their friendship was officially over.

If only Mark had listened back then, he wouldn't be in this mess today.

He parked next to the pastor and inhaled the salty tang of the Channel as they walked towards Rebecca's establishment.

The sound of voices could be heard all the way down the road and he halted, seized with fear. "I can't do this, Father, I just can't."

The priest put a hand on Mark's shoulder. "Yes, you can. I'm here."

All talk ceased and everyone stared with loathing at the interloper, when the two of them entered the sea-themed breakfast room.

"*You* again!" Rebecca stepped forward. "You're not welcome here, Mr. Boulder."

"I know. I just want to talk to Rita."

"You've done enough harm."

"Could I at least find out for myself if she's willing to talk?"

Father James smiled. "I don't think that's asking too much, is it? Then he'll be on his way."

Rita, who had been out of the room, now came in.

"Rita, love," said Rebecca, "this horrid man wants to talk to you."

She viewed Mark with apathy. "What good will talking do? It's not going to bring my – our – baby back, is it? You wanted him gone, and you got what you wanted, like you always do."

Rebecca sneered, "See? She doesn't want to talk to you. Now get out, you're trespassing on my property!"

Mark was humiliated. How low he'd sunk, to be kicked out of a bed and breakfast.

Father James touched his arm. "Go outside and wait for me, O.K.?"

Mark exited to loud cheers, and cries of 'good riddance!' and had half a mind to drive off and be rid of them all.

But Father James was the nearest person he had to a friend in all the world, and Mark was in dire need of friendship.

He walked across the village green and stood on the beach, staring dejectedly out to sea.

He'd come to St. Jude with the intention of praying to God for help again, before driving into the village to find out if Father James was still at the B&B and willing to hear his confession – the *full* version.

The church car park was full of vehicles. Assuming

Mass was being said, he went in.

But he froze in the back pew when he realised he'd walked into a funeral for his own son.

It was surreal. This couldn't be for *his* baby! He must be intruding on some other child's ceremony.

But something – or Someone – prevented him from leaving.

When Mass finished and Rita stood in front of the villagers to say a few words, Mark was galvanized into doing likewise. He had no idea what to say, but was driven to say *some*thing.

He felt vulnerable in front of all those people – at their mercy, like a criminal awaiting execution.

Then it was all over. He'd made his public confession and apologised to Rita, and that was supposed to have been that.

Now Father James was telling him to talk to Rita personally.

He felt as she did, that there was nothing to be gained by it, but an inner voice was telling him to listen to the priest. So here he was, wanting to drive away, but knowing he must stay.

A cold breeze wafted off the sea and Mark wrapped his woollen scarf twice around his cold neck, wishing he'd brought a hat – just as on the day he'd met with Rita on Dartmoor.

He shivered at his brutality. His two living children would have had a baby brother if Mark hadn't forced Rita to – what was the term used by the abortion clinics? He'd looked up women's health centres in Ruddminster, to be sure she could go to one close by, and the sites all talked about 'emptying the womb contents.' No mention of a baby, not even a foetus. Just 'womb contents.'

How could Mark have done such a thing to his own flesh and blood, or the baby's mother?

What had Father James said earlier in the churchyard? "You need to express genuine regret for the hurt you've caused others – not the hurt your actions have caused *you*."

The crafty old sod was right. Mark's quest for forgiveness *was* motivated by his desire not to feel bad about himself. It wasn't out of compassion for those against whom he had trespassed nor a yearning to heal the wounds he'd inflicted.

There flashed before his mind's eye the old people whose money he had squandered: the employees who were about to lose their jobs; the duped donors to his bogus charity; his cheated wife; and Rita, standing at their baby's empty grave.

He'd hurt so many people.

And taken a life.

How had this happened? Father James and he had both gone to the same university, yet turned out complete opposites.

I'm Father James' evil twin, thought Mark. *Does that mean I'm beyond redemption?*

"No one is beyond redemption," said a voice behind him.

"Did I say that out loud?" Mark asked.

"No, but you didn't say it – very loudly." The priest stood next to him.

Mark frowned. What did that even mean?

"Your demeanour told me what you were thinking," the priest explained.

"I don't care what you say," said Mark, "that was eerie."

Father James grinned. "Someone here is ready to

chat."

Mark turned around slowly.

"Hello, Mark," said the wraithlike figure. She no longer wore a veil and the lapels of her black coat were turned up, accentuating her long blonde hair.

"How did Father persuade you to come out here?" Mark asked.

She glanced at the priest. "He told me I needed to come to terms with what happened if I was ever going to be at peace."

Her grey-blue eyes met his, so filled with pain that Mark wondered whether he could ever forgive himself.

Swallowing hard, she looked away.

Mark longed to hold her and tell her how much he regretted his actions, but his days of holding her were over. Softly he said, "How can I help you achieve that?"

Teardrops formed on her lower lashes and her lips were trembling. "I need to know – no, I need to *feel* – that you're sorry for what you did to me and to our son. I want you to feel as horrible as I do." She looked at him full on with bitter narrow eyes. "I want you to hate *yourself* as much as I hate *myself*."

Mark expected Father James to intervene. Why wasn't he telling Rita that she shouldn't wish self-loathing on him, or even feel it herself?

But the priest moved away, leaving Mark alone to face the woman whose life he'd wrecked.

If Rita would only shout at him, he could dismiss her as irrational and walk away. But her voice was calm and he followed her logic only too well. If he'd been treated this badly, he'd have wished the same on his abuser.

She fished in her pocket and handed Mark an ultrasound. "This is what our baby looked like at three months, just before he died. He was fully formed, with arms, hands and fingers, legs, and feet with little toes."

Mark's throat tightened as he took in the details of his tiny son. If he'd seen this, surely, he wouldn't have made such a terrible decision?

Or would he? Was he truly a monster?

He wanted to yell, but only managed to croak, "Why didn't you show this to me before?"

"You didn't give me the chance. And anyway, would it have made any difference?"

Mark struggled for an answer. *I don't know, I just don't know!*

He fell to his knees in the sand and covered his head with his hands, rocking back and forth, moaning, "What have I done? O, God, what have I done?"

Blindly, he reached out his right hand. "I'm so sorry, Rita! How could I do this to you? Yes, I hate myself!"

But no one took his hand. He was alone.

He curled into a ball.

When his tears were spent, he stretched back his head to face the indifferent nothingness above.

Chapter Thirty: The Pushy Prelate
Saturday, 9th March

Father James motioned Rita to leave Mark hunched up on the sand and they walked across the village green to rejoin the reception at Rebecca's house.

"Well done, my dear, that was excellent."

"I feel mean, showing him another baby's ultrasound, Father."

"But the important thing is, you weren't lying. That's exactly your son's developmental stage when his life was terminated. And Mark needed to see it. Otherwise, he would never have grasped what he's done. He'd have kept justifying his actions to himself and never repented of them."

"What will happen to him now?"

"He'll be tried in court for his money crimes, found guilty, if he doesn't plead guilty anyway, and be charged exorbitant fines."

"What about the company? And all our jobs?"

"Time will tell, but I hope Mark will get involved as much as possible in the solutions to the problems he's caused."

They entered the breakfast room and mingled with the villagers. Father Gregory came up to Father James and asked how it had gone with Mark.

"I think he's in the big fish's belly at last."

Father Gregory grinned. "That's a good start."

"Yes, it is. You should expect him in your confessional very soon. I've warned him, you're a very perceptive confessor."

The priest's face fell. "Oh, Goodness, I really am not!"

"Have faith, Christ will give you discernment."

"I wish I had your confidence in the Lord's guidance."

"Follow His commandments, and you won't go wrong, Gregory."

Father James' mobile rang. "Excuse me, I have to take this. It's the bishop." He exited the room. "Yes, your Excellency?"

"We need to talk, James, urgently. I'm not far from King's – er – "

"Brambling."

"Yes, there. I'll meet with you and Father Gregory at the rectory in thirty minutes."

"Father Gregory needs to be out in time to preside at the Saturday Vigil Mass, Your Excellency."

"Don't be ridiculous, James, it's only noon! I'll be finished well before then. Kindly both organise to be there at 12:30 precisely."

"Of course." Father James couldn't help shaking his head. That meant the bishop expected to be fed while administering his admonishments, since there could be no reason for this sudden visit other than to chastise the two priests over some real or imagined transgression.

He returned to the reception and gave Father Gregory the bad news. "What do you have to eat at the rectory?"

The pastor's face fell. "Nothing fit for a bishop!"

"I'll ask Rebecca if we can take a plate of the food here with us. You and I can drink tea and eat biscuits while we receive our telling off."

Rebecca was predictably miffed at having to provide edibles for the bishop who'd side-lined her favourite pastor, but was eventually cajoled into putting together a bowl of Exeter stew, three slices of Devonshire apple dappy – "Two of them are for you, not all three for *him*," – and a container of fresh cream to pour over them.

"You're an angel, Rebecca," Father Gregory said.

"Just make sure you get your dappy," she said gruffly.

Father James said, as the two priests walked out to their cars, "Thank God for Rebecca's hospitality. I don't know what I'd have done without her."

"She told me what you did for her, back in the day."

Father James frowned. "I'm surprised she shared that."

"She's determined to make me understand what big shoes I have to fill."

Father James chuckled. "She's never too shy to say what she's thinking." He opened the passenger door of his Triumph. "I wish I could bring Judith. She'd love a run on the cliffs, but I don't think the bishop would approve."

"I get the feeling he doesn't approve of a lot of things," said Father Gregory.

"I think we're about to discover what some of those are." He leaned in to place the bag of food gently on the passenger floor, closed the door then walked round to the driver's side.

Out of courtesy, he followed Father Gregory in his black Ford Focus, and felt a wave of nostalgia when his old rectory came into view. It was swiftly followed by a sinking of heart at the sight of a silver Mercedes in the small parking area.

Bishop Marsden got out as the two priests approached him and stood against his vehicle, arms folded and waiting to be let in.

Father James hoped the man's mood would improve when he was served the delicious lunch Rebecca had cooked. He carried the bag close to the man's nose, with the comment, "We brought you some great food."

The bishop's expression softened at the tantalising aromas, and he eagerly entered the rectory behind

Father Gregory, who led him into the tiny dining room, leaving Father James in the rear.

"Could you pour his Excellency a drink, while I get some cutlery, please, Father?" asked the younger cleric, disappearing into the kitchen.

"What will it be, Your Excellency? Sherry, g and t, red wine, white wine?" asked Father James, not entirely sure his colleague had all those items on offer.

"I'll have red wine."

Father James joined him, and the two of them sat uneasily at the dining table until Father Gregory came in with a steaming bowl of stew for Bishop Marsden and silverware.

"Aren't you joining me?" the bishop asked.

Father James let their host explain.

"We already ate at a reception in the village."

"Oh, what was that for?"

Unsure what to say, Father Gregory looked at Father James, who took the lead. "Before my demotion, a young lady who'd recently had an abortion came to me in a distraught state, and I suggested a memorial ceremony for her deceased baby. Father Gregory took over that duty, since I'm no longer allowed to say Mass in public."

"The reception was for the villagers, who were kind enough to attend the ceremony," added Father Gregory.

Bishop Robert Marsden took a large bite of beef and chewed on it pensively. The two priests exchanged glances across the table.

The bishop swallowed, took a sip of wine, and said, "You see, James, this is the kind of thing I warned you against."

The priest was puzzled, and said so.

"Don't play dumb with me. I told you to be careful

about making women who've had abortions feel bad about themselves."

"With all due respect, Your Excellency, the memorial to honour this lady's baby wasn't to make her feel bad about herself. It had quite the opposite effect. It brought her out of her depression. Because of this morning's Mass, she's beginning to accept what happened and her part in it, and ask her baby's forgiveness. You are more than welcome to ask her yourself, Your Excellency."

"No, thank you. But didn't you say all the villagers turned out for this event?"

"Yes, but – "

"No buts, James. That poor woman was put to shame in front of all her peers, and made to feel inferior because of what she did. That's just the kind of thing I've told you to stop doing. It's exactly why you were, as you so aptly put it, demoted."

"Your Excellency," said Father Gregory, "that's not what happened. Might I be allowed to explain how the villagers came to be present?"

"I fail to see how that will change anything, but I'm listening."

How magnanimous of you! thought Father James, then quickly added, *Sorry, Lord.*

Father Gregory said, "The lady concerned was asked if she'd like a private ceremony or if she'd be willing to make it public, to encourage other mothers in the same situation as herself to come forward and have their babies acknowledged, instead of carrying their terrible burden in secret."

"In other words, she was bullied into making a public spectacle of herself."

Father James found it hard to keep his temper. "No, Your Excellency, she was given free choice."

"The choice to do what she wanted, or be judged by you two for not doing what *you* wanted her to do."

Father Gregory looked bewildered. "There was no judgement involved, Your Excellency. It was all done in the spirit of charity."

"Doubtless you thought so, Father Gregory, but Father James, you should have known better." He glowered at the young priest. "I expressly forbid you to conduct any more ceremonies of this nature, do you hear me?" A large vein pulsated in his left temple.

Father James felt sorry for Father Gregory. He'd been trying to do something kind for Rita – and what he did *was* kind – but Bishop Robert was out to punish anyone who listened to his ousted priest. His reaction had nothing to do with helping women who'd had abortions get past their sins and be open to life, should they become pregnant again. It was indirect revenge on Father James.

"Anyway," the bishop was saying, "I didn't come here to talk about your little ceremony." He steepled his fingers over the finished bowl of stew. "I've received disturbing reports that you, Father Gregory, have been following your predecessor's disobedient habit of allowing parishioners to receive Communion on the tongue."

Father Gregory gave a start and blurted, "What's wrong with that? It's been done that way for centuries out of respect for the Sacred Host! I'm very happy the parishioners here want to receive that way. Why is it wrong now?"

"*Because*, Father Gregory, it's upsetting to our Protestant brethren. The Church is moving with the spirit of the times. I don't expect you to fully understand, but Vatican II was an ecumenical council, and we have a duty to respect the feelings of our Christian brethren outside the Church."

"Excuse me." Father Gregory rose abruptly. "I need to prepare the desserts." Red-faced, he left the room.

"You've already corrupted that priest." The bishop pointed an accusing finger. "And he's been here less than two weeks!"

"How can encouraging reverence for the Sacred Presence be called corruption?" Deference compelled Father James to add, "With all due respect, Your Excellency."

The bishop eyed him suspiciously. "Watch yourself James, I can make life a great deal harder for you."

"As I am fully aware. But what exactly is my crime?"

"In a word, disobedience."

"I still don't see."

"You have not followed the spirit of the law, James. Removing you of your faculties *obviously* means that you are to allow Father Gregory to run the parish as he sees fit – without your input."

You mean, as <u>you</u> see fit, thought the priest. "With all due respect, Your Excellency – "

"You can stop saying that, James," said the bishop. "We both know you mean the utmost *dis*respect."

 "I must protest, Your Excellency!"

"You can protest as much as you like, it won't get you anywhere."

Father Gregory returned to the table in the middle of this exchange, with three dishes of apple dappy.

He put a plate in front of the bishop, who knew the young priest had overheard his last remark. "Don't mind us. Father James and I have known each other a long time, and enjoy a certain degree of familiarity. Isn't that so, James?"

"Indeed, Your Excellency."

The bishop gave Father James a sharp look and addressed Father Gregory. "Don't let this disgraced cleric lead you astray. I'm relying on you to modernise this parish. Don't let me down."

Father Gregory glanced at Father James.

"Don't look to *him* for guidance, he'll only get you into more trouble," the bishop said sternly. "Remember, the Church is moving with the times, at long last."

Father Gregory asked, "Then what makes Catholicism different from other religions? I thought she was the one true Faith, the Spotless Bride of Christ?"

The bishop sighed. "Gregory, we decry the snobbery people associate with Catholicism: we're not an elite group who think they have all the answers. There's a lot of merit in dialogue with other faiths – they all have something to offer."

Father James could see the young pastor was appalled by this speech, and impressed when he said, "If it's snobbery to say Catholicism has all the answers, then Jesus was the biggest Snob that ever lived! Do we not believe that He is the Way, the Truth and the Life?"

"Yes, yes, of course," said the bishop, "but so do the other Christian religions."

"To a much lesser extent, Your Excellency."

Ignoring that last comment, the bishop ploughed on. "We encourage a spirit of ecumenism, with an emphasis on promoting the brotherhood of man."

Father James frowned. What the bishop was saying had a distinctly Masonic ring to it and he was promoting a decidedly anti-Catholic message.

"You don't agree, James?"

"I don't recognise the Catholic Church in *any* of what you're saying, Your Excellency." May as well be hanged for a sheep as for a lamb.

Bishop Marsden sighed. "And there you have the reason why you are no longer a parish priest. You're a dinosaur, James, you need to make way for the new order."

New order, ecumenism, brotherhood of man? What on earth had happened to the Catholic Church Father James knew and loved, the Church founded by Jesus Christ?

He saw Father Gregory was also having a difficult time.

Their distinguished guest had more to say. "James, I also hear that you were presiding at Mass on Ash Wednesday, and that Father Gregory's sermon sounded a lot like something you wrote. It won't do, either of you, it simply won't do. I'm here to nip all this in the bud.

"One more infringement, James, and I'll remove you from the payroll." He wagged a threatening finger.

The priest brightened. "I'm still on the payroll, then?"

"For the time being. But that could change very swiftly." He took up his fork and spoon and surveyed the dessert. "This looks delicious. Pass the cream, would you, Father Gregory?"

Chapter Thirty-One: Sitting in the Ashes

Saturday, March 9th

Mark sat up and wiped the sand off his face. How long had he been lying there, abandoned and made a fool of?

Oblivious to his misery, an oil tanker crawled along the distant line separating sea and sky out in the Channel; the world continued to function without him.

Now I know what it's like to reach rock bottom. To be alone and without hope. To lose everything.

Worst of all, to know it's my own fault.

Everything had come easily to Mark, thanks to his good looks and ready wit. His brain worked faster than most people's and he was quick to spot the advantage. His suave manner had facilitated his use of colleagues for personal advancement, and ingratiation with his superiors without their full awareness.

God had smiled on his investment gambles, too: Boulder Enterprises was renowned for its bold strategies which paid off handsomely. That is, until He had pulled the plug.

As for personal relationships, Mark had never experienced genuine love. He'd been attracted to Mary, of course, but had married her for her diplomatic skills and influential bishop brother. His affair with Rita had been a test of his power – and a fun escape.

Mark had been invincible for decades. But now every area of his life was falling apart. Why had God withdrawn His favour?

Was this His idea of answering Mark's plea for help? Visiting devastation on him, doing unto him as he'd done to others?

The worst atrocity of all was the one he'd committed against his own son and he cringed at the thought of his baby's excruciating pain, being torn limb from limb in his mother's womb. He closed his eyes against the horrible image, but it only became more vivid.

Was there any coming back from such evil? Was Father James correct when he said no one was beyond redemption?

It couldn't possibly be true: no living being was *that* magnanimous.

So why did the priest bother with him? Mark didn't deserve his help, after what he did to the man. He wasn't fit to live among decent human beings; perhaps he *should* go to jail?

It was the perfect retreat. No decisions to make, no jilted Rita or angry wife or betrayed seniors to face. No need for the money he soon wouldn't have.

There was the loss of freedom, of course, but what real freedom could he expect outside prison? He'd have no house, no income and no car.

He lay back on the sand. Perhaps Father James would visit him in jail and they would once again have those lively debates they used to enjoy at university? Except he wouldn't be so quick to sneer at his friend's religious views.

But Father James had just walked away from him.

Looking heavenward, Mark prayed he might still have a friend in the priest.

Chapter Thirty-Two: Counting the Cost

Saturday, March 9th

Bishop Marsden turned down Father Gregory's offer of coffee and left immediately after dessert.

He climbed into his Mercedes with the parting words, "Be careful, both of you. Holy Mother Church has her eyes on you."

"He could at least have said 'thank you' for lunch," complained Father Gregory, as the two priests waved at the departing vehicle.

"That would have been nice." Father James lowered his arm. "But he's right, Holy Mother Church *is* looking at us and depending on us to do the right thing."

"You're not talking about Bishop Marsden, are you?"

"No. Although I wish I were."

"Father, what's happening to the Church? She's going in a direction that doesn't feel right."

"That's because it *isn't* right. We both know the bishop's 'spirit of the times' is Satan's agenda, whether or not His Excellency realises it. The devil is certainly having his day. I'm sorry you're caught up in this; with the present climate there's no hope for orthodox clergy to climb up the Church ranks."

Father Gregory smiled ruefully. "I now understand why you were content to be left alone in this small parish, where you could do good without hindrance." He paused then asked, "What *really* happened to put you in the bishop's bad graces?"

"What did he tell you?"

"That you were divisive and upsetting the congregation with your strong tone."

Father James was tempted to laugh, but instead inquired, "Did he describe the exact nature of my divisiveness? Or specify what's wrong with my tone?"

"No, and I'm afraid I didn't ask."

The older priest strolled with his colleague to the back of the rectory and along the coarse grass towards the cliffs. A sharp sea breeze whipped them in the face, and the priest recalled his many walks with Judith out here.

He explained how a parishioner had come to him with evidence of wrong-doing which he couldn't ignore. "What I didn't know at the time was that the criminal in this case is the bishop's brother-in-law."

Father Gregory stopped abruptly. "Oh boy! I imagine that sealed your doom."

"Yes. And because I continued to push for justice against his relative, he complained about my traditional Catholic preaching. But I wasn't about to water down the Truth."

"Any regrets?"

Father James shook his head and resumed walking. "None. In hindsight I see God's hand in all this. He was testing me, pushing me to either stand up for the Truth that I professed to believe in, and be counted, or cave in like a coward."

They'd reached the cliff tops and stood admiring the view.

Father Gregory said, "For a priest there's surely no contest."

"I'm glad to hear you say that, because the same choice stands before you."

The younger priest sighed. "It's hard, especially since we're supposed to be obedient to our superiors. Yet should we be obedient even when they're in the wrong?"

"There's the rub, Father. Do you recall Maximilian Kolbe?"

"Wasn't he the priest who offered to take the place of a stranger and die in the starvation chamber in Auschwitz?"

"The very same. He famously said on the topic of obedience that the one exception was if the superior were to command something that clearly involved breaking God's law, even slightly. In such circumstances, the superior could not be considered as faithfully interpreting God's will.

"For me, that exception has arrived."

The two men were silent for a while, watching the gulls fly in and out of their nests in the cliff face below.

Father James felt a deep sadness for Father Gregory. He himself wasn't that far from retirement. His pension may be taken away from him, but he could look back with satisfaction on a lifetime of adherence to the true teachings of the Catholic Church. Not so the fledgling shepherd by his side.

At length, Father Gregory asked, "How are you managing to stay true to your calling and pitting yourself against the bishop, who has so much power over your fate?"

The older man smiled. "By sticking to what I know is right. There is nothing so wonderful as a clear conscience. And this is merely white martyrdom, Gregory. The big test is yet to come."

"Meaning?"

"The forces of evil are gathering against the Church, from within as well as from without. Our Lady has warned seers for many years of the coming chastisement and subsequent purification."

Father Gregory looked dubious. "As Catholics we're

not obliged to believe in apparitions and private revelations. But it sounds as if you do."

"Over and over again, the same messages have been reported from Our Lord and Our Lady, making it hard for me to ignore them."

"Can you give me some examples?"

"Absolutely." He pulled out his mobile phone and tapped some words into the search bar. "This is from Our Lady Queen of Peace speaking to Pedro Regis: 'The great persecution will lead many men and women away from the path of truth. Do not retreat. My Jesus will never abandon you. Trust fully in the Power of God and all will turn out well for you. Onward in defence of the truth.'"

"Where did you find that? And how do you know this Pedro person is telling the truth?"

"Reputable writers and priests are being sent messages from many seers around the world, people who don't know each other, who speak different languages. They all say the same thing. That can't just be co-incidence."

Father Gregory tilted his head, mulling over this information. "When is Our Lady supposed to have said what you just read me?"

"Earlier this year."

"This *year*?!" He shook his head. "But people have been predicting the end is nigh ever since Jesus' resurrection. Why should we think our times are so special?"

"Because her messages are becoming more and more urgent."

Father Gregory countered, "Christ's messages were urgent two thousand plus years ago, yet He *still* hasn't returned."

"All the more need for vigilance. Our Lady is warning those of us who will listen that time is running out. The Catholic Church must boldly assert the truths Christ entrusted to her and not lapse into a generic religion indistinguishable from all the rest. Otherwise, many souls will be lost!"

"We're still administering the Sacraments, so where's the worry?"

"But are we administering them with conviction? How many of those who call themselves Catholic actually believe in the Real Presence, for example?"

Father Gregory shrugged his shoulders. "I don't know."

"Less than 30%. That means over 70% of so-called Catholics receive Holy Communion in a sacrilegious fashion. Think of the affront to Our Lord! And why do they not believe? Because we, the priests, are not instructing them."

"That's got to be an exaggeration, Father."

Father James shook his head. "Sadly not." He looked at his phone. "Here's another message from Our Lady to a seer named Jennifer: 'Where are My Chosen Sons? Where are My Priests to guide My Children in the truth? Where are My Priests to tell the world that the road to hell is becoming grid-locked with souls who have fallen into Satan's trap?[i]" Father James' voice became more forceful. "Father, *we* must be her priests. It's up to *us* to lead the flock away from the broad road and back onto the narrow path. Too many clergy in the Church are teaching a bland Catholicism that's leading the faithful to hell. But we must not do that. We must not fail Our Blessed Mother."

Father Gregory's expression was troubled as he stared out to sea.

Father James sensed his struggle. "Whether or not you

choose to believe in the messages, be assured that we priests can look forward to real persecution in the near future, possibly to the point of shedding our blood."

The young pastor's face went ashen. "Surely not!"

But Father James would not back down. This innocent needed to understand the nature of the foe, and the importance of arming himself for the spiritual warfare in which they were already engaged.

"Make no mistake, the devil is out to destroy the Catholic Church. He is approaching his last hurrah, and we priests – the real ones – must shepherd Our Lady's Little Rabble as best we can and fulfil the obligations we undertook at our ordination. Remember her words: 'Onward in defence of the Truth.'"

Father Gregory nodded slowly and the two priests stood side by side, looking out to sea.

Then they walked quietly back to the car park; Father Gregory in shocked introspection and Father James hoping he hadn't frightened the neophyte into regretting his priestly vows.

They came to the ancient Triumph and as Father James opened the passenger door, Father Gregory asked, "How do I stand firm, when the bishop is deterring me?"

"The old-fashioned way. As Our Lord said, this kind of demon can come out only with prayer and fasting."

"I hope you'll stay close and help me, Father."

Father James patted the man's shoulder. "I intend to." He climbed into the vehicle and wound down the window with a smile. "Remember: prayer and fasting beat the devil every time."

Chapter Thirty-Three: Rebecca's B & B

Saturday, 9th March

Mark urgently needed to speak to Father James.

Shaking granules of sand off his coat, he walked over to the bed & breakfast and entered the kitchen through the back door.

Rebecca was walking in with a tray of dirty glasses. She nearly dropped it when she saw the intruder.

"How *dare* you show your face again!" she cried. "Get out!" She slammed the tray on the counter and flapped angry hands at him, as though to a stray cat. "Get *out*, I said!"

"I just want to see Father James," he pleaded.

"Well, he's not here. He's gone up to the rectory. Now shoo!"

Mark retreated and Rebecca locked the door firmly behind him.

Too restless to drive, he set off on foot to the rectory. The physical exercise would do him good and he could visit the church as well as the priest, and – if he could face it – his son's memorial grave.

He'd been walking for ten minutes when he spotted Father James' car approaching. It was unmistakably his. Who else drove such a dilapidated vehicle?

The priest slowed down and waved through the open window. "Hail, fellow, well met! Where are you off to?"

"Actually, I was coming to find you."

"Excellent! Hop in."

Mark opened the creaking door and climbed in.

"Sorry about the dog hairs," said Father James.

"No problem." Mark patted the tanned leather. "This is

really comfortable. No wonder Judith enjoys riding around with you."

"Don't sound so surprised." Father James stroked the walnut dashboard. "They knew how to make cars back in those days."

"I have to agree. My BMW isn't nearly as comfy."

Peering ahead, the priest asked, "How are you doing?"

"I wasn't happy to be deserted on the beach in my hour of need."

"And yet, you're not so angry with me that you've slunk off in high dudgeon."

Mark made a sour face. "You knew perfectly well I'd be back."

"Let's just say I had a hunch you might. What can I do for you?"

How should Mark respond? He wanted reassurance that the priest was still his friend, but what grown man asks that of another?

When he didn't answer, Father James said, "I fear I was being too harsh when I refused to hear your confession earlier. If you still wish, I'm happy to do so." He glanced at his passenger.

Mark's shoulders relaxed – he hadn't realised he'd been holding them up – and a huge sigh escaped him. "Thank you!"

*

Rebecca was not happy to see him again when he walked into her bed & breakfast, through the front door this time. "What's *he* doing back here?" she demanded of the ex-pastor, not deigning to look at Mark.

"He's with me, Rebecca. And I can assure you he's feeling very repentant."

"Like I said before, you're too good for this world, Father."

"And you're very kind, Rebecca. I'll take him up to my room before anyone else notices."

Looking contrite for her benefit, Mark followed the priest up the rickety stairs and along the worn runner covering the hallway floor, to Room 33.

He smiled when he saw the number. "Did she give this to you on purpose?"

Father James chuckled. "Probably." He opened the door and Judith bounded out. "Sorry, girl, I've been gone too long. The bishop doesn't like you, so I had to leave you behind."

"The bishop?" Mark asked.

"Yes, he wanted to see Father Gregory and me up at the rectory."

"What for? Not that it's any of my business."

"You're right, it isn't, but I don't mind telling you. He told us to watch our step."

"In what way?"

"Father Gregory is to follow the laxer rules of today's Catholic Church, and I'm not to get in his way. Your brother-in-law's exact words were 'one more infringement and I will remove you from the payroll.'"

"At least you're on the payroll, then."

"It would appear so, for the time being. But that won't last long."

Mark grinned. "What infringement did you have in mind?"

"Probably my upcoming podcasts of 'non-sermons' will persuade him to cut me off without a penny. Including my pension, for sure."

"But that's dreadful!"

"I could always choose to remain silent, but that's not what God is calling me to do." He patted Judith on the head. "Now, I'm going to take this young lady for a quick walk while you gather your thoughts. When we get back, I'll hear your confession."

Mark nodded and the priest's Border Collie joyfully preceded him out of the room.

The idea of confessing had seemed a good one. But now that it was imminent, Mark began to panic. What should he say? Could he leave anything out? Or would that invalidate his confession again?

By the time Father James and Judith returned, Mark was in a cold sweat.

The Collie padded over to her water bowl and lapped up its contents, while her owner removed his heavy coat and hung it up in the tiny wardrobe. He then pulled a purple stole from the right pocket of his soutane, kissed it, and placed it around his neck with a murmured prayer.

"O.K.," he said brightly, "let's take up our positions. You sit over there, Mark, and I'll be here. I assume it will be easier if you're not facing me."

"Thank you."

He positioned Mark on the side of the bed facing the door, where he didn't have to look at his confessor.

Father James sat on the end, opposite the wardrobe. "Alright, I'm ready. May the Lord help you to make a good confession."

"Bless me, Father, for I have sinned. It has been over a month since my last confession – and longer than that since my last real one."

"Bless you for your honesty."

Mark began hesitantly, with his more venial sins – "I broke the speed limit, I thought unkindly about my wife," – stalling on his major transgressions.

But Father James patiently waited for him to name the evils he had perpetrated.

Almost half an hour later, Mark finished. "I can't think of anything else, Father."

"That was a thorough and genuine confession. Well done, I know how much it cost you. For your penance, I want you to personally apologise to everyone you've hurt."

Mark swung round, appalled. He'd expected a few Hail Marys and perhaps an Our Father. But this? It would take a lifetime to carry out!

"Surely you jest, Father?"

"I'm not asking you to have face to face chats with everyone. Although that would be wonderful, a simple email will do, to let them know you are genuinely sorry."

"But that'll take forever!"

"Better forever here than forever in Hell, wouldn't you agree?"

Mark gave a loud groan.

"How about using actual words?"

"*Fine*, Father, I'll do as you ask."

"Our Lord is the one asking you to perform this penance, not me. I'm here *in persona Christi*. Now, please say the Act of Contrition."

Mark hesitated. "Father, last time there was a cheat sheet on the confessional wall. I don't know the prayer off by heart."

"I'll lead you through it."

As Mark repeated the words after the priest, one particular phrase struck him: 'I detest all my sins because of Thy just punishments.'

Was it very shallow of him to dwell on his fear of retaliation for every sin he'd committed? Surely, he should be more concerned with loving God than fearing His punishments?

But he sincerely meant the last line: "I firmly resolve,

with the help of Thy grace, to sin no more and to avoid the near occasions of sin." He had no desire to distance himself from God anymore. It didn't work.

Father James then absolved him: "May God give you pardon and peace, and I absolve you from your sins in the name of the Father, and of the Son, and of the Holy Spirit. Amen."

Mark's eyes welled with tears – tears of relief and joy at having unburdened himself before Almighty God through the ministry of his friend – yes, for friend he'd proved himself still to be – and at having been forgiven.

Chapter Thirty-Four: A Bishop's Dilemma
Saturday, 9th March

As he departed from the rectory, Bishop Marsden saw the two priests waving at him through his rear-view mirror. He could almost hear them saying "Good riddance!"

He was furious. Things were not shaping up as planned when he put his tame priest into the disgraced pastor's shoes. The man was so compliant he'd let Father James manipulate him.

It was a shame he had to keep the ex-pastor within the diocese boundaries – as long as he was a priest, that is – and there was no way he could forbid the man from living here, in King's Whatever, either. If only!

Well, it was a matter of time before Father James put a foot wrong and was cut off the payroll. That was *some* consolation.

At the T-junction at the bottom of the hill he turned left, away from the half-moon beach on the Channel coast and back towards civilisation. The sooner he escaped this den of relics who clung to their ancient Catholicism, the better. Really, there was no reforming some people!

Look at James' car. It was a perfect example of the man's refusal to move with the times.

He drove past a sign saying "Thank You for Visiting King's Brambling! Hope to See You Again!"

"I hope I never have to come here again," he mumbled as the road narrowed and ascended steeply uphill. When he reached the crest, the thoroughfare appeared more constricted, with the addition of hedgerows on raised banks on either side. He had to concentrate on his driving; there was no room for error when passing a car coming the other way.

When he reached the exit ramp for the main highway back to Ruddminster, his mind was again free to ponder what to do with those two reprobates.

After withdrawing his support from Mark's charity, the archbishop had begun asking him awkward questions. Now that the scandals had become public, with Mark at the centre of them all, the bishop was anxious to retreat from all connections with his brother-in-law.

But that was difficult. His sister was staying at the palace, although, thank Goodness, she planned to visit her two children soon. They lived hours away, so she would be gone for a few weeks, allowing this whole mess to die down.

Being related to Mark was not good for his image, but Mary had made it clear to her brother that she'd no intention of divorcing the man. However, she would seek a formal separation. The bishop would have preferred her to be completely rid of her husband, but a separation was less scandalous than a divorce and he would have to be satisfied with that.

Now Father James was causing more trouble by corrupting Father Gregory. One option open to the bishop was to send Stryker to St. Matthew's Catholic Centre for Roman Catholic clergy, in the north. After a few months' treatment there, the priest would see the light and be more malleable. Might even be restored to public ministry and placed in another backwater parish, where he could imagine he was doing good, while not doing any actual harm.

The only problem with this plan was the man's popularity. Sending him to the infamous brainwashing institute would cause an almighty ruckus that would rock the whole diocese. Bishop Marsden couldn't afford that. He'd already seen what resulted just from local opposition – that boycott on giving to the collection.

Now Father Gregory was exhibiting disturbing signs of becoming as fiercely orthodox as the man he'd replaced. If one went to St. Matthew's, the other would have to, as well.

But if they went to the same place, they would simply contaminate each other. No, they'd have to go to two separate institutions.

Whoa! Didn't I just remind myself that the money would dry up if I sent even one of them for reprogramming?

He'd have to be careful how he handled them, especially Father James. He hoped he'd put a lid on the situation for now, but dreaded the day he was forced to stop paying the beloved priest. It might win the bishop Brownie points with his superior, but who knew what an uproar it would cause among the laity?

He'd been recently alerted to the existence of an organisation calling itself the Coalition for Cancelled Priests, and apparently the King's Brambling villagers were sending their donations there instead of placing them where they rightfully belonged – in the collection basket. How did the laity think the diocese could afford the wine and the hosts they consumed, or pay their priests, if they didn't do their bit? And what about the outreach programmes? They needed funding, too.

They were now in Lent, when guilt persuaded most parishioners into forking over more than usual.

But this Lent was not getting off to a good start, with Father Gregory not even bringing out the baskets on Ash Wednesday. Who knew what would happen at today's

Vigil and tomorrow's Sunday Masses? Would he pass the collection plate around or worry about the embarrassment of no-one placing anything in it?

He was nearing Ruddminster with these problems still unresolved, when his mobile rang on the Mercedes's Bluetooth. He sighed at the name 'Archbishop' on the screen and reluctantly pressed 'Answer.'

"Robert! How are you?" came a booming voice.

"I'm doing well, thank you, Your Excellency. How are things with you?"

"Not good. I've received reports of problems in the diocese. Is this true?"

"There have been some minor rumblings in my smallest parish, Your Excellency."

"But I trust you have everything under control?"
"Absolutely!"
"I'm relieved to hear that. Have a good evening."
"Thank you. You, too, Your Excellency."

That was a warning shot; any more disturbances and he would be in deep trouble. He needed to keep his renegade priest on a tight rein.

Chapter Thirty-Five: Casting the Pod
Monday, March 11th

That Monday, Father James felt a renewed zest for life. Today he was going to record his podcast with Rebecca's son-in-law, Dan Carlsworth.

His first 'non-sermon' was ready. His detailed hand-written notes were nestling in his trusty briefcase, a gift from his mother on his ordination, together with a leather-bound Breviary and a beautiful Rosary of onyx beads and sterling silver. He kept the latter in the pocket of his soutane and thought of her whenever he brought it out to pray the five Mysteries of the day, or recite extra rosaries, if the occasion warranted. Which these days it frequently did.

While buttoning up his heavy black coat, he glanced out of the bedroom window at the grey waves rolling onto the deserted beach. Next, he wrapped a cashmere scarf around his neck.

His consecration to the priesthood had been twenty-nine years ago, on the feast of St. Augustine. The thirtieth anniversary of that happy day was on 28th August this year. Where would he spend it? Certainly not celebrating Mass in St. Jude.

He made the Sign of the Cross and prayed, *Lord, it's in Your hands. Thy Will be done. Amen.*

He crossed himself again and pressed a black fedora firmly on his head. Picking up Judith's leash from the side table, he addressed her with, "Come on, you're invited, too."

She leapt from her bed, excited to be included. Dan's children loved dogs and it was arranged that they would play with her outside while the podcast was in progress indoors.

A gust of wind blew under the rim of Father James' hat as he was closing the garden gate. His right hand saved it from becoming airborne and he tamped it more securely over his grey hair.

"That was a near one," he told Judith.

They turned right, following the façade of houses and businesses that formed the horseshoe around the village green. At intervals he cleared his throat to rid it of phlegm.

Instead of his usual breakfast coffee, Rebecca had insisted he drink an herbal tea purporting to be good for the larynx. "I've mixed a little honey in with it," she said. "That should set you up."

Funny how he'd never worried about throat impediments during all his years of daily sermons. Was he more self-conscious because of broadcasting to a wider audience? Or was he already out of practice?

He thought back to his first Masses and how nervous he'd been about making mistakes reading the Gospel, or stuttering during his homily. He had those same jitters now.

Judith was making it clear that she needed to relieve herself, so they crossed the road to the village green. There were no other dogs or people around and Father James let her off leash, rummaging in his pocket for a poop bag.

He watched her roam the area, nose to the ground, looking for the perfect spot, and saw evidence of new growth in the dormant grass. At present only a few patches of brighter green showed here and there, but the trend was unmistakable.

Just like the Catholic Church, he mused. *She flourishes, then suffers persecution and appears to die, only to come back stronger than ever.*

He knew the Church was about to undergo a great suffering, just like her Founder and Leader. But Christ promised that the gates of hell would not prevail against her, and Father James had complete faith in His Word.

Mercifully, Judith did not make any deposits that required clearing up. Father James re-attached her lead and they crossed back over the road to Dan Carlsworth's house.

The children had been looking out for them. The priest had barely touched the bell when the door opened and three youngsters piled out of the house.

"Hello, Father! Hello, Judith!" They made a fuss of the Border Collie, whose tail wagged wildly.

Father James unclipped her lead. "Hello, all of you! Take care of her, now!"

"C'mon, Judith!" shouted the oldest, a boy of nine. "We're gonna play catch out back."

Judith and the three siblings disappeared around the side of the building, and Dan came out to greet his guest. "Good morning, Father, sorry about that. They've been driving me crazy all morning, waiting for you both to show up."

The priest chuckled. "Tactfully put, Dan, but we know who's their favourite. I hope they wear her out."

"I'm sure of it. Come in, and let's get started."

The house was as comfortable as Rebecca's and Father James could see her daughter's hand in the sea-themed décor. But among the bric-a-brac of shells, dolphins and mermaids he noticed the nautical touch: a sailor's compass, a large clock inside a miniature wooden helm and a model sailing ship with four masts.

He smiled at the blend of feminine whimsy and masculine seriousness, suggesting a good balance of personalities within the couple's relationship. He smiled:

did Dan know that his wife Anna was the happy outcome of the pregnancy Father James had talked Rebecca out of terminating?

Dan led him into his office. On the desk were a laptop, headphones, a microphone and what he was about to learn was a pop filter. He was glad to see the bottle of water.

"Sit down, Father," said his host. "I'll familiarise you with the equipment, then we'll do a trial recording. Do you have your notes handy?"

Father James pulled the sheaf of paper out of his briefcase and placed it on the desk. "Is this audio only or are we videoing at the same time?"

"If you're comfortable with going on camera, that would be great."

Father James removed his fedora, then regretted it. "Oh, dear. I've got hat hair."

Surveying the priest's dishevelled appearance, Dan replied, "Why don't you put your hat back on? It'll give you a certain gravitas."

"Do you really think so?"

"Absolutely." He then commented on the hand-written pages and Father James explained how he preferred this method because 'he felt closer to his content.'

This didn't fool Dan. "Father, please use some of the money we've given you to buy a laptop. I know you used to have one before, but I imagine it went with your previous post."

Caught fibbing, Father James reddened. "You're a kind man, Dan. If it means that much to you, I'll happily buy one."

"Good, I'm glad that's settled."

After a few minutes' orientation, a practice run and a prayer for success said together, Father James was ready to launch into the real thing.

Dan said, "I'm going to introduce you, and then you're on."

Father James felt self-conscious at first, and very unsure what gravitas his hat was adding. But he warmed to his topic and soon forgot he was on camera. The title of this first talk was *Watering Down the Faith: Has It Helped the Church?*

When he'd finished, he was exhausted, yet elated. He'd found a new outlet for the truths he needed to proclaim, and in his own small way he was still fulfilling his role as shepherd.

"Bravo!" Dan said, "that was brilliant! I'll edit it this evening, then upload it tomorrow." He smiled at the priest. "This is going to be a good series, Father. I think it'll be very popular."

"If *anyone* watches it, I'll be happy."

"I think you'll be pleasantly surprised. Anna has made us lunch. I hope you can stay?"

"If you let me take off my hat and lend me a comb."

*

Father James left the house an hour later with a full stomach and a very tired Border Collie. "I think we *both* had a good time," he told her as she walked lethargically alongside.

Once in his room, he opened his Breviary to say belated noon prayers. His dog drank greedily from her water bowl then flopped onto her bed.

When he descended for a cup of afternoon tea around 4:30 p.m. Rebecca told him how impressed her daughter and son-in-law were with his talk. "They were asking when you're doing the next one?"

Father James laughed. "I'm glad they approve. I hope to have another prepared by this time next week."

"They also said they'd told you to use the funds we've given you to buy yourself a laptop. I totally agree and I know the other villagers will feel the same."

"Thank you, I'm most grateful."

After a pleasant half hour of sipping Earl Grey and gazing at the beach view outside, the priest roused his dog and took her for a short walk before her evening meal.

That night he went to bed rejoicing that he was once again useful to the Lord.

Tuesday, March 12*th*

Dan uploaded the podcast as promised, and sent Father James the link. Rather than the usual networks, which were becoming ever more hostile to the Christian message, he'd chosen The Plain Truth Channel, a new but increasingly popular pro-Catholic alternative.

After checking out other videos on their site, Father James approved of Dan's decision. His podcast was in good company, for he recognised the names of other cancelled priests.

He'd never met them, and might never do so, but was comforted to be among such fervently loyal men determined, like him, not to be silenced.

Wednesday, March 13*th*

The next day, he couldn't help checking to see whether anyone had watched his podcast, and was gratified to see several hundred views so far. He offered up a prayer of gratitude that he was reaching an audience.

Rebecca congratulated him at breakfast and gave him an extra piece of toast to celebrate.

Father James was at peace: with the help of the Holy Spirit, he was still successfully spreading God's Word. He texted Dan to thank him for his work and let him know it was being noticed.

Happy with life, he took Judith for a walk along the beach and thought up more points to include in his next talk.

He'd just returned to his room when his mobile phone rang.

It was Bishop Marsden.

Chapter Thirty-Six: Mark Gets Busy
Wednesday, March 13th

Mark left Father James' room and walked down the creaky stairs of the bed and breakfast in a state of elation.

Which was absurd, because his external circumstances hadn't changed one bit: he was still in deep legal trouble and likely to lose all his worldly possessions, and had to report to Ruddminster Police Station tomorrow for his weekly humiliation.

But somehow none of that mattered compared to being reconciled with God and given a clean slate.

He smiled. If anyone had told him a week ago that he would feel this way, he'd have laughed in their face. God truly did move in mysterious ways.

He wasn't so naïve as to believe this state of joy would last indefinitely. But he would look back on this moment whenever he was tempted to despair, and remember that God's infinite Love and Mercy were his for the asking, as long as he continued to turn to Him in faith and humility.

If tempted to wallow in self-pity, he could rely on Father James for solace and guidance. With God and the priest on his side, whom or what was there to fear?

Hoping to avoid Rebecca, he reached the foot of the stairs, drew his coat collar around his throat and put on his woollen hat.

"Leaving already?" Rebecca barked behind him.

Slowly, Mark turned around, engrossed in pulling on his gloves. "Yes. You should be pleased."

"I'm not pleased you came here in the first place."

"I gathered as much."

"Well, gather yourself up and go, without coming

back."

"I can't promise not to return, Rebecca."

Arms akimbo, she shook her head at him. "Like I always say, that priest is too good for this world."

"I get your implication – that I'm the dead opposite, and I can't say I disagree with you. But I *am* trying to mend my ways."

She looked askance at him. "You know what they say about a leopard and his spots."

"I most certainly do." Refusing to take offence, he gave her a beatific smile. "Luckily, I'm no leopard."

He saw she was tempted to smile back, and raised his eyebrows, inviting her to give in. But it went too much against the grain. Instead, she shooed him off. "Get away with you!"

Mark's smile widened and he waved back. "God bless you, Rebecca. Good bye for now."

Outside, the sun was making sporadic appearances through the dull cloud cover. Mark had intended to drive straight back to Dartleigh, but changed his mind as he neared his vehicle.

Something was urging him to walk back to the spot where he'd broken down on the beach. He couldn't understand why this should be, but he was in no hurry to get back to his empty house and away from the only ally he had in the world.

As he strolled across the green toward the wide curve of sand, he found the rhythmic rush of waves breaking onto the shore reassuring.

Arriving at the spot where he'd been left to cry, he laughed at the difference between his anguish then and his contentment now – the switch from self-loathing to acceptance of God's Love for him.

The salty breeze blew in his face as he looked out over

the Channel waters. He was struck by the awesome majesty of Him Who created the earth and seas, and filled with confidence that Whoever did this could also bring peace and renewed hope to a wretch like him.

Checking that he was alone, he stretched out his arms and cried, "Thank you, God, thank you for all of this!"

Thursday, 14th March

Mark had arranged to meet Ronald Tibbett at his office in Ruddminster the next day, once he'd completed his obligatory check-in with the police.

Already demoralised after his time with the Devon and Cornwall Constabulary, he took a further beating during the visit with his solicitor.

Mr. Tibbet, of Tibbet, Tibbet & Treyman, had a solemn expression on his face as he invited Mark to take the seat on the other side of his massive leather-covered desk. The man made too much money.

He wasted no time launching into the main topic, for which Mark was grateful, as he was being paid by the hour.

"Our first goal is to rescue your company," he said.

Mark winced at the verb.

"If we're successful, your employees will still have a job. Which is, I imagine, very important to you."

Mark nodded vigorously, thinking about the emails of apology he had to send to all of them. If he could save their jobs, his words would come across as more genuine.

"Failing that," the man continued, "we will need to sell the company assets to pay off your creditors."

That was way worse and Mark's head drooped in shame at having brought his company so low.

"Of course," Mr. Tibbet used an upbeat voice, "we trust it won't come to that." He shuffled some papers on his desk. "We need to appoint an insolvency practitioner to take over as administrator of Boulder Enterprises." He peered at Mark over his half-moon spectacles. "It means handing over control of your company."

Not long ago, Mark would have baulked at the idea of ceding control. Now he was only too happy to do so.

"Of course," he said. "I understand. Do you have someone in mind?"

"Your auditing firm has an IP with an excellent reputation for fairness and swift execution of his duties."

Mark flinched at the word 'execution.' "Do I need to get in touch with him?"

Ronald Tibbet pushed a sheet of paper towards him. "This gives me the authority to hire an IP for you, if you would like me to."

Anything to distance himself from this mess! Mark nodded and signed on the dotted line.

The solicitor swapped that page with another printed one. "This outlines the process of administration. You can see that the IP will conduct business in your stead. His contract will run until he has done what he can to save Boulder Enterprises or use its assets to pay off your creditors, and will in any case, cease at the end of one year, when it can be renewed."

Mark took a deep breath. "What are the chances of saving the company?"

"Given that you have fewer liabilities than most companies that go – er, have issues – there is a good chance that it can be rescued. You've already paid back the investments made by your clientèle, and still have money left over, as well as a fully paid-in pension fund. I'd say there's reason to be hopeful." He coughed discreetly. "Of course, you won't be allowed back in your position as CEO."

"I know that!" Mark snapped. "But I hate to see the company die because of me. And, as you pointed out, I don't want my employees losing their jobs."

"There is, however," continued Mr. Tibbet, "the subject of lost goodwill, and whether there is any possibility of attracting new investors and *continuing* in business. Otherwise, their jobs won't be any use to your employees, will they?"

Mark sighed. Did the man *have* to bring that up? But, yes, rescuing Boulder Enterprises would be no good if new money didn't come in.

"I'm really hoping that with me out of the way, there'll be no remaining stain on my staff. They've built up good reputations individually, which will hopefully help them in the future."

"Then let's remain optimistic."

"Speaking of optimism," Mark said, "I'd appreciate it if you could give me an estimate of the likely fines I'll have to pay."

"Ah, yes," said Mr. Tibbet. "I have some information on that." He opened a desk drawer and pulled out a sheet of paper which he handed to Mark. "I've given the worst case, best case and most likely scenarios."

Mark gasped at the numbers. There was a fine for malfeasance as CEO of Boulder Enterprises and 'reckless investment of clients' funds;' a fine for misappropriation of charity funds, and a fine for bribery. It all added up to a terrifyingly large amount which Mark feared he'd never be able to pay.

He looked in distress at Mr. Tibbet, who said, "Since

you're a first-time offender – although unfortunately you've committed several offenses at once – the courts are unlikely to give you a custodial sentence."

"That's *some* comfort." Mark no longer cherished the conviction that jail would be a welcome retreat. "But how am I going to pay these fines?"

"The courts will take into consideration the fact that you've already distributed the charity funds to the seniors whose money you misappropriated. But there may be a civil suit against you for psychological damages. We'll just have to wait and see."

"But in the meantime," Mark said, "I would be smart to begin selling off my assets to create a pool from which all these fines can be paid."

Ronald Tibbet looked pained. "I'm afraid that does seem a good plan."

Mark looked to one side. *Dear Lord, I've really landed myself in it, haven't I?*

"So be it. I'll set that in motion."

*

Before making a scant dinner for himself back home in Dartleigh, Mark wrote out a list of the things he needed to do. The activity focussed him and prevented his mind from wasting energy on useless regrets.

His first action was to make an inventory of his assets and their monetary value, together with an assessment of the time needed to liquidate them.

He'd told Mr. Tibbet about his wife's request for a formal separation, and the solicitor had undertaken to draft a formal document for them both to sign. It included giving Mary half the proceeds of the house, and deciding how much to give her for daily needs.

Regarding the latter, Mark wasn't sure where that money was supposed to come from, but hoped his generous pension would be sufficient. He'd forgotten to ask his solicitor if he and/or Mary were still entitled to it. He called and left a message, asking Mr. Tibbett to let him know as soon as possible. That money was vital!

He rummaged in the fridge for something to eat. There wasn't much, as he'd been living off what Mary left before her abrupt departure, and he'd not bothered to go to the grocery store since.

She'd been gone eight days, and he vaguely recalled that one is supposed to eat leftovers within a week. That meant, strictly speaking, he should throw everything away.

Dear Lord, please don't let me be poisoned if I eat what's here! I promise to start writing those emails for my penance, if you protect me.

He poured himself a glass of red wine (at least he had enough of *that*) and heated up the remains of a stew. While the microwave was nuking it, he cut the rotten bits off the two last apples and added the only banana that hadn't gone bad for his dessert.

He sniffed at the whipping cream, hoping to drizzle it over the fruit. But it stank and he had to pour that down the sink.

Having suffered no ill effects from this meal, he fulfilled his side of the bargain with God and sat down to write the emails, beginning with his two children.

Chapter Thirty-Seven: A Bishop's Wrath Continues

Wednesday, March 13th

Father James stifled a groan as he pressed the green answer button on his mobile.

"James!" Bishop Marsden barked.

"Yes, Your Excellency?"

"It has been brought to my attention," – who were these people bringing things to his attention? – "that you have been preaching in defiance of my instructions."

"With all due respect," began the priest.

"Drop the act, James."

"In obedience to your letter, I'm not preaching from the pulpit."

"You will recall I wrote that you are no longer allowed to preach. Full stop. I didn't specify *where from*."

"But podcasts aren't preaching," Father James protested.

"What do you call them, then?"

"Spreading God's Word."

"You are no longer a fit vessel for spreading God's Word, and your disobedience has forced me to remove you from the diocesan payroll."

Father James wasn't surprised, but it was a shock all the same. Was God punishing him for trying to do His work?

"I trust you realise you've brought all this upon yourself?"

Father James dodged the question. "I'm sorry, Your Excellency, I'm trying to take all this in."

"Don't forget my offer, James. This decision is still

reversible if you attend a thirty-day retreat to spiritually heal and address the issues that led to my decree."

Father James bridled at the idea of being indoctrinated at a psychiatric institute because he'd promised obedience to his bishop. But hadn't he just told Father Gregory about the exception, if the superior commands something that breaks God's law, however slightly?

He had a duty to proclaim the Good News – the pure and unadulterated version – and sincerely believed his superior was not acting as a faithful interpreter of God's will.

With so many good priests being pushed out, surely it was vital he continue to spread the Word of God?

Striving to be polite, he answered, "Thank you. I will bear your generosity in mind, Your Excellency."

"Don't leave it too long, James. My offer won't be open for ever."

"I shall bear that in mind, too."

"You do that. In the meantime, you are still a priest – albeit side-lined – of this diocese, but I'm no longer confining you to live within its geographic limits."

"Thank you, Your Excellency."

"I hope and pray that you will rethink your position, James, and that I'll soon hear you're ready to come back into the fold."

Their conversation over, Father James slumped into the armchair in his little bedroom.

Judith turned concerned eyes towards him. "Well, old girl, it's finally happened; I'm out of a job. I can't agree to being brainwashed at St. Matthew's. My allegiance is to the one, true, holy and apostolic Church, not a modern diluted version of her, and no one is going to talk me out of it." He raised a small smile. "I think the bishop not confining me to this diocese physically is his not-so-subtle attempt to move me away from King's Brambling. I can't do that. Father Gregory needs my help or he's going to drown."

His thoughts turned to this sudden change in his finances. His parishioners were continuing to contribute to the fund for him, but he couldn't rely on their generosity forever. They ought really to be giving their money to the collection plate now. Whatever their feelings about Bishop Marsden, that money was needed to carry out missions of mercy for the poor as well as pay for the Eucharistic bread and wine.

Not only that, but he would soon receive his inheritance from Dave Miller. If he invested it wisely – he grimaced: Boulder Enterprises would have been his first choice not so long ago – he could make some income from it. But that alone would not suffice.

He must find alternative employment.

He couldn't bring himself to tell Rebecca about this new development. She'd insist on offering him food and board free of charge, and he didn't want that.

He would cheer himself up by paying Father Gregory a visit. The priest's company would be a welcome contrast to the bishop's icy reception. He picked up his Breviary so he could also recite his noon prayers in St. Jude.

Judith sat up with her head tilted to one side as he took her leash off the bed.

"Yes, you're coming, too."

*

Going to see Father Gregory proved a good move. It did indeed lift his spirits.

The young priest offered him a small sherry, which he declined. "I need to keep my head clear for noon prayers," he said.

"Perhaps afterwards I can persuade you to share a

modest lunch with me?"

"That sounds wonderful," said Father James, wishing he'd brought a food offering.

Sitting in the tiny parlour with Father Gregory, he related the details of Bishop Marsden's call. "I felt it only right to warn you about my new status. Since I'm free to live wherever I choose, I want you to have the choice to carry on here in King's Brambling by yourself."

"Father, it's up to you where you live. But if I have my druthers, I'd prefer that you stay. I need your guidance."

"About the best guidance I can give is to tell you to watch your step, lest you, too, become an ex-employee of the Church."

"I was rather hoping you'd help me with that." The young man reddened. "I have my formal spiritual director, but I did hope you might be my *informal* one?"

"To direct you through the present minefield?"

"Exactly."

"If I can find a job here in the village, then I'm more than happy to do so."

"Thank you! Will you be continuing with your podcasts?"

"I need to pray about it, but I don't see any other way to proclaim the Kingdom of God, as I'm duty bound to do."

"Good for you!" Father Gregory cleared his throat. "I want you to know that you'll always have a place to stay here at the rectory – you and Judith."

"I truly appreciate that. It's good to know if things get really bad. In the meantime, I'll stay with Rebecca while I can afford it. I've become rather attached to my little room with a view. But you'll be seeing me in church. Speaking of which, I'd like to go to St. Jude to say my prayers."

"I'll join you."

Feeling refreshed after praying in his old church and eating a simple repast with Father Gregory, Father James drove back to the village able to reflect on his situation with greater equanimity.

Dear Lord, if you mean me to stay in King's Brambling and help Father Gregory, please let me be successful in finding a job.

He parked his Triumph and walked past Rebecca's Bed & Breakfast to the Post Office next door. Pinned to a large cork board inside were scores of index cards carrying information about everything conceivable to do with village life – including available jobs.

He tied Judith to the lamp post outside, swallowed his pride and walked in.

Chapter Thirty-Eight: Making Changes
Saturday, March 16th

Mark woke up glad the weekend had just begun.

He'd gone food shopping the day before and now looked forward to a hearty breakfast of scrambled eggs (the only way he knew how to cook them) on toast, with ready-cooked sausages and bacon rashers zapped in the microwave, and a lavish serving of baked beans. Good heart-destroying stuff that Mary had always refused to make for him. Being separated had its perks.

Ronald Tibbet had called back yesterday with some good news. Mark would still receive his company pension regardless of the judge's ruling. As an added bonus, if he managed to stay out of jail, his state pension was also safe.

However, even if he *did* succeed in avoiding a custodial sentence, he still needed to find a job: he was too young to draw on either of his pensions yet. But who'd want to hire a disgraced managing director?

I'll worry about that on Monday.

As he set about creating his unhealthy meal, he glanced now and then through the kitchen window at the Devonshire hills beyond his back garden fence. The sight was glorious, even under the weak morning sun. God was in His heaven and all was well.

Within minutes, the room reeked of fat. To escape the strong odour, Mark poured himself a large mug of coffee, scooped a bottle of ketchup under his left arm, and carried the feast into the dining room.

As soon as he sat down, the house phone rang in the kitchen. He ignored it.

The caller was leaving a message.

"Mark, this is Robert. I know you're there. Pick up the

phone."

I won't, until I'm good and ready.

"Fine, have it your way," came the eerie response, "but I expect to hear from you within the hour. It's now 9:30 a.m." The phone went dead.

He did *not* want to talk to the bishop, whose diluted Catholicism he couldn't help comparing to the traditional orthodoxy of Father James and, he hated to admit, that of his wife.

Robert Marsden had moved farther away from Church doctrine the higher he'd moved up the hierarchy. He'd become less spiritual and more secular.

Power corrupts, thought Mark, then laughed wryly. *Look who's talking!*

The line between good and evil had become blurred over the years for both men.

He recalled his conversation with Robert at the club a month ago. His own morals had been too compromised to notice that at no point did the bishop mention that Mark had done anything wrong. He should have been correcting him and urging him to repent, but instead the discussion had revolved around Mark's image – on damage control, not Mark's eternal salvation.

And that damage control, Mark cringed to recall, included bribing Father James not to pursue the truth. When the priest wouldn't cave, the bishop removed his priestly faculties as punishment for being an upright man of God.

Mark had lost everything, too, but his punishment was just. Of the three of them, it was Bishop Marsden for whom Mark felt the sorriest. Like him, he had lost his way; he no longer stood up for even the most basic tenets of the Catholic Church.

Together with his sister, Robert grew up in a devout

Catholic family, believing in the sanctity of marriage between a man and a woman, and that abortion was murder. There were no blurred lines, no redefining terms or using clever euphemisms to hide the truth or present half-truths. Theirs had been a straight-forward faith, like that of Mark's own childhood.

But as Robert climbed up the Church ranks, the secular culture had obscured his proper goal of saving souls.

For Mark, the loss of direction happened at university. He'd thrown himself into a hedonistic life-style incompatible with Church teachings, which James Stryker so earnestly defended into the early hours of the morning, night after night.

Mark now understood that James' seriousness had stemmed from true friendship and a sincere desire to save his soul. For the first time, Mark grasped that saving souls was the single most important activity a human being could engage in, *should* engage in.

God was giving him a second chance to save his own soul. The Almighty had brought Father James back into his life for that very purpose; his worldly losses paled in comparison to losing eternal life.

He shuddered. *If it hadn't been for Father James!*

*

Once he'd cleared the dishes after breakfast, he forced himself to call his brother-in-law.

He checked his watch and smiled. It was 10:28 a.m. - two minutes before the hour was up. He considered waiting until 10:31, but his better nature argued against it. No point riling the man more than necessary.

"Is that you, Mark?" snapped his brother-in-law. "About time!"

"Hello to you, too, Robert. What gives?"

"I've just found out the aborted baby's ceremony in

King's Brambling was for *your* son."

"I hope you're not going to pretend you knew nothing about the abortion."

"That's not what I'm upset about, Mark. What I want to know is, what were you doing down there, fomenting rebellion in the village against the Church by supporting Father James' heretical notions of a memorial service?"

"Who told you that?"

"It was in the paper, you idiot, along with all the other bad press you're accumulating."

Mark couldn't help laughing. "Robert, since you've disassociated yourself from me, I don't answer to you anymore."

The bishop's voice took on a nasty edge. "You are still – by the skin of your teeth – a member of the Catholic Church. Any more dissention and you will be excommunicated."

Mark laughed even more loudly. "Let me get this right. You're going to excommunicate me for supporting a good priest, who follows the teachings of Christ and the true Church. You don't have a leg to stand on. Why don't you do something useful like refusing Holy Communion to this country's so-called Catholics who promote abortion? The scandal is that you haven't done it."

"Don't push me, Mark. You're a fine one to talk about scandal. I can easily put a word in high places and have you kicked out."

"Why would I get upset at being ostracized by those who purport to adhere to the Church's magisterium, yet openly flout her rules?"

"I'm warning you!"

Mark adopted a soothing voice. "I seem to be upsetting you, Robert, so I'll sign off."

"Don't you dare – !"

"Good bye." Mark pressed 'End' and took a deep breath. "That went well," he told the fridge, thinking how lucky Father James was to have Judith to talk to. Much better than chatting to inanimate objects.

Maybe he should get a dog?

Mentally reviewing his conversation with the bishop, he worried that God might be displeased. *Lord, I hope I didn't cross the line. If so, please forgive me. Amen.*

Thinking about God so often was new to him. It was comforting to know He was always close at hand, although He was obviously closer to Father James.

With that unpleasant chat out of the way, Mark took his newspaper and a mug of coffee into the sitting room where he idly checked properties for sale that fit the police criteria.

While reporting in at the police station on Thursday, Mark had explained that his marital situation was about to change. The present house would be sold and he'd have a new address.

He was told this was fine, as long as the new abode was in Devonshire and he could prove ownership.

There were several places worth considering, but he wasn't yet ready to look at new houses; it would be more useful to see about getting a cheaper car. The BMW, his beloved status symbol, must go. It cost too much to run and insure. Yet he needed transport. He drew red rings around a few possibilities in the advertisement section.

Rather than lose money on his current car through a dealership, he decided to sell it privately. He placed an ad in the online version of the paper that afternoon, hoping no one would bite.

Sunday, March 17ᵗʰ

But they did.

Ten minutes after he got home from sitting at the back of church at early morning Sunday Mass, praying no one would recognize Mark Boulder, Public Enemy Number One, in the Communion line, a BMW enthusiast called, eager to come that same afternoon and see the vehicle.

Mark was in shock: this was really happening.

He agreed to meet the man in the parking lot of the local pub as it was safer than having a stranger drive up to the house. You never knew these days.

The man loved the car.

Wednesday, March 20ᵗʰ

Over the next few days, a depressed Mark looked for an economical replacement.

Having found one, he arranged for the buyer of his BMW to meet at the dealership where he was going to buy his next – and much downsized – vehicle.

With a heavy heart, he made the last funereal trip in his luxury car. But after the exchange, he was thousands of pounds richer and shortly after that, the owner of a small used car.

As he drove it home, the image popped into his head of Bishop Marsden in his Mercedes. He fought it off with a picture of Father James' ancient Triumph, driven with such affection, and smiled.

He parked the car in his garage and made a cup of tea. While he was stirring in the milk, the doorbell rang.

The postman stood on the welcome mat holding a registered letter. "Good morning, sir, would you sign here, please?"

Baffled, Mark did as requested, and took the letter inside.

After reading its contents, he needed a friend to talk to.

Chapter Thirty-Nine: The Spirit Moves
Wednesday, March 20th

Rebecca Luckton was not happy to see Mark.

She yelled upstairs for her husband and he recalled poking fun at Mr. John Luckton, all those decades ago at university, for allowing himself to be railroaded into marrying his pregnant girlfriend instead of getting rid of the baby.

He was not looking forward to seeing the man again.

A head peered over the bannisters. "What is it?"

"Mark Boulder's here. I told him to stay away, but he wouldn't listen."

John grinned menacingly on his way down.

The gaunt man was taller than Mark, who raised his palms towards him in a gesture of truce. "Look, I'm not here to make trouble. I just want to see Father James."

"Oi'm supproised 'e's still talkin' to you. It's more 'n you deserve."

Mark had forgotten that strong Devon accent – something else he'd teased the man about.

"I keep telling him that, too," Rebecca said.

"Well, you won't foind 'im 'ere."

Mark was worried. "Why? Is he O.K.?"

"'Ow could 'e be, after what you done to 'im?"

Mark had no defence to offer. "Where's he gone?"

"He's working at the Post Office next door." Rebecca pointed to the far wall. "Thanks to you, he's had to find a new job." Mark could feel her mentally spitting on him.

Working at the Post Office?

Would there be no end to the consequences of his actions? Wherever he went, his nose was rubbed in shame.

He took a deep breath. "Thank you for letting me know. I'll be off." He turned to leave, but there was something else he needed to say. "I'm sorry for the things I said to you back at uni. It was meanspirited and hurtful, and I deeply regret it." His face was burning and he had trouble looking at the couple. "My words don't make anything better, but I want you to know that I wish I hadn't behaved so badly towards you. Your marrying was the best thing that could have happened and I envy you the strength of your relationship. God bless." He hurried out into the street.

Emailing people was so much easier than apologizing in person!

Now to face the priest turned postal worker thanks to him. Grateful for the cold air fanning his red-hot cheeks, he took a moment to compose himself with a quick prayer.

Lord, I came here for selfish reasons, because I need to be with a friend. But please help me be a friend to him.

The old-fashioned bell above the door announced his entrance into the Post Office and General Grocery. Not seeing Father James behind the postal desk, Mark walked into the shop area and spotted the priest stacking shelves. He was engrossed in arranging tins of peas in neat rows on the second shelf and had his back to Mark.

Mark watched him for a while, unsure whether he would want to be seen at this task. But his expression was serene, as if this chore were exactly suited to his abilities instead of way beneath him.

How *did* he do it?

He's an example to me, thought Mark. *Soon I'll be in his shoes, because any employment I find will be just as unglamorous.*

It occurred to him that Father James was well-loved in this community, and everyone knew it wasn't his fault that he'd landed on hard times. There was no indignity in his situation.

But Mark would be recognised wherever he went as the wicked man who didn't deserve to be given the time of day. There was no reservoir of goodwill to draw from when *he* went into the salt mines. He was universally hated.

We reap what we sow.

"Excuse me," a middle-aged woman said, "do you mind if I come past?"

"I'm so sorry." Mark moved aside and let the woman push her shopping trolley down the aisle.

Father James turned around at the sound of his voice. "Mark! Hail fellow, well met."

"Hello, Father. I'm admiring your total concentration on the job. They're lucky to have such a conscientious employee."

The priest laughed. "I *have* to concentrate. I'm not very good at this, but I'm learning."

"You make it sound very cerebral."

Father James chuckled. "Oh, but it is!"

Mark's heart ached to see the priest making so light of his situation. If only he could ease his plight! But he was in a bad place himself.

"What brings you here?" asked the pastor.

"I've been given my arraignment date and didn't want to sit at home moping about it. What about you? What brings you here?"

"I'd love to tell you I'm doing this for the fun of it, but truth be told, I've been removed from the Catholic payroll."

"Oh, no!" Mark groaned at this new aftermath of his

egotism. "Father, I don't know how to make it up to you. But how about joining me for a double celebration of our downfalls? When are you off the clock?"

"The Post Office closes in half an hour, at 2 p.m. Then I need to pop back to the B & B to let Judith out."

"I'll pick you both up there at a quarter past, if you'll please tell Rebecca not to chop off my head."

Father James grinned. "She is rather fierce in my defence, isn't she? I'll see what I can do."

*

Mark spent the intervening time walking along the beach and reconciling himself to the fact that the same level of job awaited him as his holy friend. Just as he'd had to accept downgrading his car, so would he have to grin and bear demeaning employment.

Thy Will be done, he remembered to pray, but it was hard to mean it.

Gusts of wind were pushing him off the beach and he crossed the village green towards the bed and breakfast where he was not welcome.

He opened the front door warily and peeked in to see if Rebecca was in the vicinity.

"It's alright, you can come in." She was exiting the kitchen with a tray of cutlery. "Father is upstairs." She disappeared into the breakfast room.

Relieved she hadn't driven him off the premises, Mark ascended the creaking steps and knocked on room number 33.

"Come in, Mark."

Judith jumped out of her bed when he opened the door and her greeting was so warm that Mark was again tempted to get a dog of his own. How could one's spirits not be lifted by such joyous enthusiasm?

"How did it go with Rebecca?" Father James asked.

"Whatever you said to her, it worked. She was very amiable."

"I didn't need to say much. She said you'd made your peace with her and John, and as a good Christian she would let bygones be bygones."

Mark squinted at his friend. "For real?"

"Not a word of a lie."

"Well, you're a priest, I suppose I must believe you."

"Yes, you must. And well done for achieving a détente."

Mark shook his head in surprise at the effect of his words on the Luckton couple.

Father James laughed. "It's amazing what the Holy Spirit can achieve if we give Him a chance, isn't it?"

"I'm humbled, Father, I truly am."

"And that's exactly how He's able to work through you."

Mark smiled: he was learning a lot about how God operates. He wandered over to the makeshift desk with papers strewn all over it. "Where's your laptop?"

"It was never *my* laptop."

"Would you take mine? I don't need it. I can do everything with my phone."

"That's very kind of you, but the parishioners want me to use some of the money they've raised for me to buy a new one."

"If you're sure?"

"I am."

"What are you working on?"

"A series of talks that Rebecca's son-in-law Dan is helping me turn into podcasts."

"Sounds like fun. How are you getting the word out about them?"

"Dan uploaded my first one to a Christian site and

Bishop Marsden got wind of it almost immediately. So, the word is somehow getting out."

"Is that why you've been removed from the payroll?"

"Yes." The priest smiled ruefully.

"Would you let me help you advertise it?"

"I can't pay you, Mark."

"I don't want payment. I want to help spread the truth as reparation for what I did to you. It's small potatoes, I know, but please let me start there. I've got time on my hands."

"That's very good of you. We'll talk about it, alright? "

Those kind words made Mark all the more ashamed of his treatment of the priest. If only he could undo the past.

"Now, where do you suggest we go to 'celebrate'?" asked Father James.

Mark touched the side of his nose. "Not telling. Put on your coat and don't forget Judith's leash."

Chapter Forty: Strawberry Jam
Wednesday, March 20th

"Come on, Judith," said Father James, "I've no idea where we're going, but you don't care. You're just along for the ride."

The Border Collie wagged her tail against his soutane.

"You must spend a lot of time removing dog hairs from that outfit," remarked Mark. "Shame you have to wear black."

"Good thing I have plenty of time these days to attend to the task, isn't it?"

Down at the front desk, Father James told Rebecca that his friend was taking him out for the afternoon.

"I hope you're not kidnapping Father," she said to Mark. But a smile was playing at the corners of her mouth.

"I promise to bring him back in one piece," he said.

"God willing," added Father James, putting the leash on Judith.

The three of them exited via the garden gate and as they approached the car park, the priest asked, "Where's your car, Mark?"

Father James' Triumph sat next to a vehicle the priest would never associate with his friend.

"You're looking at it." Mark took the keys out of his pocket to unlock the door of the midnight blue Mini convertible.

Father James laughed. "What, no remote opener? What happened?"

"I sold the BMW, but I still need transport. I thought of you getting around just fine in your ancient jalopy, and decided to take a chance on this old girl. One owner, comparatively low mileage, only driven to the shops and back and regularly serviced."

Mark opened the passenger door.

"Where's Judith going to sit?" asked Father James.

"On that narrow ledge behind us that's pretending to be a back row seat."

Judith chose to position her rear end on the floor behind the two men, with her front paws just missing the gear box, and her head resting on Father James' lap.

Mark switched on the ignition and winced at the loud engine. He was unaccustomed to the noise level compared to his German car.

"Sounds a lot like my old girl," Father James remarked, glancing at his friend. "Are you talking to her in soothing tones yet?"

"Does that coax a better performance out of your car?"

"It doesn't hurt for her to know I care."

Mark squinted dubiously at him. "I'll let you know if I reach that stage."

"Oh, it's a matter of 'when' not 'if.'"

Mark rolled his eyes and laughed, suspecting the priest was right.

The suspension was hard. Mark had to slow down and skirt round the uneven parts of the village road that wouldn't have bothered the BMW.

"How are you doing, Mark?" asked Father James. "Have you begun selling your assets in anticipation of those impending fines?"

"Yes. Plus, Mary doesn't want a divorce – "

"That's marvellous!"

"But she does want a formal separation. That means selling the house and giving her half."

"Oh, that makes me sad. But what about your pension? Will you still get that?"

"Yes. And if I stay out of jail, I'll get the state pension as well as the company one."

"To be shared with Mary, I presume?"

"Yes." Mark had a sudden thought. "Father, what about your pension?"

"Non-existent, I'm afraid. That went out of the window when I was booted off the books."

Mark nearly drove off the road. "Oh, Father, what have I done?"

"Look, the bishop was bound to catch up with me sooner or later. All around the country – nay, the world – priests are losing their living because they're defiantly preaching the Word of God as they're supposed to do.

"You just happened to be the instrument that brought about my ousting."

Mark grimaced. "The way Judas brought about Christ's Passion?"

Father James grinned. "Well, I can hardly compare my meagre suffering with Our Lord's, but I suppose the principle is the same, yes." He pointed an index finger at Mark. "Now, don't go committing suicide, do you hear me? Unlike Judas, you know better than to despair of God's mercy."

"I have strong empathy for that man at the moment. Everywhere I turn, I see the lives I've ruined."

"All is not lost. God makes good come out of evil for those who love Him, Mark."

"I fail to see any good coming out of what I did."

"You're feeling remorse and that's a good start. You've already paid – or plan to – pay back the seniors their money, I presume?"

"Yes, that's in the works as we speak. There's some talk about a class action against me, but my solicitor doesn't think that will amount to anything."

"Let's hope he's correct. How are you coming along with those emails?"

"I thought you weren't supposed to mention anything said in the confessional?"

"I take it that means you've not done anything about them?" deflected the priest.

"For your information, I *have*."

"Excellent! And you're bravely facing your trial and impending fines. That's a lot more than Judas did."

"Wow, thanks." Mark went on to explain the administration process for his company. "If all goes well, it could stay in business and my staff will keep their jobs."

"I shall pray it works out that way."

"Thank you. I need all the prayers I can get."

"Don't we all?"

This last part of the conversation was almost shouted over the rising engine noise as the Mini climbed the hill inland from the sea. Then the road levelled out and the decibel level decreased.

Father James chuckled. "Welcome to the less luxurious lane."

"It's going to take me a long time to get used to this new life style," moaned Mark.

"You'll learn to love it," the priest assured him. "It allows more time for reflection."

"I don't have any happy thoughts to reflect on. Do you?"

"Oh, Goodness, yes! I reflect on God's love for me and His mercy and willingness to forgive. I reflect on how He's opening doors for me to preach His Word when the usual channels are closed."

"Do you call working at the Post Office an opportunity to preach His Word?"

"Now that you mention it, it *is* a way to set the villagers an example in humility. As long as I accept my lot cheerfully, then my actions will preach the Gospel to them."

"Where on earth do you get your optimism?"

"Where do you think? Or rather, from Whom?"

"But doesn't your current situation depress you?"

"It would if I let it. But don't forget, as a priest I spend time with the Lord on a regular basis every day, which keeps Him front and centre. You should try it."

"Say the Hours? You've got to be kidding!"

"No, I mean set aside certain times of the day to talk to God. Go to daily Mass as well. It will fortify you for what lies ahead. With God you are never lonely."

"Since I've made enemies of everyone I know, that sounds very tempting."

"He's always waiting for you, especially in the Eucharist, Mark. He'd love you to come to Him every day and receive His Body and Blood. As long as you're in a state of grace, of course."

"I'll give it some serious thought, I promise."

They drove along in silence for a few minutes, then Father James asked, "Where on earth are you taking me?"

"Remember how we used to take this road from university whenever we could persuade a friend with a car to take us?"

The priest laughed. "Yes, and the vehicles we travelled in then were roughly the same vintage as our current ones."

Mark grinned. "You're right. How sad!"

They arrived at Dartmoor, and Mark followed the road to the west until he found the place he was looking for.

"Here we are. Recognise it?"

"Oh, boy, are we going to have what I think we are?"

"Yup! I can't think of a better way to celebrate our joint disgrace, can you?"

Mark parked outside a café on the edge of the moor, and Father James grinned. "We had some great times here, didn't we?"

He stayed outside with Judith, while Mark went in and inquired of the owner whether the dog could come inside with them.

"She belongs to my priest friend, and he rarely gets to go out. It would mean a lot to him."

He was relieved when she didn't appear to recognise him and said, "It's off season, I don't see why not."

Ten minutes later, Father James was sitting opposite Mark at the back of the café, with a view over the moor. Judith lay underneath the table, blending in with the dark rug.

The two men sipped tea from large china cups. On the red and white chequered table cloth were a large plate of scones, a big pot of strawberry jam and a massive bowl of Devon clotted cream.

They each took a scone, spread it with clotted cream followed by a generous dollop of jam, and bit into it.

"Mmm!" said Father James, "this environment adds something extra to the occasion. I'd like to propose a toast." He raised his teacup. "Here's to rekindling old friendships."

"To my oldest friend," said Mark, clinking his cup against the priest's, "and right now, my only friend, to whom I should have listened many years ago."

Father James smiled. "We all have our own journey to make, Mark."

"Pity I took such a horrible detour."

"But you're back on track. That's what matters."

Mark smiled and hoped the priest would help him stay on that track.

They drank their tea, relishing the over-stuffed scones and wiping jam off their faces with their chequered napkins.

Out on the moor the pale afternoon sun was casting an eerie glow over the rough grassland and craggy tors.

"First one to see a Dartmoor Pony gets the last scone," said Mark.

"You're on!"

It was a few minutes before Father James yelled, "There's one! No, three of them! Look, next to the tor."

Mark followed the priest's finger until he saw three skewbalds. "Those aren't Dartmoor Ponies, they're Dartmoor Hill Ponies."

"You're splitting hairs, Mark. I saw them first and I get the last scone."

"I said Dartmoor Ponies. Those don't count."

"Oh, yes, they do!"

Mark's mobile phone rang. "I'd better see who it is." He glowered at the priest. "This argument isn't over!"

Father James reached for the last scone as Mark pulled the phone out of his pocket.

Stunned at the caller's name, he answered, "Hello?"

"Dad? It's Joseph. I got your email."

Chapter Forty-One: The Showdown
Wednesday, March 20th

Father James took Judith out for a walk on the edge of the moors while Mark spoke with his son.

The stunned dad was glad when the priest returned, for he was dying to tell him about the talk.

"That's the best conversation we've ever had, Father. I think it's the first time we've been open with each other."

"How does it feel?"

"Liberating. Don't get me wrong, it wasn't all lovey-dovey. Joseph had some harsh things to tell me, and they needed saying. But it gave me the opportunity to apologise to him in person, so to speak, not just in an email, and that felt good."

"The person who apologises often has more to gain than the one being apologised to," said the priest. "Although I suspect you both came out the winners."

Mark grinned. "He accepted it graciously, and even went as far as inviting me to come and stay."

"Will you do that?"

He shook his head. "I'm too embarrassed to show my face right now."

"That's pride talking and you need to get over that. It's what got you into trouble in the first place."

Mark looked ruefully at the priest. "I guess if you can stock shelves at the local grocer's shop, then I can be brave enough to visit my own family. And then *I'll* be ready to stock shelves."

Father James chuckled. "I'll see if they have an opening at the Post Office store."

Mark laughed. "Please do!"

When they parted ways at Rebecca's Bed & Breakfast, Father James asked, "Will you be coming to Mass on Sunday?"

"I'll do better than that. I'll come tomorrow morning, too, so I can critique Father Gregory's sermon."

"I pity the man! Join me for breakfast afterwards."

On the way home, Mark's mobile phone rang on the passenger seat. He sighed, remembering the wonderful days of Bluetooth, when he could talk hands free. But not in this old Mini.

He pressed *Answer* and fumbled for the loudspeaker button while keeping his eyes on the road.

"Mark?"

"Yes, who is this?"

"It's Robert, you dolt. The sound isn't as clear on your phone as usual."

"Yes, there seems to be some interference. Sorry about that. To what do I owe this call?"

"I was hoping you could join me for lunch at the palace tomorrow."

Mark was stunned. Weren't they supposed to be on bad terms?

"You still there?"

"Yes, I thought I heard you invite me to lunch."

"I did. What's so odd about that?"

Mark could think of plenty of things. "What time should I be there?"

"See you at noon."

Mark pictured Father James' surprise when he told him about this invitation tomorrow.

Thursday, March 21ˢᵗ

This time the bishop's back wasn't turned on his

brother-in-law when he entered the palace dining room.

Oozing bonhomie, he walked towards Mark with his hand held out. "My dear chap, you have had a rough time of it. I hear Mary wants a separation. I'm so sorry, that's too bad."

Mark nodded and murmured his thanks. *Of course, the two of them have been talking about me.*

The bishop poured him a large whiskey and bade him sit down in the same seat as before.

They chatted about the state of affairs in the country including the rising price of petrol, and the pros and cons of exiting Europe, until their appetisers arrived.

Once the first flight of wine was poured, and the sommelier and waiter had retired from the room, the bishop said, "Now then, I understand you and Father James have become quite the pals. Interesting, given your part in his removal. What can you two *possibly* have in common these days?"

Mark sipped his drink and grinned. "Well, our time at university, for one."

The bishop's face reddened. "And what else, pray?"

Mark was enjoying this. "We've become kindred spirits due to our public disgrace."

"How can that be, when you *caused* his disgrace?"

"My behaviour might have been the instigating incident, but I didn't oust him, *you* did."

"You forced my hand," retorted the bishop, "and he knows it. I don't understand why he tolerates you and I don't care to find out."

"So why am I here?"

"To suggest, as a friend and erstwhile relative, that you reconsider your new alliance and distance yourself from James."

Mark was puzzled. "Why should I do that? And, by the

way, he is still *Father* James."

"By the skin of his teeth. Look, unless you stop this nonsense of fraternising with *Father* James, I shall have no choice but to ex-communicate you."

Mark was taken aback. "On what grounds?"

"Colluding with a demoted priest." He studied Mark's face. "I trust you understand the ramifications of what I'm telling you?" He pulled a piece of paper from the ample folds of his soutane and pushed it slowly across the white tablecloth.

Mark read: 'Loss of the sacraments, denial of attending Holy Mass and public prayers of the Church, no ecclesiastical burial, loss of canonical jurisdiction, benefices, canonical rights and prohibition of social intercourse with the faithful.'

Could the bishop really do this? Had Mark finally come back into full communion with the Church only to face the threat of being thrown out?

With supreme effort, he adopted a neutral expression.

The bishop continued. "I'll see to it that your name is mud in every parish. No priest will touch you and no congregation will accept you. You'll be a pariah in the Catholic Church, despised the same way the general public despises you now. The consolation of the sacraments will be denied you and your isolation will be complete."

One thought consoled Mark. "Father James will support me."

The bishop's tone was mocking. "You seriously believe he will, once you've become anathema to the Church? His own situation is too precarious to risk it."

An absurd side to this threat occurred to Mark. "And if he *does* support me, then what? Ex-communicate Father James? Father Gregory? Soon you'll have no priests left. You won't get a penny more from the parishioners in your diocese and you'll end up having to close most of your churches. How will your Archbishop like *that*?"

Bishop Marsden adopted a coaxing tone. "Listen, Mark. If you stop associating with that priest, I can help you get on your feet financially and build back your reputation. Making those repayments to those you've robbed has already put you on the road. I can speed up the process for you."

Even if the bishop had such power, which was doubtful, he couldn't prevent the judge from sending Mark to prison.

But Robert Marsden wasn't finished. "As you know, I have a lot of influence with my sister. I can easily persuade her to give up this nonsense about a separation, and come back to live with you in your beautiful shared residence."

He sat back to watch the effect of his words. "Think about it, Mark. You wouldn't have to sell your home and pay for two households, nor would you have to give up half your pension. Preserving the sanctity of marriage will benefit your public persona and the Church will support you again. You'll be welcomed back into the community and no longer ostracised by your entire family."

Mark recalled the earlier conversation with his son. There, at least, was one family member who'd not abandoned him.

But the thought of keeping his house and all of his considerable pension, of being able to sell that ridiculous Mini and buy a new, prestigious car – with Bluetooth – was tantalising.

Even if he *did* go to prison, his house and pension and

car would be waiting for him when he came out – not a job stacking shelves at the local Post Office, with only Father James for a friend.

He imagined being on top of the world again. He would show everyone that he'd learned his lesson: never again would he take advantage of other people. Instead, he would be a paragon of virtue, a reformed character, an example of what God can do in the lives of those who let Him in.

The people would love him once more. He would be able to walk with his head held high and his lovely wife by his side.

Heck, he'd even get a dog and take walks in the countryside.

He would, of course, go to Confession regularly and receive Communion at Mass every Sunday. He would remain in a state of grace for the remainder of his days, enjoying dinners at his club and being in the limelight at prominent social functions.

All this was his if he would only renounce his friendship with Father James.

It was such a simple choice: high profile wealth and ease versus poverty and obscurity. Only an idiot would choose the latter.

And wouldn't he be obeying the Catholic Church by going back to his wife?

The bishop's voice cut into his reverie. "Don't tell me you're having a hard time deciding! Is it that difficult to cut *one* man out of your life? You're far better off without him."

Unwittingly, the bishop had given Mark his answer.

He *wasn't* better off without Father James. The dead opposite was true. That priest was his moral compass; he supported his better nature and encouraged him to care about other people, not just himself. Mark had finally begun to like himself.

What was it Father James said back in university? "With God's grace, as Christians we can do far more good than we could possibly dream of doing on our own."

Mark had a long way to go on this Christian journey. But he liked the direction Father James was leading him in and needed the pastor as his travelling companion. He could not say the same of Bishop Marsden.

"Do you think Jesus gave Satan the wrong answer?" he asked.

The bishop frowned. "What on earth are you talking about, man?"

"You remember, don't you? Satan offered Jesus the whole world if He'd only worship him. Do you think Jesus gave Satan the wrong answer?"

"I've no idea what you mean."

Of course, you have.

A great calm engulfed Mark. "I'll be praying for you to change your mind about harming me and hope you'll see that I'm doing nothing wrong in supporting a priest who is also doing nothing wrong. For once in my life, I'm doing something right."

The bishop's eyes became green slits. "Is that your final answer?"

Mark nodded. "Yes, Your Excellency."

"Then you're finished, Mark!"

The main course arrived – steak au poivre with scalloped potatoes and asparagus tips – but Mark pushed back his chair and rose.

He folded his napkin and placed it on the table. "I may be finished in this life, but not in the next, and it's *that* life which counts."

283

I hope you enjoyed this book!

If so, would you consider leaving a review on your favourite sites? Reviews are the lifeblood of authors and help to get more visibility for our work.

Thank you and God bless,

Hilary

Further Notes

Page 226:
https://www.countdowntothekingdom.com/jennifer-where-are-my-priests/
 "Where are My Chosen Sons? Where are My Priests to guide My Children in the truth? Where are My Priests to tell the world that the road to hell is becoming grid-locked with souls who have fallen into Satan's trap?"

https://www.markmallett.com/blog/grave-warnings-part-iii/
 "Do you not see that the Church is languishing and that all her riches are buried, that her priests are inactive, are often bad, and are dissipating the Lord's vineyard?" Our Lady, powerful prophecy from Servant of God Fr. Dolindo Ruotolo (1882-1970)

Page 227:
https://www.countdowntothekingdom.com/pedro-the-great-persecution-3/
 Our Lady Queen of Peace to Pedro Regis on September 25, 2021:
 "Dear children, I love you as you are, and I have come from Heaven to offer you my Love. Do not stray from the path that I have pointed out to you. This is the right time for you to return to the Lord. You are heading for a painful future and few will remain firm in the faith. The great persecution will lead many men and women away from the path of truth. Do not retreat. My Jesus will never abandon you. Seek strength in the Words of my Jesus and in the Eucharist. Do not be discouraged. My Jesus will wipe away your tears and you will be

victorious. Trust fully in the Power of God and all will turn out well for you. Onward in defence of the truth. This is the message I give you today in the name of the Most Holy Trinity. Thank you for having allowed Me to gather you here once more. I bless you in the name of the Father, the Son and the Holy Spirit. Amen. Be at peace."

https://www.countdowntothekingdom.com/pedro-the-shadows-of-paganism/
You are heading towards a future of great spiritual darkness. The shadows of paganism will spread everywhere and many of the consecrated will go in the direction of false doctrines. Behold, the times that I foretold in the past have come. Pray. Only through the power of prayer can you attain victory. Return to Jesus: He loves you and awaits you with open arms. When you feel weak, seek strength in the Eucharist. Also accept My Appeals, because I want to lead you to holiness. Onward in defence of the truth.

About the Author

Now an American citizen, Hilary originally hails from England and lives in Hilton Head, South Carolina with her husband, and Jeeves the English Bulldog.

She is a bestselling author of Christian inspirational novels, Christian romances and short stories that transport the reader into the healing world of horses.

When not penning fiction, Hilary is down at the barn or competing in dressage with Cruz Bay, her home-bred Welsh Cross gelding.

Acknowledgements

This book, like all the others, had considerable help from my wonderful friends and readers.

A massive 'thank you!' goes to Guy Carter, who gave invaluable editorial advice throughout the whole writing process. Another one goes to beta readers Gail Gordon and Anna Rashbrook for their helpful input, and to Wendy Emblin for proof-reading the final product.

Finally, I want to extend huge gratitude to the following members of my Launch Team who were quick to post rave reviews of this book:

Julie Barrett, MaryEllen Cox, Malia Renee Lewis, Anna Rashbrook, Karen Semones and Rachael Smith.

I am constantly humbled by the people who rally round me when I need their help with a new book and make it a success.

God bless you!

Hilary

Rubesca4@Gmail.com

https://HilaryWalkerBooks.com

Discover Other Books by Hilary Walker

Available at all major ebook retailers.

For more details, visit: https://HilaryWalkerBooks.com

CHRISTIAN INSPIRATIONAL

The Jack Harper Trilogy

Riding Out the Devil (Book 1)

Riding Out the Tempest (Book 2)

Riding Out the Rough (Book 3)

Riding Out the Turbulence (Companion Short Story to *The Jack Harper Trilogy*)

The Father Michael Trilogy

Riding Out the Wager (Book 1)

Riding Out the Regrets (Book 2)

Riding Out the Wreckage (Book 3)

The Laura Harper Trilogy

Riding Out the Return (Book 1)

Riding Out the Rift (Book 2)

Riding Out the Race (Book 4) *Coming soon*

CHRISTIAN ROMANCE

Saving Prophecy: A Sinclair Island Romance (Book 1)

Dinny's Challenge: A Sinclair Island Romance (Book 2)

Friday's Folly: A Sinclair Island Romance (Book 3)

Rachel's Risk: A Sinclair Island Romance (Book 4) *Coming soon.*

Ivan's Choice: A Hilton Head Romance (Book 1)

CATHOLIC FICTION

Brittle Diamonds – a Christian Mystery Novel

A Modern Catholic Trilogy:

A Truthful Man – a Modern Catholic Novel: Book 1

A Divine Truth – a Modern Catholic Novel: Book 2 (coming soon)

A Blazing Truth – a Modern Catholic Novel: Book 3 (coming soon)

EQUESTRIAN GUIDES

A Step-By-Step Guide to Entering Your First Dressage Competition

The Beginner Rider's Guide to Stress-Free Horse Buying: *How to Purchase the Perfect Horse for a Beginner Rider without Going Insane*

AUTOBIOGRAPHY

The Horse Bumbler Series: The Autobiography of an Awful Rider with Aspirations

Part One: First Catch Your Horse

Part Two: You've Caught Your Horse: Now What?

Part Three: The Aim of All This

Part Four: What Horses Do to You

SHORT STORIES

A Perfect Christmas & Other Horse Stories (A short story collection – includes *How Not to Rescue a Racehorse*)

How I Lost My Husband's Horse

Connect with Me

Visit my website, where you can subscribe to my newsletter and download a free ebook:

https://HilaryWalkerBooks.com

Email me:

Rubesca4@gmail.com

Subscribe to my blogs:

http://christiantales.com/

http://horsetales.weebly.com/

Visit me on Facebook for Upcoming Events:

fb.me/HilaryWalkerBooks